THE EGYPTIAN MYSTERY

A Penny Green Mystery Book 11

EMILY ORGAN

Copyright © 2021 by Emily Organ

This edition © Emily Organ 2024

emilyorgan.com

Emily Organ has asserted her right under the Copyright, Designs and
Patents Act 1988 to be identified as the author of this work.

All characters and events in this publication, other than those clearly in the
public domain, are fictitious and any resemblance to real persons, living or
dead, is purely coincidental.

ISBN 978-1-8384931-5-8

This book is copyright material and must not be copied, reproduced,
transferred, distributed, leased, licensed or publicly performed or used in any
way except as specifically permitted in writing by the publisher, as allowed
under the terms and conditions under which it was purchased or as strictly
permitted by applicable copyright law. Any unauthorised distribution or use
of this text may be a direct infringement of the author's and publisher's
rights and those responsible may be liable in law accordingly.

THE PENNY GREEN SERIES

CHAPTER 1

"I really don't know where to start. I can't help thinking that I've imagined the whole thing!"

A young lady detective was sitting with me and my husband in our front room, her hands fidgeting in her lap. Brown-haired with a freckled complexion, she wore a burgundy-plaid day dress.

"It's all very strange," she continued. "Will you promise to believe me?"

"I'm not certain we can promise that until you've told us what it relates to, Mrs Worthers," responded James.

"Of course we'll believe you," I said, giving my husband a sharp glance. I had encountered this particular detective on a few previous occasions and knew her well enough to feel that I could trust her.

"The police don't believe me. They looked at me as though I had lost my mind when I told them my story. I'm coming to you because I really don't know whom else to speak to about it."

I poured out the tea and handed her a cup. "We're happy to listen without any judgement, Mrs Worthers."

"Thank you." She took the cup from me. "And please call me Beth."

I smiled. "Call me Penny. What's happened, Beth?"

"Two months ago I began working for Mr Charles Hamilton. He's an Egyptologist."

"How interesting!" I exclaimed.

"His wife is also an Egyptologist, but Mr Hamilton was my employer. Without his wife's knowledge, I might add."

"Did he want you to spy on her?" queried James.

"Yes. He suspected that she was committing adultery with his assistant."

"And was she?" asked James, his eyebrows raised in curiosity.

"Stop interrupting Beth's story," I scolded. "We'll find out in due course."

"Very well. I'm certainly interested to know more."

Beth gave an uneasy sigh. "Much of my work involves this sort of investigation. I'm forced to be a little duplicitous, I'm afraid. The husband often asks me to befriend the wife and discover whether or not she has been unfaithful to him, and this is what I was instructed to do for Mr Hamilton. I can't claim to like the man, but he offered me good money, which was much-needed at the time. I have therefore spent the past few months befriending his wife."

"How did you even begin to do that?" I asked.

"I joined the Ancient Egypt Society as an enthusiastic new member, Beth Somers, and developed friendships with a number of the ladies there. As luck would have it, Susan Hamilton and I got on extremely well. We lunched together regularly, and she told me all about her adventures in Egypt with her husband. The pair only recently returned to England after spending three years there. She adores the place and said she was looking forward to returning this coming winter."

"Impressive," said James. "But how do you do it? How were you able to forge a friendship with Mrs Hamilton, pretending to be someone else, without letting your cover slip?"

"Most of my work is undercover," she replied. "You've been placed in similar situations yourself, Penny, have you not?"

"Yes, I have done some undercover work, but to be able to keep it up for several weeks, months even, must be challenging work."

Beth gave an appreciative smile. "Yes, it is. And this case has been particularly challenging, for reasons I'll explain now."

"What do we know about Mr Hamilton's assistant, with whom she was supposedly committing adultery?" asked James.

"His name is Mr John Smollett; a charming young chap of African descent. Susan Hamilton is also young. I mention this because Mr Hamilton is quite a bit older. Almost twenty years older than his wife, I should think."

"But the charming assistant is the same age as Mrs Hamilton, is he?" asked James.

"Yes. And there is an undeniable attraction between the two. It also became apparent to me fairly swiftly that Susan was unhappy in her marriage. Mr Hamilton is rather a loud, brash man, and his manners tend to be quite coarse when he's had a drink. To be quite frank with you, the pair are poorly matched. I can't imagine why Susan's family approved the marriage. She's young and well educated, while I'm not convinced that he comes from a particularly good family, nor that he received a thorough education as a boy. However, he has acquired a good deal of knowledge about ancient Egypt and its artefacts in recent years. I suppose their shared love of the country is what brought the couple together."

My cat, Tiger, strolled confidently into the room, stopping abruptly when she noticed the unknown woman sitting on the settee. She lowered her body and swiftly trotted over to the window.

"What a lovely cat," said Beth. "Is she scared of me?"

"Just wary," I replied as Tiger jumped onto the windowsill and surveyed us. "Did you find any evidence that Mrs Hamilton was committing adultery with Mr Smollett?"

"It was soon apparent that they were fond of one another, although I never managed to determine whether or not that fondness had extended into an extramarital affair. Events rather took over, you see."

"What happened?" I asked.

"A few things, actually. Firstly, the whole situation began to feel very wrong to me. I had grown to like Susan Hamilton a great deal, and I began to feel ashamed that I was lying to her. I've worked on a number of similar cases but have never harboured such a sentiment before. I've always managed to maintain a facade and distance myself from the situation. On many occasions I have found the people I've spied on quite unpleasant, so I had no qualms about spying on them, but I had great sympathy for Susan. Her husband can be quite the bully, and I actually felt she deserved a bit of happiness with Mr Smollett. Therefore, I resolved to tell Mr Hamilton that I no longer wished to work on the case. For the first time in my career, I decided to leave the job unfinished."

"What did he make of that?" asked James.

"There was no opportunity to find out, as it was then that things took a very strange turn indeed."

CHAPTER 2

"There was an Egyptology event at the Copeland Hotel in Chelsea last weekend," Beth continued. "It was organised by the Ancient Egypt Society. The event began on Friday evening and continued until Sunday afternoon, and all the guests were invited to stay at the hotel. The Hamiltons have a home in Camberwell but chose to take a room at the Copeland for two nights. It's a pleasant hotel, and a significant discount had been offered on the usual rate. The couple had plans to travel to Paris for another event after the weekend.

"The Hamiltons invited me along as their guest. By this time I had attended several Egyptology exhibitions and had developed a genuine interest in the subject. Mr Smollett was also due to attend, and I think Mr Hamilton saw the weekend as an opportunity for me to spy a little more closely on his wife and assistant.

"I had made up my mind beforehand, however, that I would tell Mr Hamilton I no longer wished to work on the case. I was just looking for the right moment to do so. If truth be told, I was feeling rather timid about it, as I was concerned that he would be angry with me. I'm ashamed to say that I mustered up the courage on several occasions, only for my confidence to leave me at the last moment. I don't know why I felt so troubled about it; I had never felt that way before. Perhaps I've been doing this job too long. Maybe it's time for a change."

Our housekeeper, Mrs Oliver, brought a jug of hot water into the room and set it down beside the teapot. "I thought you might like to top up the pot, seeing as you've been here a while." She gave Beth Worthers a pointed glance before leaving the room.

"There was a pre-dinner drinks reception in the ballroom on the Saturday evening," Beth said once Mrs Oliver had left. "Dinner was to be served at eight o'clock, so we gathered there from seven o'clock onwards. I found myself in conversation with the Hamiltons and a lady named Mrs Chilton.

"Shortly before dinner, Mr Hamilton said he needed to return to his room to fetch some photographs. I decided this would be a golden opportunity to say that I no longer wished to continue my work, so I followed after him a few minutes later. I felt nervous, but the anguish of continuing the job when I no longer wished to do it was becoming too much for me. I hoped to encounter him as he returned to the ballroom, but there was no sign of him as I made my way up to the third floor.

"I knew the Hamiltons were staying in room 306, so I knocked at the door. When there was no answer, I tried again. Ordinarily I would have left it, but I was very determined to speak to him by that point, so I tried the handle and the door opened.

"I pushed it ajar slightly and called into the room, but there was still no reply, so I ventured further inside, calling out again. I hadn't stepped far into the room when I realised there was someone lying on the floor. I instantly knew something must be very wrong, as everything was quiet and the door had been left unlocked. As I moved closer to the person on the floor, I realised it was Mr Hamilton... and that he was quite dead."

"Dead?!" I exclaimed. "How could you be so sure?"

"He was lying face down, his head turned to one side. There was no obvious wound or any blood that I could see, but his eyes were open and unblinking, and he wasn't breathing. I touched his wrist but could detect no pulse. Although I had never seen a dead person before, somehow I just knew."

She shuddered as she sipped her tea.

"My next thought was that I must fetch help; a doctor who could somehow revive him. I bolted down three flights of stairs to the foyer and summoned the staff at the reception desk, then we all ran back up the stairs together.

"But when we reached the room, I saw that the door was closed. Perhaps I had closed it myself – I'm still not entirely sure what happened during those strange moments – though I thought I had left it open. Anyway, the door was still unlocked, but when we went inside Mr Hamilton was no longer there. He was nowhere to be seen at all."

James's brow furrowed. "Then he couldn't have been dead," he mused.

Beth sighed. "That's what everybody says when I tell them this story."

I topped up the teapot with the hot water and considered the strangeness of the incident. "Just because it seems like an impossible scenario," I began, "doesn't necessarily mean that Beth was mistaken."

"Oh, I'm sure that Beth is telling the truth about what she felt she had seen," said James, "but the man couldn't possibly have been dead. How could he have got up and left the room in the few minutes after she had gone to fetch help?"

"Someone must have moved him," I said.

James turned to Beth. "Was there any sign that there had been a disturbance in the room? Furniture that had been knocked over or anything like that?"

"None at all," she replied.

"Any sign he'd been murdered there? Blood where the body had previously lain?"

"Nothing. I now believe that the murderer must have been in the room when I went in the first time. I must have disturbed him. He must somehow have removed Mr Hamilton's body from the room while I went downstairs to get help."

"How long do you think you were away from the room for?" I asked.

"Only two or three minutes. Certainly no longer than five." She looked down at her hands. "It seems so improbable that I've begun to doubt what I really saw. I wonder if I somehow imagined it all, but I know that I can't have because Mr Hamilton is still missing."

"Then he *must* be dead," I said.

James shook his head. "How extremely odd."

"And what of Mrs Hamilton?" I asked Beth. "How is she faring?"

"Susan is also missing."

James and I exchanged a puzzled glance.

"Since when?" I asked.

"I last saw her at the drinks reception. There has been no sign of her since then."

"You haven't seen her since you decided to speak to Mr Hamilton that evening?"

"No. They've both completely vanished into thin air. I'm quite sure that Mr Hamilton is dead, but as for *Mrs* Hamilton... I haven't the first idea where she could be!"

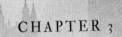

CHAPTER 3

"I'll never forget that rare view of the great jungle," said my father, leaning on his walking stick. "I'd walked for days and days, seeing little more than verdant foliage, swinging vines and tree trunks so wide that even the arms of a giant would struggle to encircle them. I had decided to try the higher ground. I knew there was a risk involved in leaving the river, but I also felt sure I would be able to find my way back to it.

"All I wanted was a viewpoint; a place from which I could orientate myself and fully appreciate the great jungle kingdom that had become my home away from home. I climbed the slopes until I found it. A rocky outcrop gifted me with a sight any man would remember for the rest of his days. I can't tell you how far away the horizon was... Twenty miles, perhaps, maybe even fifty. The jungle stretched as far as my eye could see. I felt the sun's warmth on my skin, which brought relief after labouring for so long under the thick shade of the trees. I can recall as clearly as though it were yesterday that I closed my eyes and breathed in that sweet, exotic scent one can only discover in foreign climes.

"I cannot remember taking a step forward, but I suppose I must have done, for all of a sudden the ground slipped away beneath my feet. In a matter of seconds, the most pleasant moment of my life became the very worst. I fell! I tumbled and tumbled and tumbled..."

My father paused and the stage lights dimmed. A steady drum roll began and then rose into an almost deafening crescendo, accompanied by a screech of dramatic violins. Everyone in the auditorium seemed to hold their breath until the orchestra's climactic sound had receded.

I still felt a little out of breath, having dashed to the theatre after Beth Worthers's visit, only just reaching my seat in time. I was doing my best to pay attention, but my mind kept turning over the strange story of Mr and Mrs Hamilton. We happened to be at the Royal Court Theatre in Chelsea's Sloane Square. I was tempted to visit the nearby Copeland Hotel after the performance, but decided it was probably better to wait until the morning when I could take Beth along with me.

The lights slowly came up again to reveal my father sitting in a chair.

"I had no idea how long I'd been lying there when I finally came round," he said, "and I could see very little when I opened my eyes. Just glimmers of light reaching through a dense canopy of leaves. I tried to move, but my body was paralysed. I knew then that I would inevitably die. Thirst would be the most probable cause; however, I knew only too well of the dreadful beasts that roamed the jungle at night. There was a very good chance my broken body would be mauled by a leopard or one of his big-cat cousins.

"Quite strangely, though, my mind quickly accepted this fate. I knew there was little I could do other than put my trust in the Lord Himself. It was an enormous effort for me to merely move my lips, and an even greater effort was required to find my voice, but I managed it. I was only able to utter a few words before I slipped back into unconsciousness, however. Those words included a prayer for my loved ones and a declaration that I was placing my life in the hands of my heavenly Father. His will would dictate what happened to me."

The stage lights went down again and there was another hushed silence as the audience waited for the next instalment of my father's story. When the lights came up once more, he was over on the other side of the stage, up on his feet. He began to recount how it had felt to be carried through the jungle on a stretcher, his body racked with pain. He described the foul potions the mysterious tribesmen and women had administered to him, and this section of his story concluded with a description of how he had been nursed back to health at a native camp in the middle of the Amazonian jungle.

The main lights came up for the interval, and mauve and gold curtains swung across the stage. The proscenium was painted with colourful frescoes, and I felt a sense of pride that so many people had come to this impressive venue to hear my father speak.

My sister Eliza, James and I decided to remain in our seats, while those around us bustled about, fetching drinks and ice creams.

"It's certainly a dramatic tale," said Eliza, "not that we haven't heard any of it before. The audience members seem to be enjoying it, though."

"They do indeed. And Father's clearly enjoying himself, too." I glanced down at the programme in my hand, which read: "Terrible Tales from Amazonia, as told by Mr Frederick Brinsley Green, the Daring Plant-Hunter, and his Brave Rescuer, Mr Francis Edwards."

A theatrical agent had written to my father after reading a newspaper article about his ten-year disappearance in Colombia. The agent had offered to turn it into a performance piece, and Father had been flattered by the idea. He was evidently relishing the attention on stage.

Eliza and I had found it difficult to forgive Father for his decade-long silence, although the anguish his family had suffered was unlikely to be mentioned in the performance. I had come to realise that bitterness would only lead to estrangement from my father. Having lost him for ten years, I had no wish to lose him again. I had therefore resolved to forgive him, albeit a little reluctantly at times.

"Opening night is going well," remarked James.

"Yes, it is," agreed Eliza. "All the seats appear to be filled, and I didn't notice anybody looking awfully bored. The dramatic effects certainly help, and Father appears to have developed new acting abilities, don't you think? He seems more at home on the stage than I imagined he would be. I can't imagine poor Francis being quite so confident; he never seeks the limelight. In fact, I think he's rather embarrassed about the whole affair."

"He probably feels better suited to reading books and his beloved library, but I'm sure the audience will warm to him all the same," I replied. "And they'll want to hear how he found Father. There are only four more nights of the show, anyhow. Hopefully the public's appetite for Father's stories will be satiated by then and Francis will be able to concentrate on his job again."

Eliza was quite right about Francis and his less-than-confident performance in the second half. Whereas Father was happy to stand at the front of the stage, regaling everyone with his adventures, Francis cut a more awkward figure, standing to one side, as if keen to return to the wings. He fidgeted with his spectacles and repeatedly brushed his floppy hair away from his face.

But despite his reluctance as a performer, the audience

appeared to lap up everything he had to say. After all, it was a story of bravery and endeavour, and they admired him for his incredible achievement in finding my father when no one else had been able to do so.

When we joined them in the dressing room after the performance, Father seemed overjoyed by the way it had gone.

"It was quite wonderful, don't you think? That applause at the end brought a tear to my eye. I never imagined myself standing on a stage in London, entertaining a crowd of people with my stories! I can't imagine you pictured it either, Francis."

"No, Mr Green. It's certainly proving to be an interesting experience, but I must confess that I'm rather pleased there are only four nights left."

"I'm rather disappointed about that! We could take this on tour around the country, could we not?"

"I'm afraid I would have to bow out if you did so, Mr Green. I have my employment at the British Library to consider. Perhaps you could find an actor to replace me."

"What nonsense, Francis. How could that job at the library ever be more appealing than this incredible opportunity?"

"It's very much more appealing to me, sir. I only ever agreed to take part because I knew it would be a short run."

"Not everybody aspires to tread the boards, Father," said Eliza. Her defence of Francis reminded me of her fondness for him.

Father sighed. "Very well. I understand that it isn't your cup of tea, Francis. You've made that clear from the outset. I'm so grateful that you agreed to do these five evenings with me, and I shall do my best to enjoy them while they last.

"If the audiences that gather here over the next few evenings are as enthusiastic as tonight's, I could possibly arrange a longer run of it, or at least something similar. I could employ some actors to recreate the most memorable moments of my travels. Nothing quite beats an adventure story set within a foreign clime, does it? People simply can't get enough of that sort of thing."

CHAPTER 4

I walked to Paddington station the following morning, then travelled by underground railway to Sloane Square, where I had arranged to meet Beth Worthers.

The late summer morning was growing warm as I waited beneath the shade of a tree in the square. Just a short distance away stood the Royal Court Theatre, the scene of my father's performance the previous night. A milk cart passed by on its way to serve the grand homes in nearby Sloane Gardens, and two nursery maids chatted as they pushed their large perambulators along.

"Mrs Hamilton is the most obvious suspect," James had said to me the previous evening after we had returned home from the theatre. "She went missing as soon as her husband was found dead, didn't she?"

"But she was still present at the drinks reception when Beth went off to find him," I replied.

"Perhaps Beth is mistaken with regard to the timing. Perhaps Mrs Hamilton left the reception before her."

"She seemed quite convinced of her story."

"She did, and yet it all seems rather unbelievable. I know

you feel we shouldn't doubt her, but I'm quite certain there must be some small detail she has missed. It really doesn't make sense."

"I'm sure it will once you begin your investigation."

"Investigation?"

"Yes. Beth came here asking for our help."

"It'll have to be *your* help, Penny. It's not a matter for the police."

"But a man has been murdered!"

"Where's the evidence of that?"

"Beth found him lying dead in his hotel room, James. The culprit must have moved his body."

"There was no sign of him when the hotel staff arrived in the room. The only witness to this supposed crime was Beth Worthers."

"And you don't believe her?"

"I do to some extent, but..."

"But you don't completely believe her."

"Even if I chose to believe every word of her story, the police cannot be involved in this, Penny. Not yet, anyway. There isn't enough evidence for us to examine. All we have is one woman's word."

"But Mr and Mrs Hamilton have completely vanished!"

"How do we know that they haven't disappeared of their own free will? People are allowed to vanish if they so desire."

"You don't intend to do anything about it, then?"

"It's not a matter for the police unless there is compelling evidence that a crime has been committed. I'm as concerned as you are about the fate of Mr and Mrs Hamilton, but I wouldn't be able to justify putting a team of men on the case at this stage. I'm quite sure Inspector Gresham at T Division would feel the same way."

"I shall have to find some evidence, in that case."

"You don't have to do that, Penny."

"Beth has asked for our help. Besides, no one else believes her story."

"That's really not so surprising. Anyway, she's an experienced detective. Perhaps she can find her own evidence and go to the police to request help herself."

"I don't think she would have come to us if she'd felt able to do that. She's doubting her own memory at the moment."

"I can see that you've quite made your mind up about helping her, Penny. I know from experience that this isn't the sort of case you would ever choose to walk away from."

I was still mulling our conversation over as Beth approached me in Sloane Square. She wore a smart blue flannel dress with a matching hat.

"Thank you for agreeing to meet me, Penny," she said. "I hope I won't end up wasting your time."

"You won't," I replied. "I'm rather determined to find out what has happened to the Hamiltons."

Close to Cadogan Square, the Copeland Hotel was a red-brick building that stood six storeys high. The ground floor was clad in stone, with ornately carved decorations around the windows and entrance porch.

"Is that another hotel next door?" I asked, pointing to the large neighbouring building of brown-and-cream brick.

"Yes, I think it is. The two must compete for guests!"

The foyer of the Copeland Hotel was furnished with dark wood panelling and a black-and-white tiled floor. Pots of elegant palms with spiked leaves were positioned around the reception desk.

I introduced myself to the haughty-faced man behind the desk. "I'm Mrs Penny Blakely, a journalist, and I'm investigating the mysterious disappearance of the Egyptologists, Mr and Mrs Hamilton. They stayed at this hotel last weekend."

"I'm afraid I know nothing about them."

"They were last seen at this very hotel, after which they completely vanished."

He frowned and looked Beth up and down. "You seem familiar, if you don't mind me saying so, madam."

"I'm Mrs Worthers," she responded, "a friend of Mrs Hamilton's. I'm concerned about her whereabouts."

"Would you mind if we looked around the hotel?" I asked.

"I think it would be best if you spoke with the manager," he replied. "I'll fetch him for you."

Various pamphlets advertising local events lay on the reception desk.

"There's your father!" said Beth excitedly, picking up a pamphlet for 'Terrible Tales from Amazonia'. "Have you seen it yet?"

"Yes, I saw it last night. He performed very well, actually. I think he's developing quite a taste for the stage."

The man from the reception desk returned with a tall, lean gentleman with sharp blue eyes and a thin moustache. His neat, dark hair was streaked with grey, and he wore a well-tailored burgundy suit.

"I'm Mr Edward Fortescue, the hotel manager," he said in a soft, staccato voice. "How may I help you, ladies?"

We introduced ourselves and explained why we were there.

"I remember Mr and Mrs Hamilton well," he responded.

"What can you tell us about them?" I asked.

"I can tell you that they left this hotel without paying their bill!"

"Did anyone see them leave?"

"Not that I know of."

"Mrs Worthers here discovered Mr Hamilton lying on the floor of his hotel room. She believes he was dead."

"So I recall. Yet we searched the room and found no sign of him at all."

"Did anything about them strike you as unusual during their stay? Was there anything that made you wonder if something might be off-kilter?"

"You're a journalist, are you, Mrs Blakely?"

"That's right."

"For which publication?"

"I wrote for the *Morning Express* for many years. I write for a variety of publications these days."

"I see. Well, I've reported the non-payment of the Hamiltons's bill to the police, and I really don't think there is anything else to discuss."

"I think it would be a good idea to publish an appeal asking the public for their help."

He gave a bemused laugh. "You think the public would help find a couple who failed to pay their bill?"

"I believe there must be more to this story than that. Did they leave their belongings behind?"

He adjusted the cuff of his sleeve. "Yes, they did. In fact, we still have them here in storage, awaiting collection."

"Which suggests that something untoward must have happened to them."

"I suppose if they had done a flit in the night they would have taken their things with them, at the very least," he conceded.

"Then wouldn't you agree that publishing an appeal for information might help?"

"Perhaps it would." He sighed and shook his head, as if resigning himself to becoming a little more helpful. "I only encountered Mr and Mrs Hamilton once during their stay, and that was when they were on their way to breakfast one morning. I suppose it must have been the Saturday morning, as all the attendees of the Egyptian event arrived on the

Friday evening. I greeted them, as I greet all those who stay with us, but there was no real conversation because we had a lot of guests staying that weekend, and Mr Hambridge at the Excelsior next door was causing trouble as usual."

"That's the neighbouring hotel, is it?"

"Yes. He's been making life difficult for us ever since we opened."

"What sort of trouble did he cause that day?"

"Oh, he was complaining about carriages dropping our guests on the bit of street he considers to be his. Can you believe it? He thinks he actually owns the road outside his hotel!" He gave a hollow laugh.

"And you didn't see Mr and Mrs Hamilton again after breakfast on the Saturday?" I asked.

"No. The next thing I knew, Mrs Worthers was summoning everyone in a state of panic, saying that Mr Hamilton was dead. We ran up to the room and... nothing! It was rather confusing, really."

"It was *very* confusing," agreed Beth, "and remains so."

"So while Mrs Worthers was summoning help, someone was busy removing Mr Hamilton's body from his room," I said.

Mr Fortescue laughed again. "You make it sound as though it would be easy to transport the body of a man out of this hotel without anybody noticing! He wasn't a small man, was he, Mrs Worthers? He must have stood at six feet tall, and he was broad, too. Not an easy fellow to shift, I'd say. I can see by your expression, Mrs Blakely, that you're quite puzzled by all this, just as I am. By all means publish a public appeal for information on Mr and Mrs Hamilton's where-abouts, but I simply cannot see how it will help."

"What do you think happened?" I asked him.

"While I have every respect for what Mrs Worthers says she saw, I cannot bring myself to believe that Mr Hamilton is dead. I believe he got up and flitted away somewhere with his lovely wife."

"Leaving all their belongings behind?"

"I have no explanation as to why they did that. You asked me what I think happened, Mrs Blakely, and that's all I can come up with at the moment."

"Do you mind if we look around?"

He raised an eyebrow, as if to suggest that it would be a fruitless exercise. "By all means," he replied, "but I don't know how it could possibly help to do so."

"May we see the room the Hamiltons stayed in?"

"I forget which number it was now."

"Room 306," said Beth.

"Let me check."

He stepped behind the desk and consulted a ledger. "There are guests in the room, I'm afraid. We have a number of similar rooms, but they're all occupied, too. Those rooms are particularly popular, as they're a little more sizeable than the others. We have six of them on each floor. But as I say, feel free to have a look around and see where that gets you." He gestured toward a grand staircase behind him.

We thanked him and eyed the staircase.

"Off to the Royal Court tonight?" he asked Beth, noticing the leaflet in her hand.

"If there are any tickets left, I shall be," she replied. "Mr Green the plant-hunter is Mrs Blakely's father!"

"Is he indeed? Well, that's very interesting. My wife and I have tickets for Saturday's performance, and we're very much looking forward to it! Do please take all the time you need to look around, and ask me if you have any further questions."

"We will, thank you."

"And do let me know if you come across any clues to the Hamiltons's whereabouts, won't you?"

CHAPTER 5

Beth and I climbed the wide staircase behind the reception desk. It was covered with a deep, dark carpet held in place by iron stair rods. A smart gentleman doffed his top hat as he passed us on the stairs, and a maid in a starched cap and apron bid us good morning when we reached the third floor.

Beth turned to the right. "The Hamiltons's room is off this corridor," she said, pushing open a set of heavy double doors.

The thick carpet muffled our footsteps as we walked, and the dark wood panelling made the corridor rather dingy. Etchings on the walls displayed scenes from popular London locations: St Paul's Cathedral, Trafalgar Square and the grand facade of Buckingham Palace.

"Here we are." Beth stopped outside a door with '306' affixed to it in small brass numbers.

I glanced up and down the corridor. There was nothing to distinguish this door from any of the others, aside from the number, yet this was the scene of a murder. Or so Beth claimed.

"Do you think the quickest way to leave the hotel from this room would be via the main staircase we just climbed?" I asked.

"There is a lift beside the main staircase."

"Then that route may be quicker."

"It may be, although I didn't use the lift while I was here. I don't like the thought of those things! I worry about getting stuck in one."

"Are there any other staircases?"

"There must be some back stairs for the staff to use, but I don't know where they would be."

I walked on a short way toward a recess where there was a window. Peering out, I could see that it overlooked a narrow service street and the rear of a tall red-brick building.

"Let's assume for a moment that Mr Hamilton wasn't dead when you found him," I said. "Maybe he was unconscious but somehow came round and managed to make good his escape. Could he have exited the building from here?" I slid the sash window up, creating a gap large enough for someone to climb through. Then I cautiously peered out to see a vertical drop of three storeys to the street below.

"I don't think so," said Beth. "Not unless he had a rope, anyhow, and where would he have found that? What would he have tied it to?"

"Nothing that I can see," I replied, glancing around the corridor, "and he would have been forced to leave it behind. An escape through this window seems very unlikely unless he had help from somebody else."

"Who would have helped him?"

"Mrs Hamilton, perhaps?"

"I don't see why she would have done so," responded Beth.

"On the other hand, perhaps his murderers lowered his body out of the window," I suggested.

"I can't see how they would have gone about it, but I suppose it's a possibility."

"It would undoubtedly have caught the attention of anyone who happened to be standing in the street below. It was about eight o'clock in the evening, wasn't it?"

"Yes."

"Not even approaching dusk at this time of year, in that case. Perhaps they could have got away with it at night, but not during the daytime."

"I don't think anyone could have lowered his body out of this window," said Beth. "They would have needed ropes and possibly even pulleys. I was only gone for a few minutes, so I just don't see how anybody would have got all the necessary equipment ready and smuggled him out of the building in such a short space of time."

I closed the window. "I agree. We need to consider every possibility, but none of these hypotheses seem probable at this stage, do they?"

We walked along to the end of the corridor but saw nothing other than doors leading to further rooms.

"I wonder how many guests this place can accommodate," I said.

"There are six storeys, and let's suppose all the bedrooms are on the upper five storeys," replied Beth. "I would estimate that there are around twenty rooms on each floor."

"A hundred bedrooms, then? Which means there may have been between one hundred and fifty or even two hundred guests here at the weekend."

"There were about two hundred guests at the conference. I don't think all of them stayed here, but a good number did."

We turned and walked back to room 306.

"How sure are you about the time the Hamiltons vanished?" I asked Beth.

"I checked my watch when Mr Hamilton left the drinks

reception because I wanted to see if I would have time to speak to him before dinner. It was about a quarter to eight at that point."

"And what time do you think he would have arrived up here?"

"The ballroom where the drinks reception was held is on the ground floor. Mr Hamilton would either have taken the main staircase or the lift. I think it would have taken him about two minutes, perhaps a little less if he travelled in the lift. Depending on whether he had to wait for it, of course."

"And you left the ballroom at what time?"

"Only two or three minutes after him."

"Then you would have reached his room by about ten minutes to eight."

"Yes, I should think that was about right."

"And that's when you found him on the floor, about five minutes after he had left the ballroom. Someone must have been lying in wait for him!"

"Or maybe they saw him leave the ballroom and followed him."

"Did you notice anyone leaving the room at the same time?"

"No, but it's still a possibility."

"It certainly is." I pondered for a moment before adding, "He came up to his room to fetch some photographs. Perhaps his murderer knew that he intended to do so. Did he mention why he was fetching them?"

"No. I can only imagine that he planned to show them to someone at dinner."

"Presumably someone he would be sitting with. He must have seen the seating plan and decided to show that person the photographs."

"Or that person may have asked to see the photographs."

"Yes, that makes better sense. The murderer asked to see

the photographs and Mr Hamilton went up to fetch them. But how did the murderer know when Mr Hamilton would go up to his room to fetch them?"

"Maybe he just watched and followed," said Beth.

"Or perhaps he didn't ask to see the photographs at all. Perhaps he had just been keeping an eye on Mr Hamilton, waiting for the right moment to catch him on his own. Whoever it was must have had help moving Mr Hamilton out of that room so quickly, though. How long were you away summoning help? Two or three minutes, did you say?"

"Yes. I ran downstairs, so it probably took me a minute to get from the room to the foyer, possibly less than that. Then... Well, it's rather difficult to say. When I told the staff he was dead, everyone started dashing about, asking questions all at the same time. It can't have been all that long before we found ourselves back in the room. Perhaps two or three minutes more."

"A very short period of time to get him out of there, I would say. How on earth did they do it?"

"I don't know." Beth sighed. "I'm really beginning to wonder whether I might have been mistaken. Perhaps he wasn't dead after all, and he just ran out while I was off fetching help."

"Someone would have seen him, I feel sure of it. This has to be the most puzzling case I've ever come across."

CHAPTER 6

"D id you say that the Hamiltons have a home in Camberwell?" I asked Beth as we stepped out of the hotel.

"Yes, in McDowall Road."

"Is the house empty now that the Hamiltons have disappeared?"

"There's a housekeeper there."

"Have you visited her since their disappearance?"

"I called on her, but she said she hadn't seen them."

"Is she concerned about their whereabouts?"

"No. She believes they're in Paris."

"I remember you telling us they were planning to travel there after the conference weekend. Would you mind calling on the housekeeper again, with me in tow this time?"

"Not at all."

"Good, because I should like to ask her a few questions."

We travelled by underground railway to Blackfriars, walked the short distance to Ludgate Hill station and then boarded a train that would take us south of the river to Camberwell.

Beth carried a carpetbag that wasn't dissimilar to mine. As we pulled out of the station, she took some knitting needles and a ball of yarn out of her bag. She gave me a wry smile as I watched her.

"I like to take advantage of every moment available in order to make progress with something," she said.

"What are you knitting?"

"A pullover for my nephew."

"I'm sure he'll be very grateful for it."

"I hope so. I don't see him as often as I'd like to. I hope he hasn't grown too big for it already."

We travelled over Blackfriars Bridge. I always enjoyed the views of London from the River Thames. Its wide expanse offered a respite from the narrow, crowded city streets. Smoking chimneys towered over the rooftops of south London, while ship masts and cranes cluttered the skyline of the dockyard in the east.

"What made you decide to become a lady detective?" I asked.

"I don't know if I ever made a firm decision to do so, but I worked as a store detective shortly after I left school. The father of a school friend owned a department store in Lincoln and had a terrible problem with shop thieves. He was eager to employ innocent-looking young women with a keen eye for suspicious-looking customers. I managed to fit the bill."

"Did you enjoy the work?"

"I did. You wouldn't believe the sorts of ladies who stole things! They appeared to be thoroughly respectable, both in manner and dress, yet they would happily help themselves to a pair of taffeta gloves. Some were quite professional about it, with special pockets sewn into their skirts and coats. I once observed a lady secreting a vast quantity of silk underclothing beneath her hat. She was extremely embarrassed when the store manager ordered her to remove the hat and it all fell out!

"I realised that not only was I an observant store detective, but that I was also good at disguising myself. I'm not quite sure how I achieved it. Perhaps I was so ordinary-looking that people barely noticed me. After a few years of that work, I noticed an advertisement in the local newspaper that had been placed by a lady detective. That's when I decided to set up on my own. I moved to London, reasoning that there would be a good amount of work here. Fortunately, I wasn't wrong on that count."

"I consider it a most courageous thing to do," I said.

"I don't ever think of myself as courageous."

"But you have to pretend to be someone else on occasion, don't you? I've done it once or twice myself, and I've always found it incredibly nerve-wracking."

"I suppose I've become accustomed to it. And because of my plain and forgettable looks, I'm able to assume different characters without anybody questioning me."

"I wish you wouldn't describe yourself as plain and forgettable, Beth. You're quite the opposite! What does your family make of your profession?"

"They would much rather have seen me married, of course. But as the years have passed and my sisters married, I think they realised I would much rather work than have a husband, a house and children to look after. That wasn't the life I longer for, even from a young age."

"Me neither!" I smiled. "I always knew I wanted to be a writer. Like you, becoming a wife and mother never appealed to me at all. For a number of years I felt certain I would never marry, but then I met James and my viewpoint changed. I'm lucky to have a husband who supports my desire to continue working."

"Yes, you're extremely lucky! Not only have I failed to

meet anyone I'd be interested in falling in love with, but I also feel sure that any prospective husband would want me to stop working. My job often entails working in the evenings and on Sundays. It also involves a good deal of travel. It just doesn't fit well with marriage."

"But you call yourself Mrs Worthers."

She smiled. "It looks better on my advertisements. I felt my clients might trust a married lady more. It sounds rather matronly and suggests a little more experience of life, don't you think?"

"I suppose so."

"My friends are all married now, and their lives are quite different from mine. Some have even made disapproving comments about my conduct, but I've learned not to allow their words to affect me. I'm happy doing this type of work. I enjoy it, and I never have time to feel bored."

"And when you have a moment of spare time, you knit!"

"Exactly! I find that it calms my mind."

"Perhaps I should take it up. My mother taught me how, but I can't remember now."

"Well, if you'd ever like to learn again, just let me know."

"Oh, I shall!"

We exchanged a smile.

"Maybe I'll take it up after I've got to the bottom of this case," I continued. "I can't even begin to understand it. I feel the need to know as much as possible about the Hamiltons. What can you tell me about them?"

"Where do I start?"

"Let's start with Mrs Hamilton."

"She's about twenty-five years old. Slender, dark-haired and pretty, with delicate features. She's well educated, and she met her husband in Egypt."

"When was that?"

"Three or four years ago, I believe. She told me she

had become fascinated about Egypt as a young girl and had always harboured the intention of travelling there. She taught herself about the country and its history from books, and has gleaned the rest of her vast knowledge from travelling around the country. She told me she had written articles on ancient Egypt for various periodicals."

"Did you meet any of her friends?"

"No close friends, as I recall. She only returned to England at the beginning of this year, and many of the people she introduced me to were acquaintances of hers or her husbands. The study of Egyptology seems to take up all of their time. I went along to a few lectures and events at her invitation."

"What did you learn of her family?"

"That her parents were both dead. Her father was Reverend Willis, and I believe he hailed from Rochdale."

"Is that where she grew up?"

"I think so."

"And Mr Hamilton?"

"I'd say he was about forty-five. Quite an intimidating man; tall and broad, with sand-coloured hair. The colour of the Egyptian desert, you might say!"

"You mentioned when we last spoke that he wasn't as well educated as his wife."

"That was my impression. However, he appeared to have done a good job of acquainting himself with all things Egyptian. He was extremely knowledgeable on that front, and he enjoyed collecting artefacts."

"Did he buy them or dig for them?"

"Both. There's quite a market for Egyptian artefacts, as you can probably imagine. What he didn't like was the looting of tombs and burial sites that takes place over there. He felt it was his job to find and preserve these ancient objects rather than allowing them to fall into the hands of unscrupulous people."

"You mentioned previously that you thought the Hamiltons were mismatched."

"Yes, they were. There must be a twenty-year age gap between them, and they didn't have a great deal to say to each other unless it was about Egypt. I simply cannot fathom how he charmed her into marrying him, but somehow he managed it. Some men change after marriage, don't they? Perhaps he was one of those. I sympathised with her, Penny. It can't be easy realising you've made a mistake in your choice of marriage partner."

"Perhaps she's rather relieved that he's dead, if that's the case."

"If she even knows that he is."

"Could she have murdered him, do you think?"

"No!" snapped Beth. "Never!"

Taken aback by the curtness of her reply, I chose not to pursue the possibility of Mrs Hamilton's guilt for the time being.

The Hamiltons's home stood amid a row of neat, terraced houses close to Camberwell train station. The housekeeper was a stocky woman with bulging, wide-set eyes. Her round face was framed by curls the colour of steel. She greeted Beth, then eyed me with suspicion.

"This is Mrs Penny Blakely," said Beth. "I've asked her to help me find Mr and Mrs Hamilton."

The housekeeper gave a scornful chuckle. "They don't need finding! We've already discussed this, Mrs Worthers."

"Do you know where they are?" I asked.

"They're in Paris."

"You know that for sure, do you?"

"Yes. The plan was that they would travel to Paris as soon as the weekend event was over."

"Have you heard from them since the weekend?"

"No."

"Then how do you know for certain that they're in Paris?"

She wrinkled her nose in response to this question, as if offended that I had asked it. "Because that was the plan. They were to take the train to Dover on the Sunday, and from there take the boat over to Calais. Then travel on to Paris by train."

"Do you know which hotel they were scheduled to stay at in Paris?"

"The Martinez Hotel... or *l'Hôtel Martinez*, I think they call it over there. In Montmartre, I believe. Mr Hamilton told me he'd stayed there before and found it most agreeable."

"And you assume they're staying there at the present time?"

"Yes. Why wouldn't they be?"

"Mrs Worthers found Mr Hamilton lying on the floor of his room at the Copeland Hotel. He—"

"Yes, yes. She's told me all about that." The housekeeper rolled her eyes. "As I've already explained, he'd probably had one of his episodes."

"Episodes?"

"Yes. He's prone to seizures."

I turned to Beth. "Did you know that he was prone to seizures?"

Beth shook her head. "Yes, but it didn't look like an episode to me. It seemed rather more serious than that."

The housekeeper laughed. "I once found him on the floor of the kitchen in the middle of the night. Just laid out there, he was, completely insensible. I thought he was dead myself.

It's just his way, I'm afraid." She gripped the door, as if readying herself to close it again.

"Can you explain why the Hamiltons didn't pay their bill before leaving the hotel?" I asked her. "Or why their belongings are still there?"

"They left some things there, did they? I imagine they didn't want to take everything to Paris with them but forgot to send word. I'll ask Tom to fetch their bags."

"And settle the bill? I simply cannot understand why they would leave without paying."

"Neither can I, Mrs Blakely! There must have been some sort of misunderstanding. I'll ask Tom to settle that, too. Now, is that everything? I really must be getting on."

I tried frantically to think of a way to continue the conversation, but the housekeeper was determined to be rid of us.

"Yes, that's all," said Beth.

I felt my jaw clench.

"When do you expect Mr and Mrs Hamilton to return from Paris?" I asked her before she could slam the door.

"Next week sometime." She scratched at her neck. "Although sometimes they stay on a little longer when they're travelling. That's their way."

"I see. Thank you for your time."

"Pleasure."

The door was swiftly closed.

"She's hiding something, I feel sure of it," I muttered. "How can we get the truth out of her?"

Beth shrugged. "I don't know."

"I'd like to speak to the young man you were investigating, John Smollett," I said. "Would you be able to arrange a meeting with him?"

"I'd be happy to. He still knows me as Mrs Somers, however. I haven't informed him of my true identity yet."

"I think you'll need to tell him now."

She winced. "He won't be happy to find out that I've been lying about my identity."

"I'm sure he'll understand, given the circumstances. If you're honest with him now, he may speak honestly in return."

CHAPTER 7

"I feel even more confused than ever now," I said to James after explaining how the day had gone. We were standing in our little garden and the sun had just dipped down behind the rooftops. "I'd hoped that visiting the Copeland Hotel and the Hamiltons's home would help shed some light on what may have happened to them, but it was no help at all. It's very odd that their housekeeper wasn't the least bit concerned about them."

"Well, there's one way of settling that," replied James. His shirt sleeves were rolled up and he was holding a pair of secateurs in his hand. "Send a telegram to the Paris hotel, enquiring whether the Hamiltons are staying there. If they are, there's nothing to worry about."

"I really don't expect them to be there. Nothing about this situation adds up."

"It could have been a seizure, as the housekeeper said."

"But if that's all it was, why has he disappeared? And his wife, too?"

"I can't explain that, but I do wonder whether we should so readily accept everything Beth Worthers tells us."

"I believe her, James."

"Let's suppose that she's right about him being dead. We still can't account for the mysterious disappearance of Mrs Hamilton, can we? The most obvious assumption is that she murdered him and is now on the run. Perhaps she hit him over the head with something or tasked someone else with the deed. Perhaps she found out that he had employed Beth to spy on her. We know she was unhappy in her marriage, and by all accounts attracted to another man. It's entirely possible that she murdered her husband."

"Beth is adamant that she never would have done so."

"That's because she considers Mrs Hamilton a friend and cannot imagine her doing such a thing. But there's no evidence one way or the other at this stage, so every possibility must be considered."

"How did Mrs Hamilton manage to disappear, do you think?"

"I can't imagine it would have been terribly difficult for her. She could have hopped onto a train and be just about anywhere by now. Perhaps she hailed a cab. She's had four days to make good her escape."

"Perhaps it was easy for her to disappear, as you say, but how did she hide her husband's body so quickly and easily?"

"That's the most puzzling aspect of all this. She must have had help or paid someone else to do it. At least two people must have been involved. I'm beginning to think she hired people to do it."

"It's entirely plausible that she did," I replied, "but why have there been no witness reports of a group of men making their way into Mr Hamilton's room and, more importantly, making their way out of there with a dead body?"

"Yes, that is a puzzle. If you're sure the only access point is the main staircase or the lift, they wouldn't have been able to slip out without being seen. They may not have looked suspicious, however. They may even have been there for the Egyptology event."

"Colleagues of Mr Hamilton, you mean?"

"Yes, they may have been."

James examined some new growth on one of the rose bushes. "I think we're approaching this the wrong way around," he mused as he lopped off a faded flower head. "We've got ourselves too caught up in the logistics of how the murder – if indeed there was a murder – was committed. What we need to look out for is someone with a motive. Mrs Hamilton is the most obvious one, but there may be others, of course."

"And to establish who had a motive, we need to learn more about the Hamiltons," I added.

"Definitely. What has Beth Worthers told you about them?"

"Not a great deal."

"Then she needs to tell you more."

"I don't think she does know much about them, to be perfectly honest. She only worked for Mr Hamilton for two months."

"Then it sounds as though you have a bit of work to do if you're to discover what they're really like. This entire thing could still be a ruse, however."

"What do you mean by that?"

"Perhaps Mr and Mrs Hamilton found themselves in a spot of bother and decided to fake Mr Hamilton's death."

"What sort of bother?"

"I don't know. Money troubles, perhaps. Maybe Beth is in on it."

"You seem determined not to trust her!"

"I just feel we need to be cautious about believing her version of events."

"Why would she approach us for help if she were in on it?"

"To make it seem more plausible, perhaps."

"It just doesn't make sense to me."

"All possibilities must be considered, Penny."

"I suppose you're also about to remind me that isn't enough evidence for the police to get involved at this stage."

"I'm afraid so."

"But the Hamiltons left the hotel without paying their bill. That's a crime, isn't it?"

"And the hotel manager has presumably reported it, Penny, but I can't imagine the Metropolitan Police spending a great deal of time on that. If they can't track down the chap and his wife, there isn't a great deal they can do about it. They're hardly about to start searching London for the pair when they've so many other things to be getting on with."

I shook my head. "I shall carry on with my enquiries," I said. "I'm determined to get to the bottom of all this, even if it is a ruse."

"Very well. But remember, trust no one."

"Beth Worthers, you mean?"

"I mean *anyone*, including Mrs Worthers."

"I've made the mistake of trusting the wrong people before, and I accept that it's a risk I shall have to take once again. But having started looking into this, I shan't be able to rest until I've found some answers."

James smiled. "Why doesn't that surprise me, Penny?" He cut one of the new blooms from the rose bush and handed it to me. "For the vase in your writing room."

CHAPTER 8

I went to the Holborn Restaurant the following day to meet Beth Worthers and John Smollett. They were seated in a corner and I had to weave my way between the tables of chatting diners to reach them.

Mr Smollett stood to his feet as I approached. "You must be the journalist Miss Somers was just telling me about," he said.

I gleaned from this that Beth hadn't yet revealed her true identity. "That's right. It's a pleasure to meet you."

He was dark-skinned with arched eyebrows, prominent cheekbones and thick, dark whiskers covering his jawline. His blue suit seemed a little ill-fitting, as though he were unable to afford a tailored one.

As we seated ourselves, I began to explain to Mr Smollett why I wished to speak with him.

"Miss Somers has already explained quite a lot," he politely interrupted. "To be honest, I had no concerns about Mr and Mrs Hamilton until now. I wondered why they left the hotel so suddenly, but I simply assumed there had been a disagreement that had left them both in a bad humour. My next assumption was that they had travelled on to Paris as planned."

"Maybe they did," I responded. "I've already sent a telegram to the hotel, so I should soon receive confirmation one way or another."

"I certainly hope that's where they are," he said. "I can't begin to entertain the thought that Mr Hamilton might be dead and that some awful fate may also have befallen his wife. It's too awful to even consider!"

"Hopefully the reply will confirm that they are safely arrived in Paris," I replied. "In the meantime, you mentioned that Miss Somers has explained a lot of this to you, but I think there's something quite important she needs to add before we continue our conversation."

I glanced over at Beth and saw her swallow uncomfortably. Mr Smollett turned to her, his brow furrowed.

"I didn't really want to do this," she began, "but I suppose it's for the best."

A short while later, after a sizeable glass of red wine, Mr Smollett appeared to have recovered himself.

"I had no idea at all," he said. "I'm ashamed and embarrassed to know that Mr Hamilton suspected that I should have any romantic interest in his wife! He's helped me a great deal, and I would never do anything to betray his trust. I wish he were here right now so I could tell him that nothing untoward has ever taken place between Mrs Hamilton and myself."

"But you're fond of her?" I asked.

"Yes, very fond. I certainly haven't ever committed adultery, though." He turned to Beth. "I think your decision to leave his employment was a sensible one. You never would have found evidence of anything unseemly between us."

"At the present time, I regret ever entering into his employment," she replied. "But there's nothing I can do about that now."

"Mrs Hamilton will be very disappointed when she finds out your true identity," said Mr Smollett. "She considered you a friend."

Beth looked down at her hands. "I realise that, and I feel terribly bad about it."

"Perhaps you could tell us a bit more about Mr and Mrs Hamilton," I said to Mr Smollett. "How long have you worked for them?"

"About nine months. I answered an advertisement I found in a newspaper last October. Mr Hamilton was looking for an assistant. He wanted someone who would be willing to travel and could sketch well. Bed and board were provided, but no salary was offered. I was struggling to find employment at the time, and it sounded like a very interesting job. I didn't mind the fact that I wouldn't be paid; I enjoyed sketching and wanted to travel.

"I met Mr Hamilton at a public house in Bermondsey, and he offered me the position. I was absolutely delighted when I discovered I would be spending time in Egypt. I rushed home to bid farewell to my mother and began the journey to Cairo with him the following day."

"And it was in Cairo that you met Mrs Hamilton, was it?"

"Yes. She was staying at Shepheard's Hotel. That's where everyone stays in Cairo before they travel up the Nile. We spent a few days there, and I visited a museum and a bazaar. The museum was extremely interesting but the bazaar wasn't so very different from Petticoat Lane market! It was just as crowded but a little more colourful, with more interesting smells. I had never come across some of those foods and spices before.

"Mr Hamilton hired a dahabeeyah – the type of boat they

use on the Nile. It's like a wide barge with a canvas canopy over the upper deck and two large sails. I've certainly never seen anything like it on the Thames! We sailed to Amarna, almost two hundred miles up the Nile from Cairo, and it was there that we worked on a dig with Joseph Bagshaw."

"Who's he?" I asked.

"Another Egyptologist. He and Mr Hamilton wanted to dig at the same location in Amarna, so they decided to work together."

"It sounds as though he would be an interesting person to speak to." I retrieved a notebook and pencil from my bag. "What's the best way to contact him?"

"I'm not sure of his address, but I know that he spends a lot of his time at the Cavendish Club."

I made a note of this information. "I shall write to him there. How long did the dig last?"

"We were there for much of last winter; almost three months in the end. I enjoyed it a great deal, and I'm hoping to go back. Mr and Mrs Hamilton are planning to travel out there this autumn, and I shall be accompanying them if all goes well."

"What sort of work did you carry out for Mr and Mrs Hamilton on your return to England?"

"I finished off my drawings and sketches, then painted several watercolours from them. I've also been cataloguing the treasures we found at Amarna, as well as various artefacts Mr and Mrs Hamilton had acquired from previous digs. They're all kept in storage now. I've also been assisting Mr and Mrs Hamilton with their day-to-day work. You know, managing their correspondence, assisting with speaking engagements, organising travel itineraries and that sort of thing. I enjoy it." He gave a broad smile that faded as quickly as it had appeared. "I can only hope that no harm has come to them. The Hamiltons are decent employers and have been paying me a salary since we returned to England, which means I can afford to rent a room now. I sincerely hope we hear from them soon."

"Why do you suppose Mr Hamilton suspected that you and his wife were committing adultery?"

"I really don't know." He rubbed his brow. "As I've already said, I feel ashamed that my friendly manner toward her seems to have been misconstrued."

"Is Mrs Hamilton happy in her marriage?"

"Yes." Mr Smollett seemed to think better of this reply and rubbed his brow again. "Actually, not always. Mr Hamilton has a temper, and it upsets her from time to time."

"Does she confide in you?"

He gave an awkward laugh. "Only in a manner that would be considered appropriate for a married lady."

"I'm not sure whether that means she did or she didn't."

"She has never behaved inappropriately."

"Has she ever confessed to being unhappy in her marriage?"

"She has hinted, on occasion, that she isn't entirely happy with her husband, but that's usually because he's just lost his temper about something. He's not a pleasant man to be around when that happens."

"Does it happen when he drinks alcohol?"

"Yes, sometimes."

"Does he drink often?"

"That's not for me to say! He enjoys a drink, and sometimes he takes a turn for the worse after consuming a fair bit. He's always been good to me, though, and I do enjoy my work. It's quite distressing to discover that he suspects my intentions. I wish he were here so I could allay his fears. I truly hope you're mistaken about him being dead, Mrs Worthers."

"How did Mrs Hamilton seem at the weekend?"

"Her normal self."

"And Mr Hamilton, too?"

"Yes."

"Neither appeared to be concerned about anything?"

"No."

"Had they argued at all?"

"Not that I know of."

"So their manner seemed completely normal to you. There was nothing out of the ordinary?"

"Completely normal."

"The Hamiltons's housekeeper stated that Mr Hamilton sometimes suffers from seizures. Have you ever witnessed it?"

"Seizures?" He raised his eyebrows in surprise. "No, that's not something I was aware of."

"Even though you were on a dig together for three months?"

"Perhaps he kept the truth from me. It's not something a man would be proud to admit, is it?"

"Is it possible," I ventured, "that Mrs Hamilton murdered her husband and then ran away?"

"No!" He scowled. "It's not at all possible! Have you ever met her, Mrs Blakely?"

"No."

"I thought as much. If you knew Susan – Mrs Hamilton, I mean –you'd realise she's completely incapable of doing such a thing!"

The heat of Mr Smollett's anger surprised me as he spat these words across the table. I felt relieved when the waiter arrived with our lunch and brought the conversation to a close.

I spent my return journey on the omnibus wondering how truthful Mr Smollett had been over lunch. *Had he told me everything he knew? Or did he have something to hide?*

A telegram was waiting for me when I arrived home, and I immediately saw that it was from the Martinez Hotel. Perhaps I shouldn't have been surprised by its contents:

Mr and Mrs Hamilton are not staying with us.

Had they booked another hotel instead? Or had they never arrived in the city at all? Was Mr Hamilton dead, as Beth claimed?

Another day had passed, yet few of my questions had been answered.

CHAPTER 9

"So what you're really saying, Mrs Blakely, is that a dead man somehow got up and ran out of that hotel." My former colleague at the *Morning Express* newspaper, Edgar Fish, steepled his fingers and regarded me with his small, beady eyes.

"No, that's not what I said at all."

"But you implied it," he replied. "Somehow you're still managing to find these fascinating stories even though you're no longer a news reporter. Why don't I find them? I'm currently writing an article about a new chapel at the Royal Asylum!"

"You had a good one yesterday," commented another former colleague, Frederick Potter.

"Did I?"

"About that chap who was caught stealing cabbages in Woolwich."

Edgar tutted. "I think it's time I looked for a new job."

"A new job, Fish?" We jumped as the editor, Mr Sherman, strode into the newsroom with papers in his hand, the door slamming behind him. His shirt sleeves were rolled up and he wore a blue serge waistcoat. His black hair was oiled and parted to one side.

"Oh, I didn't see you there, sir," said a flustered Edgar, his face colouring. "I was only joking."

"That's a shame," Mr Sherman responded. "You raised my hopes for a moment there. How's that article about the chapel coming along?"

"It's meandering along, sir."

"Well, it had better hurry up. I only need three hundred words. Do you have a picture?"

"Picture?"

"Yes, you know I want more pictures these days. Isn't there a sketch of the chapel we can use? Surely the Royal Asylum has commissioned one and will permit us to publish it. Find out, please." He turned and gave me a rare smile. "Mrs Blakely! It's always a pleasure to see you here. I can only guess that you have a story for us."

"She's got more than a story, sir," said Edgar. "It's a fantastical tale."

"Is it indeed? Let's hear it, then." He checked his pocket watch. "It had better not take longer than two minutes. I need to go downstairs and scold the compositors."

I told him, as quickly as I could, about the disappearance of the Hamiltons. "They're still missing," I added. "I think we should publish an appeal asking the public for help."

Mr Sherman stroked his chin. "So we have a man found dead in his room who subsequently vanishes, and then his wife vanishes, too. But the police aren't investigating because there's no evidence he's dead, you say?"

"That's right."

"What about that husband of yours?"

"He's very interested, but his hands are tied because there's no official evidence that any crime has been committed. Other than Mr Hamilton not paying his hotel bill."

"Rather impossible to do so if one is dead."

"How is that schoolboy inspector of yours these days?" asked Edgar with a grin. "Do pass on my regards."

"I'm sure he'll be extremely grateful to receive them," the editor responded. He turned back to me. "Something's clearly afoot here. How long is it since they were last seen?"

"Five days, sir."

"And they never arrived in Paris?"

"They're not at the hotel where they had planned to stay."

"Interesting. It's certainly an intriguing story, and I think our readers would very much enjoy learning about it. Knowing you, Mrs Blakely, you're already making attempts to get to the bottom of it all."

"I am indeed, sir. I'm hopeful that someone who reads the story may be able to help. Someone who knows the Hamiltons, or who was staying at the hotel at the same time and may have seen something significant."

"How did your friend come to be involved? You said she was with Mrs Hamilton while her husband was supposedly being murdered, and then found Mr Hamilton dead. Is that right?"

"She's a private detective, sir. I'd prefer to keep her name private for now, as she doesn't want too many people knowing her true identity."

"Working undercover, was she?"

"Something like that."

"I presume you've ruled her out as the culprit?"

"I haven't even considered her as the culprit, sir."

"Have you not? That's rather unlike you, Mrs Blakely. Don't you think there's a possibility she might have come up with this unusual story to cover her own tracks?"

I faltered. I felt sure that Beth would never do such a thing, but it seemed foolish to assume so when Mr Sherman put it like that. "What I need to do is gather more information, sir. I need to speak to more people who know the Hamiltons. The people I've spoken to so far haven't really imparted much useful information."

"You're a good journalist, Mrs Blakely, so I'm sure you'll find someone who can be a little more helpful before long."

"Would you be willing to publish an appeal for information?"

"I'd want five hundred words on the disappearance, and then we can put an appeal at the end. Dead men don't just walk out of hotels; we need an explanation. I'm disappointed in the police, though. I'd have thought they'd want to solve this one."

"It's possible that the Hamiltons purposefully disappeared. Mr Hamilton may even have faked his own death."

The editor rubbed his hands together. "Excellent! That would be a wonderful story, wouldn't it? The Egyptologist who faked his own death. If that's the case, you really must track him down. This could turn into quite the saga."

CHAPTER 10

"I noticed that you and Mr Blakely had nothing to keep your teapot warm," said Beth the following Monday as she handed me a soft parcel wrapped in brown paper and string. We were walking along the riverside in Battersea Park, a short distance from Beth's home.

"That's very kind." I stopped and examined the parcel in my hand. "Is this one of your knitting projects?"

She smiled. "Why don't you open it and see?"

Inside was a knitted tea cosy with bright orange and yellow stripes.

"How very thoughtful of you! Thank you. It must have taken you some time to make."

"Not really. I've made lots of them for friends and family. Now your teapot will stay warm for a little longer."

"It will indeed!"

I tucked the gift inside my carpet bag and we continued on our way.

The morning breeze rustled in the trees, and families and couples promenaded around us. On the opposite riverbank lay Chelsea; its rooftops and chimneys peeking through the tree-lined embankment.

"What is your opinion of Mr Smollett?" I asked Beth.

"I think he felt rather ashamed that Mr Hamilton should suspect him of committing adultery with his wife, and he was doing his best to pretend that there was no attraction between them."

"I suppose he wouldn't want to admit it. He's probably rather embarrassed that his feelings for Mrs Hamilton were more obvious to others than he had realised. Do you consider him to be trustworthy?"

"Yes, although I think he was trying to protect his reputation. And Susan's, too. I imagine he'll continue to deny that they had any affection for one another."

"What evidence did you see of their mutual affection?" I asked.

"Oh, certain glances and smiles between them, and they sometimes took walks together when Mr Hamilton wasn't around. I never caught them in a fond embrace or found any romantic notes. That said, I felt increasingly reluctant to report any unusual activities to Mr Hamilton as I found my sympathies turning toward his wife."

"Did she confide in you about any affection she might have had for Mr Smollett?"

"Shortly before she disappeared, Susan told me she enjoyed Mr Smollett's company and wished to spend more time with him."

"How did she envisage doing that while she was married to another man?"

"She didn't get a chance to explain. I suppose it was a confirmation that she was considering a love affair with him."

"But you didn't impart this information to Mr Hamilton?"

"No. I felt she deserved to enjoy some happiness with Mr Smollett, and I had no desire to scupper her chances of it. I had resolved to leave my employment by that stage, and no longer felt duty-bound to report back to Mr Hamilton on everything I saw. I considered telling Susan her husband suspected her, but that would have meant unmasking myself as a detective. I simply couldn't face it. She thought I was a friend. She trusted me!"

"It was brave of you to take on a job that required such..."

"Deception?"

"I was going to say dedication."

"But it was deceptive. I've done a good many jobs like this in the past and never felt guilty as a result. But the reality is, I did on this occasion. I like Susan because she reminds me of my sister. I wasn't prepared for my feelings to interfere with my work. And now I desperately want to find her and tell her the truth, but the reality is..." She turned away to look at the river. "I may never see her again."

"But you might well do," I responded, keen to reassure her. "We're trying to find her, aren't we? I shan't give up until I can find out exactly what has happened to Mrs Hamilton and her husband."

She turned back to face me and smiled. "Thank you, Penny. That's why I asked for your help."

"We must remain hopeful. Do you think there's any chance that Mr Smollett knows where she is?"

"Do you think he was lying to us?"

"It's a possibility. Perhaps he helped her get away somehow. Maybe he even helped her hide Mr Hamilton's body."

"No, that's quite impossible. He would never do anything of the sort. And that also implies that Susan would do such a thing, and I've already told you that's impossible."

I decided not to pursue the idea any further, as it seemed to irritate her every time I suggested such a thing. "We really must find her," I said. "I need you to tell me everything you know in case there's a hidden clue somewhere. We'll need to talk to friends and family members, and find out about locations that are important to her, such as the area she grew up in and the places she liked to visit."

"She mentioned that her parents were both dead. I don't remember her mentioning any other family members."

"You said that she hails from Rochdale in Lancashire, did you not?"

"Yes, but I don't think she had been back there for a long time."

"The Willis family, is that right? I remember you saying her father was a clergyman. That gives us a starting point at least."

"She didn't talk about herself a great deal."

"It's possible that she may have gone back to Rochdale, isn't it?"

"I suppose so, but I'm not sure why she would go there if her parents are both dead. She didn't mention any other family members, but perhaps she has an aunt or uncle there. Or cousins, maybe."

"What else did she tell you about herself?"

"Not a great deal. She changed the topic relatively quickly after mentioning that her parents were dead, so I suspected she had been very hurt by their loss. I felt it would have been inconsiderate of me to ask too many questions about them. I was interested, of course, and I suppose I assumed I would ultimately learn more about them as I got to know her better.

"She wasn't the sort of lady who was interested in idle gossip. We only really talked about meaningful matters; events we'd read about in the newspaper, for example, and Egyptology. That topic is a passion of hers, and she enjoyed sharing what she had learned with me." Beth paused and looked out over the river again. "There were many times during those conversations when I longed to tell her who I really was. I feel so awfully guilty about it now."

"You were just doing your job."

"I know." She turned to look at me again. "But she thought I was a friend."

"And you were. You considered her a friend, too, didn't you?"

"Yes. But friends should always be truthful with one another. Otherwise there's no trust, is there?"

"You can explain all this to her when we find her."

"I hope we can."

"Did she tell you how she met her husband?"

"They met on a boat trip up the Nile and fell in love."

"That sounds rather romantic."

"It does, although I struggle to imagine Mr Hamilton being romantic in any way. In fact, I'm not sure how he appealed to her at all. I imagine she was feeling the loss of her parents rather keenly and he offered her comfort at a time when she needed it most. They were both extremely interested in exploring Egypt, and I suppose their shared interest was what brought them together."

We reached Albert Bridge, which spanned the Thames between Battersea and Chelsea. From there, our path turned away from the river and into the park. I began to feel more confident now that we had enough information to start our search for Susan Hamilton.

"A trip to Rochdale would likely tell us a good deal more about her past," I said. "Perhaps we might even find her there." I paused to consider the article I was working on for the *Morning Express*, as well as my work for various other publications. "It'll be difficult to find the time, though. A visit would take up two days at the very least."

"I have the time to go," she responded. "I haven't taken on any more work since this upset with the Hamiltons."

"Are you sure?"

"Of course."

"And you don't mind travelling alone?"

She laughed. "I know it's not the usual custom for a lady, but I'm quite used to it."

"It would be extremely helpful if you were able to go," I said. "I'm sure it wouldn't be too difficult to find someone who knew Reverend Willis and his family. Perhaps Mr and Mrs Hamilton even married there. Parish registers should be able to tell you more."

"I shall send off a letter to book my hotel accommodation as soon as I return home this afternoon," she said. "I suppose I'll need to take a train to Manchester and then another on from there."

"I imagine it would be about five hours of travelling," I said. "Are you sure you don't mind the journey?"

"Not at all. I'm quite accustomed to travel. I can while away the time with my knitting. In fact, I'm quite looking forward to it!"

CHAPTER 11

I wished Beth luck on her journey and made my way across the river to Chelsea. Once over the bridge, I walked the short distance to the Copeland Hotel.

I paused outside the building and surveyed its exterior. Surely someone had seen something suspicious the night Mr Hamilton was reportedly murdered. Eight days had passed since the supposed crime and I felt frustrated by our lack of progress. I could only hope that Beth would have more success during her visit to Rochdale.

The attendant behind the reception desk was occupied with a group of guests, so I took the opportunity to walk through the foyer and up the staircase without having to explain why I was there.

Once up on the third floor, I strode along the dingy corridor toward room 306. Before I reached it, I stopped beside a maid's trolley outside room 304.

I peered in through the open door. "Hello?" I called out.

A young maid wearing a starched cap and apron appeared. She had a duster in her hand. "Can I 'elp you, madam?"

"Have you heard about the disappearance of Mr and Mrs

Hamilton?" I asked. "The Egyptologists who left without paying their bill?"

Her brow dropped. "Yeah, I remember all right, but I ain't got time ter talk. I gotta get the rooms clean."

"A shilling for your time?"

She half turned her head toward me and observed me out of the corner of her eye. "Who are you?

"My name is Mrs Blakely and I'm a friend of the Hamiltons. I'm worried about their disappearance and am trying to gather as much information as I can about what happened that night."

"You'd best talk to the manager. Fortescue's 'is name."

"I already have, but there were a few small details I asked him that he wasn't able to help me with. He's a busy man, isn't he?"

Her face softened a little. "That 'e is."

"Were you working here the night the Hamiltons disappeared?"

"Yeah, I work 'ere all the time."

"Did you come across them?"

"What about that shillin'?"

I retrieved my purse from my carpet bag and handed her the coin.

"I ain't got long, as I say. And I ain't allowed to stop an' chat."

"I'll make this as quick as possible. Did you see Mr and Mrs Hamilton during their stay?"

"Yeah, jus' comin' and goin'."

"Did anything strike you as unusual about their time here?"

"'Ow d'you mean?"

"Any items in the room you weren't expecting to see? Perhaps they had more luggage or belongings than you might expect for a few nights' stay?"

"Nothin' like that, no. I remember thinkin' they was nice. Mrs Hamilton was, any'ow. Polite lady, she was. Spoke nice to us maids. A lot o' them treat us like we're nothin', see. But she was nice, and I remember thinkin' it were strange that a lady like 'er would do a runner. There jus' ain't no tellin' with some folk."

"They left all their belongings in the room, did they not?"

"Yeah."

"And there was no sign that they'd taken anything with them?"

"I dunno if they took anyfink with 'em or not. From what I seen they left most o' their pers'nal belongin's. Clothes in the wardrobe and toothbrushes on the washstand. We packed everythin' up all careful. The cases are proberly still in the storage room for all I know."

"Their housekeeper told me she would send someone to collect them."

"P'raps they 'ave. I wouldn't know."

"You gathered up their belongings on the Sunday morning, did you?"

"Yeah, it would've been the Sunday."

"Did it appear as though the Hamiltons's bed had been slept in the previous night?"

"Nah, it 'adn't been. The bedcovers 'adn't been turned down, neither.

"Are the covers usually turned down each evening?"

"Yeah."

"Then why weren't the covers on the Hamiltons's bed turned down that Saturday evening?"

"They told us not to."

"You saw them in their room that Saturday evening, did you?"

"Didn't see 'em, as such. Just 'eard 'em through the door."

"What time was this?"

"Lemme think. We normally start turnin' the covers down around eight o'clock. We did the rooms on the first and second floor afore we come up 'ere."

"What time might that have been?"

"'Bout half-past eight, I s'pose."

This didn't make any sense to me. Beth had found Mr Hamilton on the floor of his room at around ten minutes to eight. "So you heard Mr and Mrs Hamilton in their room at half-past eight?"

"Yeah."

"Did you speak to them through the door?"

"That's right."

"How can you be sure that it was them?"

"It must've been. Who else could it've been?"

"And it was definitely room 306? It couldn't have been guests from another room?"

"It 'ad to be 306 'cause I remember thinkin' everythin' was all right again after they thought 'e was dead."

"What was the nature of their conversation? Did it seem normal to you, or did you hear raised voices?"

"No raised voices. It was all jus' normal."

"Did you hear Mrs Hamilton's voice?"

"Yeah, I fink so."

"And which of them spoke to you through the door?"

"Must've been Mr 'Amilton. It was a man's voice. Told me 'e didn't want 'is covers turnin' down."

"And the next time you visited the room was when you were asked to pack up their belongings, was it?"

"Yeah."

I wondered if the maid was aware that Beth had raised the alarm after finding Mr Hamilton's body.

"A friend of mine, who was here with the Hamiltons, told me she knocked on the door of room 306 at about ten minutes to eight that evening," I explained. "When there was no answer, she tried the handle and found the door unlocked. She went inside and found Mr Hamilton lying on the floor. She went to fetch help, but by the time she returned to the room with assistance it was empty."

"Sounds about right. Everyone was rushin' round for ten minutes, but 'e weren't on the floor and the room was empty. We 'ad a look round the 'otel for 'em, but there weren't no sign."

"And yet you say that you heard them in their room about half an hour later?"

"Yeah, they was back in there by then."

"But you didn't actually see them."

"Nah."

"Did you think it odd that they wouldn't let you into the room to turn down the bedcovers?"

"I didn't fink nuffink of it. Guests don't always want us in their rooms, see. Any'ow, I gotta be gettin' on now, madam. Nice talkin' to yer."

The maid's story didn't tie in with what Beth had told me. I felt my brow furrow. "Just a couple more questions, please." I rummaged around in my purse and pulled out another shilling, which I handed to her. "When you packed up their belongings the following morning, were there any signs of a struggle in the room?"

"Things knocked over, yer mean?"

"Yes. Or perhaps something out of place. Something that hadn't been put back in its correct position."

"I didn't notice nuffink like that."

"Any sign of any rugs or carpets having been cleaned? Or walls wiped, perhaps?"

"Why'd someone wanna do that?"

"To tidy up after themselves."

She shook her head. "Nah. We packed their cases, dusted

like we always do, swept the rug an' changed the linen. There weren't nuffink broken or out o' place."

"What do you think happened that evening? My friend is quite adamant that she found Mr Hamilton lying on the floor."

"P'raps she did. He must of recovered in time, I s'pose."

"But then he and his wife disappeared."

She shrugged. "I dunno, madam. All I know's what I saw and 'eard, and that's what I've told yer. I'll be in trouble if I keep talkin' any longer."

"Of course."

I thanked the maid for her help and went on my way.

On my way out, I encountered the tall, lean hotelier, Mr Fortescue, standing beside one of the spiky palm trees. I felt an uncomfortable twinge in my stomach. *Would he be annoyed to see me inside his hotel again?*

"Can I just say, Mrs Blakely, how much I enjoyed your father's performance at the weekend?" he said. "He was wonderfully entertaining, and I've been recommending the show to all my guests. I believe tonight is the final show, is that right?"

"Yes, I think so."

"I hope he's able to put more on soon. Do please let him know, won't you? Tell him that Mr Fortescue, manager of the Copeland, and his good wife had a thoroughly enjoyable time."

"I will do. He'll be pleased to hear it."

"Have you solved the Hamilton mystery yet?"

"I'm afraid not."

He shook his head. "Most odd. Mind you, I mustn't grumble about them any longer. The Hamiltons's house-keeper arranged for their bill to be paid and sent a man to collect their belongings. As far as we're concerned, the matter's over and dealt with."

"But my friend is convinced that she saw Mr Hamilton dead in his room."

"I understand. And we did everything we possibly could to deal with her concern at the time. We searched the place from top to bottom, but there was no sign of him! It really is a puzzle."

CHAPTER 12

"That's an interesting hat," commented James when he saw Beth's gift lying on the table that evening. "Or is it a bonnet of some sort?"

"It's a tea cosy."

"An outfit for the teapot!" He gave a bemused smile. "Shall we see if it fits?"

He picked up the tea cosy and walked into the dining room, where the teapot was sitting on the sideboard. I followed behind him.

"It fits perfectly," said James, pulling the woollen cosy over the teapot. "And very colourful, too!" He stood back to admire it.

I couldn't resist a giggle.

"What's so funny?" he asked.

"I never thought I'd see you so enamoured with a knitted tea cosy."

"I've never seen one I like quite so much! It's cheering me up after a tedious day at the Yard."

"Perhaps I should ask Beth to knit us some more!"

"I'd like one for each day of the week." He grinned.

"She'll have time to knit at least one more while she's travelling up to Rochdale."

"Why Rochdale?"

"That's where Mrs Hamilton comes from. There's a possibility she may have gone back there."

"Is that right? Let's hope Beth finds her, in that case. We'd certainly have a few questions answered if so, wouldn't we?"

"Yes. At the moment it seems as though the more questions I ask, the more confused I become."

As we moved into the front room, I told James about my conversation with the chambermaid. Tiger was asleep in James's favourite chair, so he had to make do with the settee.

"How could Mr Hamilton have been dead at ten minutes to eight, yet heard chatting to his wife at half-past eight?" I asked once I had finished summarising the conversation. "It makes no sense."

"Either Beth or the maid must be mistaken. Perhaps the maid was thinking of the previous evening. Or another pair of guests entirely."

"It's possible. She seemed adamant that it was the same room and the same evening, however. She recalls the search for Mr Hamilton after he had supposedly been found dead in his room, and she told me she had felt reassured when everything seemed all right again afterwards."

"Except that it wasn't all right, was it? The Hamiltons had vanished."

"They had indeed."

"Perhaps they're both alive and well in Rochdale."

"Beth is certain that Mr Hamilton was dead."

"Yet everything she's told us so far has been contradicted by the chambermaid."

I sighed. No one had been able to corroborate Beth's story. *Was it possible that I was being too trusting of her?* "I still believe her," I added.

"You *want* to believe her."

"Yes, I do! Perhaps I'm being foolish, but at least her story gives us something to work on. If it turns out to be a lie, well…" I shook my head. "I shall work out how to cope with that if I discover it to be so."

"It'll be interesting to see how she gets on in Rochdale."

"Yes, it will. In the meantime, I'll set about getting my article for the *Morning Express* finished and arrange to speak to Mr Bagshaw."

"Who's he?"

"Another Egyptologist, whom the Hamiltons spent some time with on a dig. I'll write him a letter now."

James checked his pocket watch. "Aren't we supposed to be having dinner with your father this evening?"

"Yes."

"And don't we need to leave in half an hour?"

"Yes. I'd better get on with it!"

CHAPTER 13

"The shows have come to an end," said my father over dinner. "I had a wonderful time, but I'm sorry there will be no more performances at the Royal Court Theatre for the time being."

I glanced across the table at Francis Edwards and noticed that he didn't appear particularly sorry.

"Mr Fortescue, manager of the Copeland Hotel, told me to inform you that he thoroughly enjoyed the show," I said.

Father smiled proudly. "Thank you, Penny. That's wonderful to hear. And actually, I have some more good news. Mr Hoddinott, our director, would like to take a similar show on tour around the country. How wonderful is that?"

"You won't be going with him, will you, Francis?" asked Eliza.

"No. I have my job at the library to attend to."

"I thought so." Eliza seemed relieved by this.

"We've discussed all that," replied my father. "Mr Hoddinott says we can substitute Francis with an actor. He's also suggested a few additions that could make it a little more entertaining."

"And what might they be?" asked James.

Father shifted in his seat and gave a nervous cough. "Well, Mr Hoddinott has asked whether Malia and the children could be involved in the show."

"To be paraded around on stage?" I queried.

"Yes, that's the idea."

My father's common-law wife Malia and their children were currently en route to England from South America. Father had decided not to return to Amazonia just yet, so had arranged for his family to join him on British soil instead. It alarmed me to think of them appearing on stage as a novelty act; not dissimilar to the popular human zoos staged at large fairs, in which unfortunate people described as natives were paraded around in their traditional costume to be marvelled at by strangers. I thought of the misery I had seen in their faces.

"That can't be right," I said. "The show is about your adventures. It wouldn't be fair on your family to force them to participate. Especially not the children."

"I agree about the children," said Father. "I don't think they should be made to go on stage at this present time, and it's important for them to attend school. They'll find themselves dwelling in quite a different culture here, and I need to ensure that they're able to learn the language and earn themselves an education. But Malia may be intrigued by the proposition."

"But will she really know what it would entail? She would be brought on stage as a novelty for people to stare at."

"She's more than a novelty. She's my wife!"

"She is to you, but what of the audience? They will be there to stare at her, and I think she might find it an uncomfortable experience."

"Well, Penny, I'm afraid that's for myself and Malia to decide," replied my father, "and that's all there is to it. The audience may well come to stare, but they'll be paying good money to do so. It's expensive to maintain a good standard of living for five children, you know."

"*Seven* children if you include Penny and me," commented Eliza.

"Yes, but you both have your own income. You had the sense to marry and divorce a rich man, Eliza. And Penny has earned her own money. At least I don't need to worry about you two."

"There was never any danger of that," said Eliza a little sourly. No doubt she was thinking of his endless travels abroad followed by ten years of silence while he was missing, assumed dead.

"I'm sure you and Malia will be able to come to an agreement, Father," I said cheerily. "In the meantime, James and I have been given rather a puzzling case to work on." I briefly described the strange disappearance of Mr and Mrs Hamilton.

"Goodness me! That really is rather puzzling," said Eliza once I had finished. "Although I don't see why you need to get involved, Penelope. I think you should leave your friend to it. You're busy enough as it is!"

"But I want to be involved," I replied. "And she asked for my help."

Eliza rolled her eyes. "I had hoped marriage would calm you down a little, but it seems you still have these little whims—"

"It's not a whim!" I snapped. "Two people have vanished, one of whom has possibly been murdered. My friend has been caught up in it and needs my help!"

"It's certainly an interesting case," said James calmly, trying to defuse the tension as Eliza and I glared at each other. "And Penny has done some excellent work on it so far. She's a skilled investigator, you know."

"Thank you, James," I replied. "Although I realise you're bound to say nice things about me given that you're my husband."

"Egyptology," mused Francis. "I must admit that ancient Egypt is one of my favourite topics, too. If you need any help with that side of things, just let me know."

"Don't encourage her, Francis," scolded my sister.

"Oh, I say encourage her," interjected my father. "I think it all sounds excellent. Let's drink to the health of the ancient Egyptians!"

He held up his glass and we all did the same.

James and I exchanged a baffled glance at the unusual toast. I knew he often found dinner with my family amusing, and tonight was no exception.

CHAPTER 14

A lady called Mrs Palmer contacted the *Morning Express* office as soon as the article about Mr and Mrs Hamilton was published. She suggested we meet for lunch at a restaurant close to Fleet Street.

"What a mystery!" she proclaimed once I had introduced myself. "Who'd have thought the Hamiltons could disappear like that?"

She was about sixty years of age and wore a lavender dress and a large matching hat with shiny artificial fruit glued to it. Her lips were stained a deep purple, which I found myself becoming a little distracted by as she spoke.

"How well do you know Mr and Mrs Hamilton?" I asked.

"Quite well. They both happen to be members of the Ancient Egypt Society I helped found. They've attended a number of meetings and events over the past year or so, and I've also spent time with them out in Egypt, of course. Have you ever been to Egypt?"

"No, I haven't."

"Well, you simply must go. It's a wonderful place. The historical monuments are absolutely astounding! Did you know that the Great Pyramid is more than four thousand years old? It was constructed before the birth of Abraham. Its base covers more than thirteen square acres, and the pyramid is estimated to contain more than half a million stones. To think that an ancient civilisation was able to build such a thing!

"Now is such a tremendous time to explore Egypt, because it's recently become a British protectorate. My fellow society members and I were delighted when the Khedivate fell and Egypt became our playground! There really is no excuse not to go, Mrs Blakely."

"I should like to go one day. When did you last see Mr and Mrs Hamilton, Mrs Palmer?"

"At the drinks reception just before dinner on the Saturday evening of our event. Mr Hamilton left the room, then his wife followed him, but no one appears to have seen either of them since. The hotel manager was rather angry that they left the hotel without settling their bill."

"Doing so was out of character for them, was it?"

"Yes! Mr Hamilton would never usually do such a thing. He's not a gentleman, I should make that clear," she gave a polite laugh, "but he has made an effort to educate himself, and his manners are perfectly acceptable. I should add that nobody is ever refused membership of the Ancient Egypt Society on account of their background. Our members are admitted based on their demonstration of a knowledge and passion for the subject. That's why I personally admitted Mr Hamilton to the society. I very much hope he'll be found safe and well."

"A friend of mine believes that she found him dead."

"Yes, so your article said. Her name was Miss Somers, was it not?"

"That's right."

"Well, I can't say I understand that at all. Perhaps the

young woman had a little too much wine at the drinks reception!" She laughed again. "There was a brief hullaballoo overheard from the lobby and then the evening's frivolities resumed. I did think it odd that the Hamiltons never arrived for dinner, but I felt they must have had their reasons. It was no business of mine!"

"Was there any indication that Mr and Mrs Hamilton were upset about anything?"

"Such as?"

"Anything to suggest that they weren't their usual selves?"

"They were their normal selves, all right. Mr Hamilton was rather loud and enthusiastic. Cantankerous at times, too. He can be quite argumentative when he chooses to be. Mrs Hamilton was quiet, demure and terribly pretty. Awfully clever, too. I'd even venture to say that she's cleverer than her husband, although she doesn't show off about it. She hides her light under a bushel, so to speak."

"Do you think them mismatched as a couple?"

"What an odd question! What do you mean by that?"

"There's quite a difference in age between them. About twenty years, I believe. And their backgrounds are also very different."

"Like chalk and cheese."

"Yes."

"Nothing wrong with that, though. I always think it dreadfully boring when a husband and wife are too similar."

"When did you realise that their disappearance was a cause for concern?"

"Only when I read your article in the *Morning Express*! I had no idea they hadn't turned up in Paris, or that they had left all their belongings at the hotel. That really is rather puzzling, and I'm worried some sort of harm may have come to them. The whole affair has quite shaken our little society.

"It's such a shame, because the event went extremely well.

We had a delightful dinner on the Friday night and a day of fascinating lectures on the Saturday. Everything ran like clockwork; the hotel did such a fabulous job.

"It all came about after the hotel owner, Mr Fortescue, approached me and asked if I would consider hosting an event with him. He offered us an excellent discount on the hall hire and room rates. If I'm honest, I think he had some sort of ulterior motive. He's rather keen to create a loyal customer base, I suspect. There's a fair bit of competition between him and the hotel next door, you see. Between you and me, I think he'd been losing out on business.

"Anyway, he did an excellent job of hosting us, and one could argue that the Hamiltons ruined it a little by leaving without paying for their room. On the other hand, if they came to any sort of harm... Well, it seems rather unfair to blame them for that. But the whole affair is rather an ink stain on what seemed to have been the most perfect weekend."

"Is it possible, do you think, that Mr and Mrs Hamilton have travelled to Egypt on a secret expedition?" I asked.

"An expedition they wanted no one to know about, you mean?"

"Yes."

"Impossible! No one gets to do anything in Egypt these days without someone hearing about it. If one wants to travel, one has to hire a boat and people to sail it. If one's on a dig, one needs people to haul buckets of sand and earth, and what have you. One also needs people to see to one's everyday needs, such as food and drink. And one couldn't possibly stay at Shepheard's Hotel, because absolutely everybody stays there. One would be spotted immediately."

"Could someone stay in Cairo without being noticed?"

"Possibly, but I should think it very unlikely for Mr and Mrs Hamilton. Their faces are well known about the place, you see. And besides, why go to Egypt in the extremely hot summertime? The best time to travel there is from October onwards. No one in their right mind would go digging up the desert at this time of year."

I tried to ignore the distracting purple lips and remain focused on my questions.

"You mentioned that Mr Hamilton could be rather cantankerous. Is it possible that he upset someone?"

"Of course it is! He's always upsetting people. He isn't a gentleman, as I've said."

"Do you know whether he fell out with anyone while he was staying at the Copeland?"

"No one that I know of, but I can tell you now that he almost certainly will have done. He's that sort of a fellow. Perfectly pleasant and entertaining, but he doesn't half irritate people. He'll have made up with them again afterwards. That's just his personality, I'm afraid."

"Is there anyone he often falls out with?"

"If I were pushed to think of someone who probably wouldn't invite him to a dinner party, I'd have to say Joseph Bagshaw."

"I've heard his name mentioned before. The two spent time together on a dig, is that right?"

"Yes, and they really did fall out with one another. Bagshaw is just as grumpy as Hamilton can be sometimes, so it's difficult to know who was really at fault there."

"I've already written to Mr Bagshaw to request a meeting with him."

"I hope he agrees to speak to you. We haven't seen him at our society meetings for a little while, and I've been far too busy to contact him because I've had such a lot to manage since your article was published. Various members of the society have contacted me to ask me what our position is."

"And what is it?"

"It's a position of concern for two of our well-respected members. May they both be found safe and well. Our members are rather upset about the whole affair."

"Could you please let me know if any of your members are able to shed light on the whereabouts of Mr and Mrs Hamilton?" I gave her my card.

"Of course."

CHAPTER 15

eth Worthers returned from Rochdale that evening.
She had sent a telegram ahead of her departure to let
me know, so I decided to wait for her at Euston
station. I hoped she would have some useful information to
tell me, as her telegram had imparted frustratingly little about
how her search for Mrs Hamilton had gone.

My lunch with Mrs Palmer had felt like a waste of time.
She appeared to enjoy the attention more than anything else,
and had suggested at the end of our lunch that I write an
article about the activities of the Ancient Egypt Society for
the *Morning Express*.

Shortly after seven o'clock, the express train from
Manchester pulled in to platform nine. I peered at the throng
of people making their way through the clouds of steam,
eagerly searching for Beth. She eventually appeared wearing a
light-brown travelling coat and a plain bonnet. Her face
appeared tired and disappointed.

"Any luck?" I asked hopefully.

She shook her head.

. . .

"Perhaps I got it wrong," said Beth as we dined on mutton chops and sipped tea in the station dining room. "Perhaps it wasn't Rochdale she came from after all."

"But you were sure Mrs Hamilton had told you she grew up there, weren't you?"

"Yes, quite sure. But I couldn't find anyone who had heard of a Reverend Willis there, and I asked a great many people. I found a couple of families with the surname Willis, but they weren't aware of there being a reverend in their family. Neither did they know of any reverend's daughter who had travelled to Egypt. It's quite puzzling."

After the wasted time I had spent with Mrs Palmer, this came as another disappointment. I sipped my tea and tried to feel some sympathy for Beth. She seemed weary and had clearly tried to find some clue as to Mrs Hamilton's whereabouts. *But had she tried hard enough?* I began to wish I had accompanied her. *Perhaps I would have been able to track Mrs Hamilton down myself.* Then I felt ashamed of myself for doubting Beth's investigating abilities. She had worked as a private detective for years. Surely she was skilled at it.

"I feel like I've let you down," she said, as if she were reading my mind.

"No, of course you haven't! You did your very best with the limited information we had. Cases like this can be frustrating, and dead ends are unavoidable."

"I suppose so."

"I spoke to a maid at the Copeland Hotel a couple of days ago," I ventured. "She told me she heard Mr and Mrs Hamilton in their room at half-past eight the evening they went missing."

She frowned. "That's impossible."

"I realise that. Perhaps she was mistaken about the time. She didn't see them, however, so perhaps it wasn't the Hamiltons at all. I'm beginning to wonder if what she heard were the voices of the people who murdered him."

"The only person in that room at ten to eight was Mr Hamilton himself," she replied, "and he was dead. I don't know how the maid could possibly suggest that he was alive and well forty minutes later."

"Me neither." I decided not to push the issue any further, given that Beth was clearly tired and fed up following her fruitless trip to Rochdale. "I think we need to speak to Mr Smollett again," I said. "He must be able to tell us something more. Would you mind asking if he'd be willing to do so?"

"Of course."

"I have another idea, too," I continued. "Go home and get some rest, then meet me tomorrow at ten outside the British Museum."

Beth looked a lot brighter the following day. A bit of rest and the morning sunshine appeared to have helped lift her mood.

"Are we here for the museum or the library?" she asked.

"The library, of course!" I grinned. "And more specifically, a place that's almost as comfortable to me as home: the reading room."

"I've never been in there before. You're hoping to find something that will help with our investigation, are you?"

"Yes. We'll to look for records relating to a Reverend Willis. You don't have a reading ticket, so we'll have to ask Francis Edwards very nicely if he'll let you in."

"Before I forget..." Beth reached into her bag. "I knitted this for your cat."

"For Tiger?"

She handed me a small parcel wrapped in brown paper and string. "You can open it now if you like."

I did so and found a little grey knitted mouse inside. "Thank you, Beth! She'll love it. It's very kind of you."

She shrugged. "My pleasure. It was a long train journey!"

"I shall be in big trouble if the head librarian finds out," whispered Francis as he regarded Beth with a frown.

"We won't be long," I responded. "He won't even notice that Mrs Worthers is here. We need to look up a vicar, Francis."

"*Crockford's Clerical Directory*? I recall you looking for vicars in there before. Makes me wonder what a respectable man of the cloth could possibly have been getting up to."

"There's no evidence that the one we're looking for has committed any wrongdoing."

"Well, that's a relief. Is he an Anglican?"

"I don't know."

"If you don't know, you'll probably want to look in the *Catholic Directory Ecclesiastical Register and Almanac*."

"He has a daughter. Surely that means he can't be a Catholic priest."

"One would hope not. You could try the nonconformists, though. The *Baptist Handbook* or *The Congregational Year Book* may be of use."

"It sounds as though we've quite a few directories to look through."

"You may be longer than you expected." He gave Beth another suspicious glance. "Can I trust your friend? She looks like a bit of a troublemaker."

Beth gave him an indignant look.

"I'm joking of course," he swiftly added with a grin. "Do you remember where the directories are, Penny?"

"Yes."

"Just don't do anything that might lead to the head

librarian wanting to check your reading tickets. I'll be done for if he does."

"You have my word. Thank you, Francis."

Beth and I found a desk as far away from the head librarian's dais as possible. Looking through *Crockford's Clerical Directory*, we found twelve entries with the surname Willis, but none with any link to Rochdale.

"Perhaps we should look in the other directories Francis suggested," I said.

Within half an hour we had identified and made notes about a fair number of clergymen named Willis, but Rochdale still wasn't listed alongside any of them.

"I suppose we'd better write down the place names we don't recognise and look them up in an atlas to find out if they're anywhere close," suggested Beth.

I found a weighty atlas of the British Isles and returned to the desk with it. It was at this point that the head librarian began a tour of the reading room. A plump, round-faced man, he sauntered around with his hands clasped behind his back.

My heart began to pound. "Keep your head down and don't look at him," I whispered to Beth.

How this would help us I wasn't sure, but it seemed the most sensible thing to do.

We remained silent and scribbled furiously in our notebooks as the head librarian walked slowly past. He paused for a moment and observed us before walking on.

"Thank goodness for that," I whispered.

It took us a while to look up the location of each Reverend Willis. The closest match we found was a minister in Blackburn, which was roughly twenty miles from Rochdale. We imagined he was probably too old to be Mrs

Hamilton's father given that he had been ordained in 1820. We appeared to have reached another dead end.

"Is it possible that Mrs Hamilton wasn't completely truthful about her past?" I asked Beth.

"Why should she lie about her father?"

"I don't know. I just cannot understand why we've been unable to find any record of him. Not only is he missing from these directories, but you were unable to find a single person who knew him or his family in Rochdale. It makes me wonder whether she invented him entirely."

"I don't see why she should do such a thing."

"Are you certain the name was Willis?"

"Yes."

I returned to *Crockford's Clerical Directory* and examined similar surnames, including Wilkinson, Wilmot and Wilson, just in case.

"Nothing," I said, slamming the book closed a little more forcefully than I had planned.

The noise caught the attention of the head librarian.

"Oh dear. I think we'd better pack away our papers," I muttered to Beth. "He's coming this way."

We weren't quite quick enough, however, and he was upon us before we could make our escape.

I looked across the room to see Francis casting a nervous glance in our direction.

"May I see your reading tickets, please, ladies?" asked the head librarian. "I recognise you, miss..." he said to me, then, turning to Beth, added, "but you don't look familiar."

My mouth felt dry. Although he was shorter than me, he had an authoritarian air that I found intimidating. *How could I convince him we both had a ticket?*

"I—" I began.

Beth quickly interrupted me. "I don't have one," she said. "I know it was very wrong to persuade my friend Mrs Blakely here to admit me to the reading room, and she tried to say no, but I was rather insistent. I take full responsibility for my actions."

The librarian opened then closed his mouth again, seemingly taken aback by Beth's candour.

"I shan't do it again," she added.

"No, you shan't!" he scolded. "And neither shall Mrs Blakely!" He turned back toward me, his face red. "I have no option other than to confiscate your reading ticket for the next ten days."

"Very well." I had feared a much longer confiscation. Ten days seemed fairly manageable.

I found my reading ticket in my carpet bag and held it out to him. He snatched it away with his stubby fingers.

"Now please leave," he added, "before I change my mind and impose a harsher penalty!"

CHAPTER 16

Joseph Bagshaw's tall, narrow townhouse stood in Hans Place, a wealthy square in Chelsea.

"What a beautiful morning," stated Mr Bagshaw. "Ra travels high in the sky once again!" He was an animated, large-nosed man with thick lips and a small chin. His wavy grey hair reached his collar, and thick eyebrows and mutton-chop whiskers framed his face.

"Ra is some sort of god, isn't he?" I queried, vaguely recognising the name.

"The sun god of the ancient Egyptians! We must celebrate each morning as he is reborn after battling the monsters of the underworld while travelling on his night boat."

He must have mistaken my raised eyebrows for interest, because he continued. "The greatest foe of all in the underworld is the enormous serpent Apep, who is so large that his roar alone can cause the earth to move. Fortunately for Ra, he has help in his fight against Apep every night in the form of Set, the god of storms, war and chaos! Ra and Set's battles with Apep are legendary. I've seen depictions of them myself on the walls of the tombs at Deir el-Bahri. I see that you're quite taken with this room, Mrs Blakely."

I felt momentarily overwhelmed by the combination of Mr Bagshaw's fervent storytelling and the decor of the drawing room. It was an ostentatious pastiche of an Egyptian tomb or temple, or perhaps a combination of both. Plaster columns decorated in rich red, blue and gold, which presumably served no structural purpose, lined one wall of the long, narrow room. An enormous fireplace surround was flanked by a pair of statues depicting seated men in loincloths with long beards and pointed hats. Their painted features regarded me in a stern manner.

Every inch of the walls was covered in hieroglyphics and pictures of ancient Egyptians going about their daily business. Although impressive, the decor was a little too much within a domestic setting.

Mr Bagshaw gestured for me to sit on an elaborate settle bench upholstered in gold velvet. He seated himself in a colourful wooden chair with painted wings on either side and carved lion paws for feet. It resembled a pharaoh's throne.

"Those scripts are taken from the Book of the Dead," he said, pointing at the hieroglyphics.

"That doesn't sound terribly cheery."

"It all depends on the way one views them. Personally, I think they're quite wonderful. They're the spells that were written on the walls of their tombs to help the dead navigate the afterlife.

"A German gentleman, Mr Lepsius, published a complete translation about forty years ago. He wouldn't have been able to achieve such a feat without the marvel that is the Rosetta Stone. Found by Napoleon's forces in 1799, it provided us with the very first translation of the obscure hieroglyphs. Up to that point, the language and secrets of the Egyptian Empire had long been confined to history. A thick layer of dust had settled upon it, and it is only now, through our extraordinary work in that great land, that we are finally uncovering those secrets once again. Blowing off the dust, as it were!" He blew on an imaginary object in front of him and majestically swept away an invisible layer of dust.

I managed to suppress a giggle. The sight of him sitting on his pharaoh's throne was amusing enough.

"Mr and Mrs Hamilton—" I began.

"Oh yes, them. You're looking for them, you say?" He glanced down at my calling card, which lay on the gold side table next to him. "It says here that you're a journalist."

"That's right."

"Do you intend to publish any of our conversation?"

"No, not at all."

"I'm glad to hear it. Although if you wish to interview me about my travels and work, I should be more than happy to lend you some of my time. I shan't even expect payment for it! I think it extremely important that the great general public learns more about our wonderful ancient civilisations."

"Thank you, I shall bear that in mind. Now, there's a suspicion that Mr Hamilton may have been murdered."

"A woman claimed to have found him dead in his room, didn't she? Some funny business going on there, if you ask me. Makes you wonder what she was doing there in the first place!"

"She was a friend of his, and she wished to speak to him about something."

"That's her story, anyway!" He gave a cynical laugh.

I felt my teeth clench.

"Mind you," he continued, "no one else ever saw him dead, so it's rather difficult to believe her story."

"Have you any idea where Mr and Mrs Hamilton might have gone?"

"Me? Why should I have any idea about that?"

"Perhaps there's a clue in something they mentioned to you at some point. A particular place they had connections to or enjoyed visiting."

"I can only think of Egypt," he replied, "but I suspect we would have received word by now if they were there. How long is it since they were last seen?"

"Ten days."

He exhaled through his rubbery lips. "Someone really should have come across them by now. Doesn't look good, does it?"

"I heard that you spent time with Mr and Mrs Hamilton on a dig."

"Yes, I did. Never again!"

"May I ask why, Mr Bagshaw?"

"We both happened upon some interesting sites at Amarna in upper Egypt. The city was built by Pharaoh Akhenaten on the eastern bank of the Nile. Both Hamilton and I wished to carry out excavations there, and I actually got there first. He disputed that fact, however. He had a tall story about having visited the place some months previously and making preliminary excavations. I gave way to him in the end; that's the sort of chap I am.

"I had the natives on my side, as I always work on setting up a good rapport with them... something Hamilton always overlooks! It's important, because one needs their help with pitching tents, digging, hauling sand and soil about, looking after the finds and so on. Hamilton has no organisation skills on that front, so I did it all. It was an uneasy arrangement, but I realised we were faced with two stark choices: bicker until the cows come home or get on and work together. After all, in that part of the world there's usually a Frenchman hot on one's heels, ready to snatch a bit of glory for himself.

"Hamilton thinks rather highly of himself, and is keen to consider himself the expert. I occasionally had to pretend that I deferred to his greater intellect, but I think we both knew that I was in charge. There's no doubt he has a detailed understanding of ancient Egypt, although to be completely frank there are so many books on the subject these days that any chap of reasonable intellect could acquire such knowledge by spending a few days at the library."

"Or lady."

"Lady?"

"A lady could also acquire such knowledge."

"Oh, yes. Of course."

"How did you find Mrs Hamilton?"

"Perfectly delightful. She's a pretty young thing, and funnily enough I believe she has read a good few books on Egyptology. Very knowledgeable about the subject indeed, she is. The fact of the matter is that I would have preferred to excavate on my own. I have no need for other Englishmen to help me. Or English*women* for that matter."

"There were disagreements, were there?"

"Naturally. Hamilton and I had different ways of doing things. I agreed to compromise because I didn't see any use in wasting time arguing."

"Did you attend the Ancient Egyptian Society event at the Copeland Hotel, Mr Bagshaw?"

"I certainly did. The hotel is only a short walk from here, so it was extremely convenient for me."

"Did you speak to Mr and Mrs Hamilton at the event?"

"No, I did not." His lips thinned.

"May I ask why not?"

"We fell out. I'd rather not go into the details."

"Why's that?"

He gave me a sullen look. "That's a private matter between myself and Mr Hamilton."

"Their disappearance seems so out of character that it

sounds as though someone else must be behind it, wouldn't you say?"

"You don't believe that crazy murder story your supposed friend cooked up, do you?" He snorted contemptuously.

"I can't say that I really know what to believe just yet. Perhaps they were kidnapped."

"If that had happened, surely those responsible would have been in touch with ransom demands by now. And if they were murdered, what on earth would the motive be?"

"Perhaps Mr and Mrs Hamilton had been getting in the way."

"Of what?"

"Of someone else's work, perhaps."

He gave me a dark look. "Are you talking about someone like me?"

"Isn't there a bit of competition to become the most renowned Egyptologist?"

"Do you honestly think a chap like me would murder Mr Hamilton just because he was getting in the way of my work?"

"That's not what I said."

"You implied it, though." He continued to stare at me icily from his pharaoh's throne.

I was beginning to find him less amusing, and my heart was beating a little faster. I sat still and in silence, cautiously waiting for him to speak again.

His rubbery lips formed a smile. "I must admit, Mrs Blakely, that there were times out in the heat of the desert when I might have been tempted to murder the old chap." He gave a dry laugh. "However, it would have done me no service at all. Although there is a touch of rivalry between us, I regard it as a healthy rivalry. Even now I can imagine us in our dotage sharing a nice glass of whiskey and fondly recalling our days in Egypt. That's how these things usually end up, isn't it?

"I couldn't honestly comprehend the thought of murdering a rival. Or murdering anyone, for that matter. And to be honest with you, Mrs Blakely, I'm rather offended that you should consider me capable of such an act."

"I'm not suggesting that you are. I'm merely trying to consider all the possibilities. I do apologise for offending you, Mr Bagshaw."

"You didn't really offend me," he said, laughing it off. "It would take a lot more than that to offend me, that's for sure! Thutmose III wouldn't have been easily offended, either. He's the pharaoh I identify with most. A military genius who never lost a battle, he was. His exploits are recorded on the walls of the great temples in Karnak. You're familiar with Cleopatra's Needle, are you?"

"The obelisk on the Victoria Embankment?"

"The very same! Gifted to this great country in 1819, it was, although it has only stood on the embankment for seven years or so. It's almost three and a half thousand years old, can you believe it? Thutmose III arranged for it to be built, along with various others, in the city of Heliopolis."

"It has nothing to do with Cleopatra, then?"

"Only a little. She ordered the obelisks to be moved to a temple she had built in Alexandria."

"What do you think might have happened to Mr and Mrs Hamilton, Mr Bagshaw?"

"I can only imagine that they've headed off on a secret expedition. I can picture Hamilton returning to British shores with a great many ancient artefacts and boasting to high heaven about them. In fact, I'm rather annoyed that I never concocted the idea of a secret expedition myself. It won't remain secret for long, of course. We'll hear of it soon enough."

CHAPTER 17

"These are my drawings from Amarna," said Mr Smollett, leafing through his sketchbook. "Mr Hamilton wanted me to sketch every find."

We were seated in the Holborn Restaurant once more.

"You're such a talented artist, John," commented Beth.

"Not especially," he responded, scratching at his neck. "I just happen to sketch a lot, and that's all there is to it."

Rows of objects were depicted in neat pencil drawings on each page. They were small statues of birds and animals, many incomplete with the edges knocked off. There were also bowls and vases; the more detailed items drawn from a front and rear view.

"I'll show you some of my favourites," he said, turning a few pages over. "I particularly like this one."

It was a drawing of a stone tablet with detailed etchings. Two eyes stared out from the top of the tablet and several rows of hieroglyphics followed beneath. At the foot of the tablet was a seated figure with a stylus of some sort in its hand.

"Is that a scribe?" I asked.

"Yes, it could be," he replied. "He's holding what I think is a pen made from reed."

Other drawings depicted scenes from Amarna: temple ruins with broken columns and walls standing proud in the desert. Huts and tents nestled in the shade of tall palms.

"I should like to travel there," said Beth.

"I should as well," I agreed.

"It's a beautiful place," said Mr Smollett, "I'd like to go back there myself, preferably with Mr and Mrs Hamilton." His face fell. "I can't understand why there has been no word from them. It makes no sense at all."

I told him about my visit to Joseph Bagshaw's residence the previous day.

"Was there any obvious conflict between Mr Bagshaw and the Hamiltons?" I asked.

"Yes, there was," replied Mr Smollett. "They often disagreed with one another."

"What a lovely picture!" Beth had continued leafing through the sketchbook and the page she was looking at showed the head and shoulders of a beautiful young woman. Her eyes were large and dark, and her wavy hair was pinned loosely at the nape of her neck. She was gazing off to her left, as if surveying some distant scene. A great deal of time had clearly been spent on the drawing. Each stroke appeared delicate and softly applied.

Mr Smollett gave a bashful smile, his dark skin flushing slightly at the top of his cheekbones.

"Is that Mrs Hamilton?" I asked.

"Yes, and John has captured her perfectly," said Beth.

Mr Smollett's hands began to fidget, as if he should have liked to take the sketchbook from Beth and fold it closed again. I sensed that the picture reflected his deep affection for Mrs Hamilton; an affection he had tried to keep hidden during our previous meeting.

"Did you draw Mr Hamilton as well?" I asked, partly out of curiosity and partly to ease his discomfort.

"Yes." Mr Smollett took the sketchbook from Beth and flipped through the pages. "This was just a quick sketch I did one evening."

The rough sketch depicted a stocky man sitting in a chair next to a tent. Although hastily drawn, the picture conveyed heavy features with small eyes and a wide, stern mouth.

I resisted the temptation to mention that Mr Smollett had clearly spent far less time creating this portrait. Instead, I told him about Beth's fruitless trip to Rochdale.

"Did Mrs Hamilton ever mention Rochdale to you?" I asked once I had finished.

"Yes, she did. She told me her father was a vicar there."

"Is it possible she lied about that?" I asked.

This question prompted a puzzled look from both my companions.

"Why would she do that?" asked Beth.

"I don't know. I'm just a little confused because we haven't been able to find out anything more about her."

"She wouldn't have lied," said Mr Smollett. "I've only just forgiven Mrs Worthers for being untruthful about her identity, but Mrs Hamilton? She would never do such a thing."

"You don't like the idea of her lying to you at all, do you?" I asked.

"No!" he responded. Mr Smollett appeared to be upset at the very idea that she might have been deceptive.

"Susan Hamilton had no reason to lie," said Beth.

"How do you know that?" I asked. "She wasn't even aware of your true identity."

"You know full well that I already feel ashamed about that!" she snapped.

I sat back in my chair, disappointed that both Beth and Mr Smollett were irked with me.

"What can we do to find her?" I asked. "What else did she tell either of you that might lead us somewhere?"

My two companions exchanged a blank look.

"Honesty will be a big help to us," I said, giving Mr Smollett a pointed look. "*Complete* honesty."

There was a moment's silence, and I stared determinedly at him until he felt compelled to respond.

Eventually, he cleared his throat. "All right, I admit it," he said. "We had a love affair." He paused, as if relieved by his honesty. "I'm ashamed of my actions, of course. I had no intention whatsoever of falling in love with a married lady, but we have such a great deal in common. And Mr Hamilton... although he's a respected Egyptologist, he's not a very pleasant husband. I felt sorry for Mrs Hamilton being married to him. We had a short spell of happiness together. I so wish I knew where she was." He rubbed his brow.

"You must be very worried about her," I said.

"Yes, I am! It's a relief to be able to tell you how concerned I am, in fact. I've been looking for her myself, and have already called at her home several times, but the housekeeper has heard nothing of their whereabouts. I even called in at the police station and they told me to pop back if she doesn't turn up soon. That's not much help, is it? The constable I spoke to seemed to think she had gone somewhere with her husband. Maybe she has."

"Her husband's dead," said Beth.

"Well... I... I just don't know what to think." His shoulders slumped and he took a long sip of wine, as if he hoped the drink would help in some way. "If I'm to be completely honest with you, I suppose I should admit that I also travelled to Rochdale. Mrs Hamilton mentioned to me that she had family there. I made lots of enquiries but was unable to find anybody who knew her or her family. I simply cannot understand it. I can't begin to think where she might have gone."

"Had you planned to run away together?" I asked.

"We never made serious plans, but we talked about it. I hoped that one day..." He rubbed his brow. "I just hoped that one day the situation would be different. I can still picture the last time I saw her. It was at the drinks reception, and we caught each other's eye from opposite ends of the room. I had ended up speaking to rather a dull gentleman and was desperately trying to leave the conversation. Once I had managed to do so, I looked around the room again but Mrs Hamilton was no longer there. I assumed she would soon reappear, but then... she never did. I sincerely hope she hasn't come to any harm! I'm so worried about her. I haven't heard anything at all, and that's what worries me the most."

I felt sorry for Mr Smollett. He appeared to genuinely care for Mrs Hamilton.

Unable to offer him any great consolation, I decided to find out what I could about the Hamiltons's dig with Joseph Bagshaw.

"You mentioned there were regular disagreements in Amarna," I ventured. "Were you referring to disagreements between Mr Hamilton and Mr Bagshaw?"

"Yes."

"May I ask what they were about?"

"They seemed to disagree about most things. There were several minor arguments while we were sailing on the dahabeeyah, and then the atmosphere worsened during the dig. The pair had differing opinions on how everything should be done. I quietly carried on with my sketches and stayed out of it as much as I could, although matters came to a head when a few of the artefacts went missing."

"Someone took them?"

"Mr Bagshaw believed that Mr Hamilton had taken them."

"He thought Mr Hamilton had stolen them?"

"That's what Mr Bagshaw accused him of. And he accused Mrs Hamilton, too. Oh, I shall call her Susan from now on, because that's what she liked me to call her. Perhaps the items weren't really stolen, as such. Perhaps it was all just a misunderstanding."

"Tell us more," I said.

"I will," he responded, "but not here. I'll tell you tonight if you can meet me again."

"But why?"

"I have my reasons." He opened his sketchbook and tore off a slip of paper. Then he retrieved a pencil from the pocket of his jacket and wrote down an address. "I'll meet you there after nightfall."

CHAPTER 18

"I'll wait here," said James as we stepped out of Loughborough Junction train station that evening. "If anything goes wrong, run back here as quickly as you can. Or just shout my name as loudly as possible."

"Thank you, James," I said, "but Beth and I will be fine. There's nothing intimidating about Mr Smollett."

"That doesn't mean he's incapable of mischief, Penny."

"I can assure you, Mr Blakely, that John Smollett is not someone we need to worry about," said Beth.

"I'd like to know why he's so keen to meet two ladies after dark beside some railway lines in south London!"

"We're about to find out," I replied, "and I'm quite certain there's nothing untoward about it. Besides, there are two of us and only one of him."

"Can you be sure of that?" asked James. "Perhaps he's invited some friends along."

"I can't see why he should. Is it nine o'clock yet?"

James checked his pocket watch. "Yes."

"Then Beth and I had better go and wait outside the Green Man public house, as we arranged."

"I shall keep step behind you," said James.

"You said you would wait here outside the station."

"I've changed my mind. It looks as though there are a few unsavoury individuals around here, and it's already dark."

"All right, but don't let Mr Smollett see you. He may not agree to our meeting if he finds out there's a police inspector close by."

"You think he's up to no good, do you?"

"I have no idea. I just don't want to run the risk of him seeing you."

"Right. Well, I shall be invisibly close by."

"Thank you, James."

Mr Smollett was waiting for us beneath a gas lamp outside the Green Man. He doffed his hat and gave us a cautious smile. I noticed he was carrying a small paraffin lamp in one hand.

"I'm prohibited from entering the place we're about to visit without Mr Hamilton," he began. "But if he's gone for good..." He shrugged. "I don't know what else can be done."

"Well, thank you for bringing us here," I said.

"I'm not sure if it'll help us find him or Susan, but it can't do any harm. Follow me."

We crossed the road and walked down a narrow alleyway that ran alongside a row of shuttered railway arches. The railway line ran over a viaduct high above our heads. The paraffin lamp flickered against the brickwork, and before long I noticed another row of railway arches to our right.

"We're in between the railway lines here," I said.

"That's right," responded Mr Smollett. "Three railway lines converge at this point, and we're standing on a little triangle of land that sits between them. It's the perfect hiding place."

"Whatever for?" asked Beth.

"I'll show you. Mr Hamilton only ever came to this place after dark. He didn't want anyone to know it was here."

"Apart from you," I said.

"Yes. And Susan, of course. The three of us knew about it."

The darkness seemed to intensify all of a sudden. *Had James been right to worry?*

Unpleasant odours lingered in the air and Beth gasped as the bright eyes of an animal flickered in the lamplight.

"It's only a cat," Mr Smollett said reassuringly. He moved toward the row of arches to our right and approached one with a paint-splintered door. He held the lantern out to me. "Would you mind holding this for a moment, Mrs Blakely? I need to unlock the door."

I held the lamp while Mr Smollett retrieved a key from his pocket. Then Beth and I waited patiently as he turned the key in the lock. A train rumbled heavily overhead as he pushed the door open. Taking the lamp back from me, he led us in through the darkened doorway.

It was impossible to make out Beth's features in the dark. *Was she as concerned as I felt?* I tried to convince myself that Mr Smollett was to be trusted, fervently hoping we weren't being led into a trap.

The interior smelled musty and damp. The flickering light illuminated numerous shelves laden with boxes and bundles of paper and sacking.

"What is this place?" I asked. My voice sounded muffled in the small space.

"Mr Hamilton's treasure trove," replied Mr Smollett with a note of pride in his voice.

He lit another paraffin lamp, then hung both lanterns on the wall, giving us a clearer view of the shelving units and the countless items stacked upon them.

"Are these all Egyptian artefacts?" I asked.

"Not all of them," he replied. "Mr Hamilton is quite a collector, so there are other items here that he has gathered over the years. I haven't had anything to do with quite a bit of it. I've just been cataloguing the objects on these shelves." He stepped over to a shelving unit on the right, which appeared to have fewer cobwebs covering it than the other shelves. "I'll show you the items there was some dispute over with Mr Bagshaw."

My nerves began to settle as he untied the string around an item wrapped in sacking. He pulled the outer layer away to reveal a thin blue vase with a fine handle.

"Made from glass, would you believe?" he said.

"Is it really from ancient Egypt?" I queried. "It looks so modern!"

"It's about three thousand years old." He wrapped it up again, then showed us another artefact. Made of yellow stone, it was a broken fragment of the lower part of a woman's face. "I like to think she was a queen," said Mr Smollett.

"May I touch it?" I asked. There was something irresistibly smooth about the object. Its surface was cool and pleasing to the touch.

"It's made of yellow jasper," Mr Smollett explained as he carefully rewrapped the fragment. "And this here is the find we were all particularly fond of."

The package was a little over a foot in length and almost the same in width. He pulled away the wrapping to reveal the torso of a statue. The arms were missing and it had hieroglyphics carved into its front and rear.

"Limestone," he said. "The complete statue must have been really quite impressive."

We were interrupted by a train thundering over our heads.

"Did Mr Bagshaw accuse Mr Hamilton of stealing these treasures from him?" I asked once the noise had faded.

"That's right."

"And had he?"

"There's no doubt that he spirited them away rather quickly. I assumed there had been an agreement between the two men to transport them back to Britain, but perhaps I was wrong."

"If Mr Bagshaw believes Mr Hamilton stole these treasures from him, he must be very angry about it."

"No doubt he is."

"A possible motive for murdering him," suggested Beth.

"Oh, but I couldn't imagine him doing that," said Mr Smollett.

"Well, someone did," she retorted, "and it sounds as though Mr Bagshaw had a grievance against him."

Mr Smollett showed us some of the other items lying on the shelves, including pieces of pottery, jewellery and papyrus. He seemed proud of the collection and honoured to have been asked to help look after it. *Had he brought us here solely to show off this collection?* I couldn't see how our visit would provide us with any clues as to Susan Hamilton's whereabouts.

Mr Smollett paused for a moment, then peered closely at the shelf upon which the torso had been resting. He frowned.

"Is something wrong?" I asked.

"The goblet," he replied. "It's usually kept here." He looked around at the shelves close by. "I can't see it... How strange! It's made of alabaster and is quite beautiful. I can't see where it's got to."

He began to search a little more frantically, retrieving one of the lanterns from the wall and shining it into every corner of the shelving unit. "It's not here..." he muttered to himself. "I swear it's not here!"

"When did you last visit this place?" I asked.

"About a week ago. I came by just to see if there was any sign that Susan had visited. I don't understand..."

"Was the goblet in its usual place at that point?"

"Yes. Just next to the torso."

"Who else has a key to this place?" asked Beth.

"Mr Hamilton, myself and Susan."

"No one else?"

"No one else even knows it's here!"

"Then either Mr or Mrs Hamilton must have taken it," I said.

"But why would they? This is where we store everything."

"Was there any indication that the goblet was of particularly great importance to either of them?"

"No more so than any of the other objects we store here."

"Was it one of the finds from Amarna?"

"No, it was something they had acquired before that."

"Perhaps they needed money," I suggested. "Maybe they took it so they could sell it on."

"Is there any possibility that the keys might have fallen into the hands of someone else?" asked Beth.

"I always keep mine very securely, and Mr and Mrs Hamilton are the same."

"Well, either one of the Hamiltons took the goblet or the keys were stolen from them and the goblet was taken," I said. "Does it look as though anything else is missing?"

"Nothing else immediately obvious, but I'll need to check through everything. I can only speak for the items I've been cataloguing, of course. As for the other items stored here, I couldn't possibly say."

"Why should someone wish to take the goblet?" I asked. "What's so special about it?"

"I don't think there's anything special about it at all. That's why I'm so baffled by the fact that it's gone missing. It's quite an attractive piece, so I suppose it would look rather smart on someone's mantelpiece, but there are far more valuable items here. And there's no sign that anyone has broken in. Regular thieves would presumably have taken as much as possible. As much as they could carry, perhaps."

This new development was a puzzle.

"You visited this place a week ago," I said, "which after Mr and Mrs Hamilton vanished. One of them must have come back here, or perhaps they both did."

"Or maybe they gave the key to someone else," said Beth, "and asked that person to take the goblet."

"No, I must just be mistaken," said Mr Smollett. "It must be here somewhere. But even so, who could possibly have moved it?"

I glanced around the room and considered how strange it was that Mr Hamilton should wish to store all of his treasures inside a railway arch. *Why all the secrecy? Why couldn't he have donated them to a museum instead?*

The shelves over on the other side of the room caught my eye. *What was stored on those?* I couldn't resist walking over to them.

"What are you doing?" Mr Smollett called out, his voice cracking with concern. *Was there something he didn't wish me to see?*

"Just having a look," I said.

"But Mr Hamilton forbade me from touching those things!"

"Do you have any idea why?" I called back.

"He didn't say."

I pulled away a piece of sacking to reveal a glimpse of dull, tarnished gold. As I pulled a little more, I saw what appeared to be a candlestick. The object next to it was wrapped in dusty paper. I peeled some of that away to see what appeared to be an ornate jewellery box.

I realised these weren't treasures imported from Egypt. They were something else altogether.

I returned to Mr Smollett.

"I hope you don't mind," I said, "but I should like to involve my husband at this point."

"Your husband?"

"He's an inspector at Scotland Yard."

"But why? I've done nothing wrong!"

"I'm sure you haven't, Mr Smollett."

"And neither has Mr Hamilton!"

"I'll let my husband be the judge of that."

"But you can't do that, Mrs Blakely. I showed you this place in good faith. You can't go reporting it to the police!"

"If Mr Hamilton has done nothing wrong, Mr Smollett, there will be nothing for you to worry about."

CHAPTER 19

Mr Smollett was even more perturbed to discover that James had been waiting close by all along.

"There's absolutely nothing for you to worry about," James said reassuringly as he inspected a few of the items on the shelves I had been examining.

I could have sworn the young man was shaking.

"B-but if... if Mr Hamilton finds out..." he stammered.

"I'm afraid he may never come back," responded James bluntly. "I realise that's a distressing thought for you to consider, but it also means that you're unlikely to find yourself in any trouble with him. What can you tell me about the items in this room?"

"I only know about the Egyptian artefacts. Mr Hamilton forbade me from looking at those other items."

"I think I can understand why," said James, lifting one edge of a piece of sacking to reveal a patterned vase. "These look like the sorts of things that would belong in a stately home. Did Mr Hamilton tell you anything at all about these objects?"

"No, nothing. Only that I shouldn't look at them."

"I shall inform P Division at Camberwell Green," said James. "We need to get some men down here to start looking through this lot. It all looks rather suspicious to me."

"What do you mean?" asked Mr Smollett.

"Stolen goods. We need to look through our records of any pilfered items and work out if any of them show up here." James scratched the back of his head and grimaced. "It'll be quite a task."

"Mr Hamilton isn't a thief!" protested Mr Smollett.

"Can you be absolutely sure of that?" I asked.

"I trust him!"

"Ah, but he didn't trust you, did he?" replied James. "That's why he employed Mrs Worthers here."

"If the police are to be involved," began Mr Smollett, "can you please start looking for Susan?"

"Susan?"

"Mrs Hamilton," I explained to James.

James nodded. "I shall speak to the superintendent at Camberwell Green station."

"You said, Mr Blakely, that you don't believe Mr Hamilton will be coming back," said Beth. "Do you now believe that he was murdered, as I previously told you?"

"I'm increasingly believing that to be the case, yes," said James.

I noticed Mr Smollett shifting uncomfortably from one foot to the other.

"Having been shown this little cave of treasures," continued James, "I'm now rather suspicious of Mr and Mrs Hamiltons's conduct. Their disappearance, and indeed their possible murder, should be properly investigated."

"The police are finally going to get involved!" I said with great relief.

"Let me speak to my colleagues first, Penny."

Mr Smollett piped up, "Well, if the police are to take an interest, I should like to report a theft."

"Of what?" replied James.

"An alabaster goblet. It was stored here and now it's gone. It's shaped like a white lotus flower and is engraved with the names of King Amenhotep IV and Queen Nefertiti."

James moved closer to one of the paraffin lamps and made a note of this in his notebook. "A stolen item has been stolen again, eh?"

"They're not stolen!" protested Mr Smollett. "Mr Hamilton either found or purchased all these items. I know he brought some of them back from Egypt last winter, but he also liked to buy artefacts from Mrs Miller."

"Who's Mrs Miller?" I asked.

"An antiquities dealer in Mayfair."

"Would she be able to verify that she sold him these things?" James asked.

"I should think so."

James made some more notes.

"The disappearance of the goblet is intriguing," I said. "It appears to have been taken after Mr and Mrs Hamilton were last seen. But they are the only ones who have keys to this place. Apart from Mr Smollett, that is."

"Very interesting." James pondered this for a moment. "Which means at least one of them has been in here since they vanished."

"How much do you know about Egyptian artefacts?" I asked Francis after I had joined him and Eliza in St James's Park. It was a pleasant late-summer afternoon and several children were feeding the ducks on the lake.

Eliza laughed. "You're consulting him as though he were a living encyclopaedia, Penelope."

"He is, though, isn't he?"

"I wish I were!" replied Francis. "I'm sure I could make some good money out of it. Egyptian artefacts, you say? So many of them are being found these days that it's difficult to keep up. We have some excellent publications in the library, of course. How's your French, Penny?"

"Reasonable."

"In which case, you might enjoy *Voyage dans la Basse et la Haute Egypte* by Mr Vivant Denon. 'Travels in Upper and Lower Egypt' is what it translates as, but you probably knew that. Mr Denon travelled around Egypt as part of Napoleon's expeditions there at the end of the last century. Then there is *Description de l'Égypte* – a series of fascinating French publications that were printed a good fifty or sixty years ago, but are very informative all the same. How's your German?"

"Not as good as my French."

"Same here. It's possible you'll be able to make some sense of *Denkmäler aus Aegypten und Aethiopien* or 'Monuments from Egypt and Ethiopia' by Mr Karl Lepsius. I wouldn't advise reading it all in one go, mind you. It's twelve volumes long and would probably take you several years to plough through."

"Isn't there anything written in English?" asked Eliza.

"Well, one really can't go wrong with *Manners and Customs of the Ancient Egyptians* by Mr John Gardener Wilkinson. That's only six volumes long, and a revised edition came out just a few years ago. A more entertaining read is *A Thousand Miles Up the Nile* by Amelia Edwards. No relation of mine, by the way. And not an academic text, either, but very informative all the same."

"All that should keep you busy, Penelope," said Eliza.

"What about alabaster goblets?" I asked Francis. "Have you come across any mention of them?"

"Not specifically, no."

"I should like to find out whether they are valuable artefacts."

"I can certainly read up on them for you, Penny. I always enjoy learning something new."

"Thank you, Francis. The particular goblet I'm interested in is engraved with the names of…" I pulled my notebook out of my carpet bag and turned to the page where I had made notes on the subject. "King Amenhotep IV and Queen Nefertiti," I added.

Francis nodded. "The names are familiar to me, but I'll need to consult the relevant textbooks before I'm able to give you any further information about them."

Eliza sighed, visibly bored by our conversation.

I decided to change the topic of conversation. "Any word yet on when Father's wife will be arriving?" I asked my sister.

"*Common-law* wife," she corrected. "In about two weeks' time, I think. I suppose we shall soon be meeting our half-brothers and half-sisters, Penelope. Don't you think it all rather odd?"

"It will certainly feel rather strange to meet them, but I'm determined to do my best to make them feel welcome. I imagine they'll find it rather different here from their home in Amazonia. I just hope Father decides against putting them on the stage. I don't think that would be good for them at all."

"I can readily agree that the stage is not a nice place to find oneself," said Francis. "I'd rather read all twelve volumes of *Denkmäler aus Aegypten und Aethiopien* than go through that again!"

After leaving Eliza and Francis, I walked a short distance to the Victoria Embankment to see Cleopatra's Needle. I had passed the monument a number of times without paying it much heed. Now that I knew its age and had more interest in the country of its origin, I found myself rather enthralled by it.

The obelisk stood at almost seventy feet high and was carved with hieroglyphics on all four sides. Two large bronze sphinxes guarded it, and there was a plaque to commemorate the six men who had lost their lives trying to save the crew of the obelisk's ship during a storm in 1877.

It was difficult to imagine how old the monument was or to believe that it had stood for so long in a foreign land before making the long journey to London. I felt drawn to the beauty of the hieroglyphics and was beginning to see why

so many people became enchanted by the wonders of ancient
Egypt.

CHAPTER 21

'Mrs. L. J. Miller, Antiquities' were the only words
that adorned the brass plaque outside the smart
red-and-cream-brick building in Mayfair.

I pulled the bell rope and was admitted by a young woman
wearing a fashionable blue bustle dress.

"What can I help you with?" she asked.

We were standing in a wood-panelled office containing a
large mahogany desk with a typewriter on it. I deduced that
the woman was Mrs Miller's secretary.

I introduced myself and gave her my card, which stated
that I was a journalist. Then I added, "I'm looking for Mr and
Mrs Hamilton, the pair of Egyptologists who have disappeared. I should like to speak briefly with Mrs Miller about
them."

The woman disappeared through a door beyond her desk.
I surveyed some lithographs of classical scenes on the walls as
I patiently waited.

"Do please come in!" came a brash voice from the other
side of the door. I turned to see a woman wearing a crimson
bustle dress that was even more fashionable than her

assistant's garment. The bodice was tightly corseted with gold trimming. She was dark-skinned and her lustrous black hair, pinned into waves, was garnished with a red ribbon. Her attire seemed better suited to a night at the theatre than to everyday usage.

I needed a moment or two to take it all in, which caused me to hesitate a little.

"I'm afraid I don't have very long, Mrs Blakely."

There was a slight accent to her voice. *Was she Egyptian?*

I wasn't sure, and I decided it would be impolite to ask. "Indeed. Thank you for seeing me." I hurried into the room, feeling rather underdressed in my plain jacket, blouse and skirt.

Mrs Miller showed me to a seat opposite her enormous desk. Her dress rustled as she sat down.

"I do appreciate your time," I said. "I hear you deal in antiquities."

"I most certainly do, although I suspect you're not here to buy or sell any."

"I'm investigating the mysterious disappearance of Mr and Mrs Hamilton. There's a possibility that Mr Hamilton may have been murdered."

"Yes, I've heard." Her dark eyes widened with interest.

"Do you know the Hamiltons?"

"I met them once, a few months ago now. They hadn't long since returned from Egypt. We met at a dinner hosted by a mutual friend, and they were very pleasant company. Quite the experts on Egypt, the pair of them."

"Have they ever bought anything from you?"

"No. As I understand it, they like to find objects themselves. We discussed the idea of me buying a few items from them. They were planning to bring them in, but it never came to anything. Sherry?"

"Thank you," I responded before the offer had properly

registered in my mind. It wasn't yet ten o'clock in the morning.

Mrs Miller got up from her seat and opened the door of an elegant drinks cabinet. Having only agreed to a drink in order to establish a rapport with her, I didn't relish the idea of consuming sherry at such an early hour.

"You must know a good number of the Egyptologists," I commented.

"Oh yes, lots."

"Do you know Mrs Palmer?" I asked.

She nodded in reply.

"Mr Bagshaw?" I probed.

"A very knowledgeable chap. You wouldn't want to get stuck with him, though. He could talk the hind leg off a donkey."

"Have you bought artefacts from many of them?" I asked.

"I buy items that interest me, but I turn down a great deal, too. Egyptologists do approach me, as do other gentlemen who have been off exploring remote parts of the globe and have picked up some antiquity of interest. And I stress the word *antiquity*." She handed me my glass of sherry. "I'm not interested in mere *antiques*. Let's drink to the health of the Queen."

She raised her glass and I followed suit. Then she took a sip and returned to her seat.

"Why don't people just give antiquities to museums?" I asked.

"Some do, but others are chasing the money. They've often travelled to far-flung parts of the world at great personal expense. Why not bring back a little something they can make a bit of money on?"

"Who usually buys from you?"

"Oh, all sorts of people. The only thing they have in common is their wealth!" She laughed. "I once had a chap buy a whole range of objects so he could pretend to his friends that he'd picked them up on a Grand Tour. I don't think he ever set sail from this country, but he was keen to create the impression that he had! I'm quite discerning with regard to whom I sell to, of course. I like proper introductions. I have to be rather careful, you see. I can't just show off my collection to everybody and anybody, as the items are exceptionally valuable. I don't keep any of them on these premises, by the way."

She picked up a catalogue from a neat pile on her desk and slid it toward me. I picked it up and began to leaf through.

"Only when I can be certain that a customer is serious about conducting business with me do I show them one of these. I've probably turned away many genuine people in the mistaken belief that there may be something rather crooked about them."

"Has anyone ever tried to sell you something you suspected might be stolen?" I asked.

"I usually only accept items from people I'm well acquainted with. If, for instance, you were in possession of something like... Oh, I don't know, a bronze statuette of a pharaoh for example, standing so high..." She gestured about three inches above her desk. "Three thousand or possibly three and a half thousand years old... I would be extremely interested, but I would still need to assess your credentials first. I would want to know how you came by it and what your motive for selling it was. I would also endeavour to find out what dealings you might have had with colleagues of mine, and whether they could put in a good word for you. I go about my business extremely carefully, Mrs Blakely. I certainly wouldn't want to be caught up in anything untoward. More sherry?"

"No, thank you."

Mrs Miller got up to refill her glass.

"Has anyone offered you a goblet recently?" I asked.

"What sort of goblet?"

"Made of alabaster," I said, "and shaped like a lotus flower. The one in question is engraved with the names of King Amenhotep IV and Queen Nefertiti."

"It sounds like a beautiful object." She returned to her seat with the replenished drink. "I haven't been offered that, no."

"It appears to have gone missing from a collection belonging to Mr and Mrs Hamilton. Did they ever mention the goblet to you?"

She shook her head. "No, I don't recall hearing about it. I can certainly let you know if anyone offers it to me. I should like to see it."

"It would be very helpful if you could do so. Thank you."

"I'm not sure how any of this might help with your search for the Hamiltons."

"It's possible that at least one of them is in the possession of the goblet," I replied. "Do you ever seek out specific items?"

"What do you mean?"

"Perhaps a trusted customer of yours is after a particular object. Might he or she approach you and ask you to acquire it?"

"Occasionally, yes."

"And how would you go about acquiring the desired item?"

"I would speak to my acquaintances, and if they couldn't help I might put a private notice in a newspaper. People in possession of such items usually know where to look."

"Would you be interested in trying to acquire the goblet I mentioned? Well, not actually acquire it, but make some enquiries about it and then let me know if anyone contacts you?"

She frowned. "It would look a bit odd if I were to request that particular item. The Hamiltons would immediately become suspicious."

"Perhaps you could make your request a little more general. Maybe alabaster items or ancient Egyptian goblets?"

She sat back in her chair and gave this some thought. "I might be deluged with responses! I don't have time for all that."

"Would you really be, though? I can't imagine many people being in possession of such things."

She leaned forward across her desk. "I was referring to people who wish to waste my time, Mrs Blakely. There'd be hordes of them."

"You could state in your advertisement that you wouldn't consider any time-wasters."

She threw back her head and laughed. "The sort of people who are in the habit of wasting my time wouldn't pay any heed to that!"

"If we can find the goblet, we may just be able to find Mr or Mrs Hamilton."

"Mr Hamilton's dead, though, isn't he?"

"We think so... Unless it was an elaborate ruse."

"If they're in hiding, they're unlikely to reveal themselves even if they hear that I'm after the goblet."

"They might be in desperate need of the money. They may have taken it with the sole intention of selling it to fund their escape."

Mrs Miller fixed her eye on the far wall and appeared thoughtful for a moment. "I suppose Mrs Hamilton could have murdered her husband, then taken the goblet to sell so she could pay for a ticket to the continent."

"That's a possibility."

"In which case, I'll help you."

Her immediate acquiescence came as a surprise to me. "Are you sure? Well, thank you, Mrs Miller!"

"It would help you solve the mystery, wouldn't it? She might even approach me in disguise. That would certainly be interesting!"

"Thank you. I'd be happy to pay you for your trouble."

"There's no need for that!"

"But—"

"I won't hear of it, Mrs Blakely! I don't need the money, but I do like the idea of solving a mystery."

CHAPTER 22

"You again, Mrs Blakely! What would your husband say if he knew how often you were visiting me?" Joseph Bagshaw gave me a rubbery-lipped smile before seating himself in his pharaoh's throne.

"He knows I'm visiting you, Mr Bagshaw. He's investigating the disappearance of Mr and Mrs Hamilton himself."

"He's investigating as well, is he?"

"Yes. He's an inspector at Scotland Yard."

"Is he, indeed? Well, I hadn't realised that. How can I help you, Mrs Blakely?"

"Why didn't you mention the items Mr Hamilton took during your time in Amarna?"

He lowered his chin and glowered at me from beneath his thick eyebrows. "There was no need for me to dredge up that unpleasant business."

"It would have been useful for me to know."

"Why? It has nothing to do with his disappearance or murder... or whatever it is that's happened to him."

"But it might do."

He uncrossed and recrossed his legs. "Here we go again,

Mrs Blakely. You're going to accuse me of murdering him again, aren't you?"

"I've never accused you of that."

"I think 'implied' was the word I used last time. You suggested there was competition between us Egyptologists and that perhaps we would set about murdering each other as a result."

I ignored his exaggerated take on my words and consulted my notebook. "You found a blue glass vase... a fragment of a statue's face made from yellow jasper and... a torso from a statue. Limestone, I believe."

"Yes, that's quite correct!" he snapped. His eyes never left my face. "How did you know that?"

"I've seen them."

"*Seen* them?" He sat up and leaned forward in his throne, quite forgetting that he was supposed to be fixing me with a menacing stare. "Then where *are* they?"

"I'll be happy to tell you, Mr Bagshaw, if you're willing to tell me what happened on the dig in Amarna."

"There isn't a great deal to tell." He scratched the side of his large nose.

"Other than the fact that Mr and Mrs Hamilton stole from you."

"They did!"

"When did you discover that?"

"At the end of a dig, all the finds are laid out in the tents and we decide what to do with them. That's what we did in Amarna, and we decided that a few would remain in Egypt for the Egyptians to put in their museums." He gave a despairing shake of his head. "Rather primitive museums, if I may say so. They have grand plans for some new ones in Cairo, but they'd better get on with it, as there are a great many treasures to be housed. Anyway, we agreed which ones should stay, and then Mr Hamilton and I began to discuss who would take home which treasures. It was during this conversation that I realised three of the finds we had been most proud of were missing."

"The ones I just mentioned?"

"Yes. It's a great relief to discover that you know of their whereabouts, Mrs Blakely."

"You challenged Mr Hamilton about the missing items, did you?"

"Yes, and he denied all knowledge of having anything to do with it! Blamed it on the natives, he did. Can you believe it? I've had hundreds of natives help me on every dig I've ever done, and I can confidently say that every single one of those men was as honest as the day is long. I've never once had a problem with anyone stealing from me. Not until I met Hamilton, that is!"

"Is it possible that he was innocent?"

"No! He's the only person who could have taken those objects... with the exception of his wife, of course. In fact, I shall blame the pair of them. I'm quite certain they would have worked on it together."

"You have no evidence that he and his wife took the items, but you're certain it was them."

"Yes, that's right. Where were they found?"

"Among some of his belongings."

Mr Bagshaw slapped his thigh and gave a loud laugh. "There you go, Mrs Blakely! There's your evidence. I knew he had taken them!" He jabbed his forefinger at me. "I knew it! When will I get them back?"

"That would be a discussion for you to have with the police."

He groaned. "What do they have to do with this?"

"They're taking a look through Mr and Mrs Hamilton's belongings."

"And when will they be finished?"

"I have no idea. They've only just begun."

"I want it known that those three objects are my rightful property! I expect them to be returned to me as soon as the police have finished their search. Why are the police involved, anyway?"

"The Hamiltons have been missing for more than two weeks now, and the police have decided it's time to investigate. By the way, if you believed those three objects had been stolen from you, why didn't you inform the police?"

"I didn't want to make a big hoo-ha about it. I trusted the matter could be resolved between us."

"And how did you attempt to resolve it?"

"Through simple discussion, of course."

"And how did that go?"

"Not well at all. Until Hamilton was willing to admit that he had taken the items, no progress could be made. I decided to ensure that..." His voice trailed off.

"Ensure what?"

"Never mind."

"You were going to tell me something but then changed your mind. Why?"

"It doesn't matter."

I folded up my notebook and placed it back inside my carpet bag. "Thank you for your time, Mr Bagshaw, and for speaking to me about the stolen items."

"Whom do I contact about them?"

"I'm not sure." I stood up to leave.

"What do you mean you're not sure?" He rose up out of his throne. "You said that you would tell me where the items were if I helped you. Now where are they?"

"I shall be happy to tell you when you're prepared to be honest with me, Mr Bagshaw. When it came to Mr Hamilton and the stolen items, you decided to ensure... What was the rest of that sentence?"

He bared his teeth and stuck out his chest. "I decided to ensure that I would make life as difficult as possible for him until he admitted that he had taken them. That was all I was going to say."

"And how did you go about making life difficult for him?"

"I never got the chance! He vanished... or was murdered. One or the other."

"I see. One more thing before I go. Have you ever come across an alabaster goblet shaped like a lotus flower?"

"No, I don't think so. Egyptian, I presume?"

"Yes. It's engraved with the names of a king and queen."

"Which ones?"

"King Amenhotep IV and Queen Nefertiti."

His face lit up. "Ah, yes! Akhenaten. He changed his name, you see. The founder of Amarna, nonetheless! That sounds like a very interesting object. Why do you ask about it?"

"It's gone missing."

"From where?"

"It seems someone has stolen it from Mr Hamilton's collection."

"Oh dear! Did they indeed? Someone has stolen from the thief himself." He gave a low chuckle.

"Could you let me know if you hear any mention of it?"

"Of course. Now, whom do I speak to about getting my belongings back?"

I had no desire to burden James with the inconsequential demands of Mr Bagshaw. "The superintendent at Camberwell Green police station," I replied. "He should be able to help you."

CHAPTER 23

"I visited Mr and Mrs Hamilton's home today," said James that evening as he took off his jacket. "There's something rather odd about the place; it's rather spartan inside. I realise they haven't been living there for long, but it struck me as odd all the same. Perhaps Mrs Hamilton is more interested in pursuing her work than making a home – and I'm not passing any judgement on her for that, Penny, before you suggest that I am." He smiled. "I'm merely stating a fact."

"How did you get on with the housekeeper?"

"She didn't give much away at all."

"Is she still adamant that there's nothing to worry about?"

"She doesn't seem unduly concerned, but she did acknowledge that she hasn't heard anything from them for more than two weeks now."

"And presumably she considers that unusual?"

"Yes, she does. She wasn't particularly happy about us looking around the house. I had a couple of men from P Division with me, which didn't help. What struck me as quite peculiar was the fact that we found barely any personal papers. Most people keep their correspondence and documents in a locked writing desk. We asked the housekeeper to unlock all the drawers and cupboards, but we found nothing of any great interest."

"Perhaps they've hidden them somewhere."

"They must have, but why? And where? There are no papers in that Aladdin's cave of Mr Hamilton's, which, incidentally, the housekeeper knew nothing about."

"Really?"

"Or at least she claimed not to. It's difficult to tell with her, really. She doesn't give much away."

"You'd think she would want to be helpful."

"You would indeed! I wouldn't describe her as obstructive or uncooperative, but she certainly didn't go out of her way to help us. I asked about her employers, but she doesn't know a great deal about them, either. She hasn't worked there for long; just four months or so."

He removed his revolver from its holster and locked it inside one of the writing table drawers.

"It fits a pattern, doesn't it?" I said.

"What do you mean?"

"No one seems to know much about them, and there are very few clues or personal papers in their house. Even the scant information we have about Mrs Hamilton has come to nothing. It makes you wonder whether they're really who they say they are."

James loosened his tie. "Impostors, you think?"

"I don't see why they should be... But here we are, two weeks after their disappearance or possible murder, and we still know so little about them. Even Beth and Mr Smollett haven't learned much about Mrs Hamilton, despite their having been friendly with her. We've spoken to a lot of people but still know almost nothing. In fact, I don't think anybody has been able to tell us a thing about their lives that occurred more than two years ago. We don't even know when they married."

"It can't have been too long ago. Mrs Hamilton is fairly young, isn't she?" said James.

"Beth said she's about twenty-five years of age."

"And Mr Hamilton is about twenty years older, is he not?"

"Apparently so."

"We need to find someone who knew them before they travelled to Egypt. How long were they there?"

"A few years, I think."

"And where did they meet?" he asked.

"I have no idea."

"They seem to have just appeared out of nowhere, and their staff have only recently been employed. Everything points to Mr and Mrs Hamilton having adopted false identities."

"Perhaps Mr Hamilton staged his death, in that case. Perhaps he somehow managed to lie there on the floor of his room and convince Beth that he was dead."

"It seems like a strange thing to do, but it's not beyond the realms of possibility. And then they escaped somewhere, you think?"

"Yes, having retrieved a valuable item from their collection to sell. The proceeds must have been used to fund the start of a new life somewhere."

"I do hope that goblet comes to light soon enough. I'm very pleased you managed to persuade Mrs Miller to help us on that front."

"If the Hamiltons sold it to someone, that person may be tempted to sell it on to Mrs Miller."

"That would be the ideal situation for us, wouldn't it?"

"It would indeed. But if Mr and Mrs Hamilton are not who they say they are, who are they really? And why would they lie?"

"I have no idea," replied James. "But we need to work that out if we're to have any hope of finding them."

CHAPTER 24

"I refuse to believe anything of the sort!" snapped Beth the following day. "Why would Susan lie about who she is? She's always been so genuine and honest with me."

Dark clouds were rolling low over the top of Primrose Hill, where we were taking a walk, and I could feel light spots of rain in the air. Two children skipped past us, pushing hoops.

"She would probably say the same of you, yet you were also pretending to be someone else," I replied.

Beth offered no reply. Instead, she shook her head sadly. "We were just fooling one another, then."

"It seems that way."

"Let's suppose that she did lie to me about her identity," said Beth. "Why would she do so?"

"I think she and her husband must have been involved in something untoward. They stole three artefacts from Mr Bagshaw, after all."

"You mentioned that before, but you've only heard Mr Bagshaw's side of the story. Perhaps there was a misunderstanding between them."

"I suppose there may have been, but you have to admit that Mr Hamilton's cave of treasures seems rather suspicious. How did he come by all those precious items? And why is everything hidden away like that?"

"It does look suspicious, I agree. But maybe Mrs Hamilton knew nothing about it."

"Mr Smollett says she had a key."

Beth sighed. "I truly believed they were who they said they were. I was so easily fooled."

"Everyone was fooled by them. We haven't told Mr Smollett yet. What do you suppose he'll think?"

"He'll be quite upset. Isn't it odd to think that both Susan and I were pretending to be different people? I don't feel quite so guilty for lying about my identity now. I wish I could discuss all this with her, and... Oh, I don't suppose she's a particularly nice person after all, is she? If she and Mr Hamilton were stealing from people, they must be criminals. That's what I find so difficult to believe. Perhaps I could grow accustomed to the idea of her having a false identity, but considering her a criminal? That's much more difficult."

"Do you think Mr Hamilton might have been a criminal from what you know of him?"

"Yes, I can picture that. But not Susan; she was simply too nice. I think he must have persuaded her somehow. Threatened her, even. How awful to think that she had no choice in the matter! She may have been trapped in a marriage in which she was made complicit in her husband's crimes. I forgive her already, Penny! I can see how she must have been forced to do her husband's bidding. And I feel happy for her if she managed to get away."

"Maybe she planned it all well in advance," I suggested.

"She may well have done."

"Perhaps she wished to ensure that she was well and truly free from his control."

"I'm quite sure that's what she would have wanted."

"She may have wanted him dead."

"Please don't suggest such a thing, Penny. I really don't want to believe that!"

CHAPTER 25

"I'm beginning to feel quite convinced that Mrs Hamilton murdered her husband because she no longer wished to be married to a criminal," I said to James in the garden that evening.

"An interesting theory," he replied. "She no longer wished to be associated with a criminal, so she secured her fate by committing a murder."

"Well, we already know that murderers often have rather distorted reasons for committing their crimes."

"True. Reasons that make sense to them but to no one else. You think she murdered him, then made her escape and stole the goblet, do you?"

"Yes."

"That doesn't explain how she managed to hide Mr Hamilton's body within a matter of minutes. How did she get him out of that hotel?"

"Perhaps John Smollett helped her," I suggested.

"Yes," James said thoughtfully. "I like that theory. He's admitted that the two were involved in a love affair, hasn't he? It would seem that she had more than one reason to be rid of her husband. Firstly he had forced her to lead a criminal life-style and secondly she had fallen in love with another man. Do you think Smollett has been lying to you all this time?"

"I think it's possible. It took him a while to admit to their affair, though I can understand why. He clearly didn't want to be accused of plotting with Mrs Hamilton against her husband."

"Do you think he knows where she is now?"

"He must be a very good liar if he does."

Tiger joined us in the garden and began rubbing her face against one of the terracotta plant pots.

"Perhaps Smollett gave her that goblet to sell," suggested James. "The two of them could somehow have disposed of Hamilton's body, then visited the Aladdin's cave together and taken the goblet. P Division has a man making enquiries in the vicinity of that hideaway under the arches. They want to ascertain who has been seen coming and going recently."

"That's an excellent idea. I hope someone saw something."

"What do you think of the rudbeckia?"

"Which one's that?"

"This one here with the bright yellow flowers."

"It's lovely. I thought it was a type of daisy."

"I think they're relatives of one another. Cousins, perhaps." He opened his secateurs and began removing faded flower heads. "P Division has made an excellent list of all the items the Hamiltons had hidden away," he said. "I've checked it against a ledger we keep at the Yard, which lists all the items stolen in the burglaries we've investigated. As you know, we often get called out to the bigger robberies at the large villas and country houses, and I've made some inter-esting discoveries. A five-light bronze candelabra found within Hamilton's treasure trove bears an uncanny resem-blance to a French, neoclassical, gilt-bronze candelabra stolen from Lord Manningham's home in Epsom, Surrey, four years ago."

"Really?"

"And a silver cup with a domed cover sounds rather similar to a Georgian silver cup stolen in the same burglary. There's also a silver inkstand fashioned in the shape of a ram. I've seen it myself and cannot understand why anyone would want it on their desk, but Lord Manningham clearly did, and now we've found it for him."

"Does this mean that the Hamiltons have been burgling homes?"

"Either that or they fenced the items. Perhaps they bought them from the thieves. Although why the Hamiltons kept them for so long, I'll never know. Maybe they were waiting for the trail to go cold before selling them again."

"So before they became Egyptologists, they were involved in the theft of valuable items. Was anyone ever arrested for burgling Lord Manningham's home?"

"It's interesting you should ask that, Penny, because that was precisely my thought, so I looked up the case. One man, Jack Tremmel, was arrested but all the other gang members got away. There are items in the Hamiltons's treasure trove from other burglaries, too: silver plate that appears to have once belonged to Lady Cooper-Burns and some jewellery taken from a vicar's wife in Middlesex."

"I don't usually associate vicar's wives with valuable jewellery."

"Neither do I, but she appears to have had quite a bit of it. Until Hamilton got his hands on it, that is."

"Is there any possibility that he came by these objects innocently?"

"I very much doubt it. Why would he hide them in a cave if he had?"

"It's not a cave. It's an archway under a railway line."

"A man-made cave, then." He smiled.

"I agree that it does look terribly suspicious."

"There's no doubt about it, Penny. Hamilton either stole those items or bought them from thieves. I don't think there's any possibility that he's completely innocent. And as for Mrs Hamilton, she undoubtedly knew about his nefarious dealings and was probably involved in them, too. It seems she decided to leave her husband and then had him dealt with. Smollett may have helped, but I'm beginning to wonder why the two of them didn't run away together if he was part of it."

"Maybe she wasn't really in love with him," I suggested.

"Maybe. Another possibility is that she employed someone to murder her husband and used the alabaster goblet as payment."

"That sounds plausible. I can only hope that Mrs Miller is able to lure the owner of that goblet in. Whoever it is may wish to exchange it for money."

"I'll pay a visit to Jack Tremmel and see if he's willing to tell us about his accomplices. He may need some sort of incentive to talk, so I'll speak to the governor at the jail about the possibility of a few days' parole in return for his assistance. I'd also like to speak to John Smollett again. We need to work out whether he knows more than he's letting on."

CHAPTER 26

Although I couldn't rule out the possibility that John Smollett had been instrumental in Mr Hamilton's death, I felt rather sorry for him as James, Beth and I crowded his little room in Pimlico. It was only slightly larger than the room I had once occupied in Mrs Garnett's home.

Mr Smollett sat on the end of his bed with a forlorn expression on his face, having just received the news that Mrs Hamilton was not the person she had said she was.

"Susan wasn't a thief," he said. "And if she'd known those items in the storage room were stolen she would have informed the police, I'm sure of it. She was a good person."

"Do you have any idea why she might have used a pseudonym?" asked James.

He shook his head.

"Mr Hamilton obviously forced her to do so," said Beth from the only chair in the room. "Don't you agree, Mr Smollett? She really wasn't a devious person."

"No, she wasn't," agreed Mr Smollett.

"But she was unfaithful to her husband," said James.

Mr Smollett flinched, as though he had been hit. "She had a reason to be!" he exclaimed bitterly. "Although I respected Mr Hamilton in many ways, he wasn't a good husband."

"Do you think there's any possibility that she knew her husband had employed Beth to spy on her?" James asked Mr Smollett.

"I think she would have spoken to me about it if she had."

"Perhaps she was too upset," suggested James. "Perhaps she made the discovery the day she went missing. Already unhappy in her marriage, it may have given her the final impetus to leave him."

"Now I feel even worse about what I did!" protested Beth.

"There's no need to feel guilty," I said. "You were merely doing the job you had been employed to do. If Mr Hamilton hadn't hired you, he simply would have found another lady detective. You cannot be responsible for the unhappiness of the Hamilton marriage or the actions of either party."

"If only I could find her and explain everything!" she responded. "I want the chance to tell her that I didn't want to work for her husband any longer. I was so fond of her as a friend. How I wish I'd been able to tell her who I was before all this unpleasantness began!"

"I realise now how little I really know about her," said Mr Smollett, his eyes resting on the faded hearthrug. "As soon as she went missing I did what I could to find her. I think I'm beginning to understand why she mentioned so few friends and family members to me. Even the father who was a vicar in Rochdale must have been a lie." His eyes grew wide and sorrowful. "She didn't have to lie to me! She could have told me the truth and I wouldn't have minded it at all. I would have kept her secrets if that's what she had wanted. She should have been able to trust me."

"Did Susan Hamilton ever mention wanting to harm her husband?" James asked Mr Smollett.

"No! She would never have done that."

"But she had expressed her wish to leave him?"

"Yes."

"What was the reason for that?"

"She didn't love him."

"Did she love you?"

"She never quite said that word, but we were very fond of one another."

"If she had wanted to get rid of her husband, would you have helped her?"

Mr Smollett's eyes narrowed. "Get rid of him? Do you mean *murder* him?"

"I'm not suggesting that she committed the act herself, but she could have arranged for someone else to do it on her behalf."

Mr Smollett shook his head vehemently. "Impossible!"

"He forced her into a life of crime," continued James. "And he was short-tempered, especially when he had been drinking alcohol. Then he employed someone to spy on her. It would have been very difficult for her to leave him and even harder for her to petition for a divorce. The man was a criminal. I never met him, but I imagine he had very few redeeming qualities as a husband. Who can blame Mrs Hamilton for wishing her husband dead?"

"She never expressed any such desire."

"But she may have thought about it, or planned it even. Many would sympathise with her."

"She may have thought it in a moment of desperation," conceded Mr Smollett. "But I don't believe she ever would have done it."

"Perhaps not. It would have been far easier for her to find someone else to do the deed, I suppose. Someone who would accept payment in the form of an ancient Egyptian artefact."

"The alabaster goblet?"

"Possibly. What do you think?"

"No."

"Do you think it completely impossible?"

"Quite impossible."

"But not completely?"

Mr Smollett rubbed at his brow. "Not completely, no."

"Poor Mr Smollett," I said to James as we travelled home on the omnibus. "Not only has the woman he loves gone missing, but he's also discovered that she had been lying to him. He was still trying to come to terms with that while you stood over him firing one question after another at him!"

"I'm a detective, Penny. It's my job."

"Don't you at least have a little sympathy for him?"

"I do, but I cannot allow emotion to get in the way of my work. Besides, he may not be as innocent as he appears."

"Do you think he might have had something to do with Mr Hamilton's murder?"

"He may well have done! Don't be fooled by the man's soft nature, Penny. He may be young and wide-eyed, but we have no idea what he's capable of."

CHAPTER 27

O n returning home, Mrs Oliver the housekeeper informed us that a guest was waiting for us in the front room.

"He insisted on waiting," she added.

As we stepped into the room, Joseph Bagshaw got to his feet. "You must be Inspector Blakely!" he said, holding his hand out toward my husband. "And good evening to you, too, Mrs Blakely."

"What are you doing here?"

James's response wasn't a particularly polite one, but I could see that he was rather perplexed by the sudden appearance of the Egyptologist at the end of a long day.

"I do apologise for imposing upon you like this, but I'm merely attempting to recover my belongings. Your delightful wife suggested that I contact the superintendent at Camberwell Green police station, but despite having done so, I have still not been reunited with the items Mr Hamilton stole from me. I believe they were found in a storeroom below some railway arches. These items are accustomed to warmth!

It will do them no good to be kept in the damp and cold like that. I would like them returned to me immediately!"

"Identifying all the items in that storeroom is proving to be quite the task," replied James. "Each one is being carefully recorded and researched to ascertain whether it has ever been listed as stolen. A good number of the items found there have."

"Why doesn't that surprise me? Hamilton's a crook!"

"Did you report those items as stolen, Mr Bagshaw?"

"Actually, I didn't. They were stolen in Egypt, you see, and the Egyptian police are completely hopeless at anything like that."

"Perhaps you should have reported the items stolen once you knew they had arrived in England."

"I could have done, I suppose..."

"It would have helped us reunite you with them. At the moment we have no record that they were ever stolen from you at all."

"But they were!"

"You'll need to report the thefts at the police station."

"Right." Mr Bagshaw looked a little deflated. "I shall do that right away."

"While you're here," said James, "you may be able to answer one or two questions I have about Mr and Mrs Hamilton."

"I've already told your delightful wife everything I know."

"We have a theory now that Mr and Mrs Hamilton may be impostors."

"Impostors of what?"

"We suspect that Hamilton was not their real name, as we have been able to find out so little about them. Is there any information they let slip about themselves that we could use to track them down?"

He gave this some thought. "Nothing that immediately

springs to mind, but I shall continue to think about it. I struggle to believe that they're not who they said they were. Why would they do such a thing?"

"They were thieves. It's fairly common for those leading that sort of life to change their names."

"I suppose it would be."

"Will you let us know if you recall them telling you anything at all about themselves? The smallest of clues could potentially help us find them."

He nodded. "Of course. And my belongings?"

"Report them as stolen first, Mr Bagshaw, and then the police will begin the process of returning them to you. They may ask to see some proof that the items truly belong to you."

"Proof? How can I provide proof? I dug them out of the ground in a foreign land!"

"Then perhaps you'd like to ask yourself whether those items are truly yours!"

CHAPTER 28

"Penny!" My father greeted me with a wide grin as I arrived at my former lodgings in Milton Street. He still lived in the room I had occupied for many years in Mrs Garnett's house. "You received my telegram, then?" he said, leading me through to Mrs Garnett's parlour. "Thank you so much for making the journey here. I know how busy you are with those missing Egyptologists and the rest of it."

Mrs Garnett was sitting at the table in her parlour. Although she greeted me with a smile, she didn't seem her usual cheery self. A bottle of Vin Mariani coca wine stood on the table but very little of it had been drunk.

My father offered me some, but I declined. "It's a little too invigorating," I added. "I find it makes my heart race."

"That's exactly why I drink it!" replied my father. "One needs a little vigour when one gets to my age. That's why I'm surprised you didn't want any today, Mrs Garnett."

"Are you suggesting that I'm the same age as you, Mr Green?"

"Yes..." His reply was cautious. "Aren't you?"

"I don't know how old you are, but I don't think you have

any business speculating about my age! It's not gentlemanly conduct!"

"No, I suppose it's not." He turned to me. "Take a seat, Penny. There's no need to stand around like that."

I did so, sensing an unusually tense atmosphere in the room. I watched my father refill his glass of coca wine and give the two empty glasses a sad glance.

"The truth of the matter is, Penny, I need a little bit of help," he said.

"You're not going to ask your daughter the same thing you asked me, are you?" said Mrs Garnett.

"I need help! And I can't say that you've given me much assistance, Mrs Garnett."

"What do you expect me to do, Mr Green? Evict my current tenants? They're good people. They're respectable and always pay their rent on time. I've never been so lucky with my tenants before."

She gave me a sidelong glance, as if to remind me of the few occasions when I had been unable to afford my rent.

"The problem I have, Penny," said my father, "is a lack of space."

"Space for what?"

"My family. They're currently sailing across the Atlantic and I have nowhere to put them!"

"Perhaps you should have thought of that before you arranged for them to make the trip," said Mrs Garnett.

"I *did* think of it! I simply assumed it would be all right to—"

"To take over my house!"

"For want of a better description, yes. Let me tell you part of the problem here, Penny," said my father. "Mrs Garnett doesn't want my wife—"

"*Common-law* wife."

"We were married in the jungle!"

"Not at a wedding recognised under English law," snapped the landlady. "When she arrives on these shores, she will be your common-law wife."

"And this is the problem I face," said Father. "Mrs Garnett won't allow Malia to live here with me."

"Not in the same room," she clarified. "I will not tolerate an unmarried couple living together as man and wife."

"Despite the fact that we did so in Amazonia," muttered my father. "It would make matters far easier, of course, if I could marry Malia here, and so formalise our union in the eyes of the English law. But in order to do that I must first divorce your mother, Penny."

Mrs Garnett made a disapproving sucking noise with her lips.

"This is the quandary in which I find myself," continued Father. "I can petition for a divorce, but it takes a good while. In the meantime, Malia and the children must be housed somewhere."

I finally realised what he intended to ask of me. "You want them to stay with me and James?" I asked.

Father gave me an apologetic smile. "Would you mind?"

I stared back at him.

His grey eyebrows were raised hopefully above his bright, pleading eyes. I sensed Mrs Garnett watching me, interested to hear my answer to this preposterous request.

"I... I would need to speak to James about it."

"Thank you, Penny. That's very kind of you." He leaned forward and rested his hand on mine. "I'm extremely grateful."

By not replying with an immediate refusal, I had given him hope that we would agree to it. In fact, he seemed to think I had already agreed to it and that the proposed discussion with James would be a mere formality.

I stumbled over my words as I tried to correct my mistake. "I didn't mean to imply that it would be possible."

"Oh."

He withdrew his hand and I immediately felt guilty.

"I need some time to think about it," I continued. "Your request has taken me quite by surprise, you see." I knew it was impossible, yet I struggled to directly refuse him.

"You knew my wife and children were on their way here."

"Yes, but I assumed you had arranged accommodation for them."

"I would have done so had it not been for that rather troublesome chap."

"Which troublesome chap?"

"The one I mentioned to you before. He claims I failed to fulfil the terms of some agreement relating to an expedition undertaken in '73. I was initially told he had no leg to stand on, but it seems he was right in some respects. Now he's laid claim to that rather tidy little sum I had sitting in the bank on Lombard Street."

"Which means you have no money," I replied.

"Ah, but I will have! I shall make an enormous sum with this tour around the country! The debtors will be paid off and—"

"*Debtors?* There's more than one?"

"Just a few little outstanding matters I hadn't quite cleared up before my unplanned ten-year stint in the jungle. But the money from the tour will soon come in, and then I shall have everything paid off and be able to rent a large home, too. Perhaps I'll even have enough to buy one! I shall have money for the divorce, and then Malia and I can have a wonderful wedding and a huge celebration. The children will go to the best schools in the land and we shall be wonderfully happy. It'll all be possible in just a short amount of time; I just need a little help to get me there. Can I rely on you, Penny?"

CHAPTER 29

"**A**bsolutely not!" exclaimed James when I explained Father's request that evening. "I hope you made that abundantly clear to him!"

"Almost."

"Almost?! What do you mean *almost*? There is no possible way we can have his common-law wife and five children living under our roof! We have three bedrooms and one of those is your writing room. Where do you propose to put them all?"

"I'm not proposing anything. I just need to find a way to tell him it isn't possible."

"Yes, you do. The gall of the man! Fancy making such a request of his daughter. Can you imagine what the neighbours would say if we let six members of an Amazonian tribe move into their street?"

"I'm not particularly interested in the opinion of our neighbours."

"Neither am I, usually. But they would stand outside the house and stare! Is that what you want?"

"No, and I know that I need to turn down his request. The difficulty is, I simply don't know how."

"You just need to tell him straight, Penny. That should be the end of the matter."

James poured himself a whiskey. Once he had calmed down a little, he told me about his visit to Wormwood Scrubs prison earlier in the day.

"I was the guest of Mr Jack Tremmel there," he said. "A former associate of Charles Hamilton."

"I hope he was a good host," I replied with a smile.

"Not too bad, considering that convicts don't tend to like policemen as a general rule."

"I wonder why…"

"It's rather a puzzle, isn't it? Anyway, I think he might have warmed to me a little given that I managed to negotiate five days of parole for him in return for helping me with my investigation. He's been incarcerated for four years, and seems to be a well-behaved inmate."

"What did he say about Mr Hamilton?"

"He knew him as Robert Higgins."

"Is that his real name?"

"I doubt it, somehow. He told me Higgins liked to consider himself a gentleman, despite his humble beginnings. He put on airs and graces, and apparently went around telling people he was descended from a French marquess."

I sniggered.

"It might be true, Penny!" He winked. "Anyway, Tremmel painted a picture of a man who liked to think he was a little better than he was. He envied the large homes of the landed gentry and aspired to be just like them. Tremmel told me Higgins was a clever man, with the ability to absorb knowledge. He took a keen interest in the arts and regularly went to the theatre, concert performances and lectures. In the brief time Tremmel knew him, Higgins managed to significantly elevate his status."

"Although he was actually a thief."

"Yes. We've come across gentleman criminals before, haven't we? Although I'm not quite sure Higgins ever managed to fully acquire the genteel manners of the upper classes. Tremmel told me that Higgins spent a great deal of time touring villages close to London and looking up the homes of wealthy folk. He read the newspapers every day, looking out for any mention of where affluent families might reside, and he attended auctions, taking a keen interest in the ownership of items being bought and sold. He prided himself on the depth of his knowledge, and Tremmel admitted that he admired Higgins for it.

"Once a house had been identified as a target, Higgins would watch it for a number of weeks and accustom himself to the household's comings and goings. Sometimes he would befriend servants or, failing that, bribe or blackmail them for information. When it was time for the robbery to take place, he would inform the gang about every single outbuilding and loose dog on the property, as well as the location of every tree, shrub and any other suitable hiding place. He would also tell them which valuable items could be found in the house and where they were likely to be located."

"He appears to have been a highly organised man."

"You could say that. He recruited gang members and gave them their orders. And he paid them in cash, so they didn't receive any of the stolen items."

"Why did he keep so many of the items he stole?"

"We're not exactly sure how many he did steal. If he was as prolific as Tremmel says he was, the bits we found in Aladdin's cave probably only account for a small proportion of his takings. I suspect those were the most difficult items to sell. And I suspect he also had a good deal of pride about the haul he had accumulated over the years. If he couldn't be a rich man living in a stately home with a vast collection of valuables, why not store a collection of valuables beneath a railway line in Camberwell? It was as close as he could get to his dream.

"Tremmel suspects that Higgins had to answer to someone else. A more senior criminal, as it were. He doesn't know the identity of this man, and Higgins rarely mentioned him. But Tremmel suggested that some of the stolen items had been specifically requested by another person."

"Interesting. What made Higgins decide to become Mr Hamilton the Egyptologist?"

"He wasn't able to tell me that. It all happened after Tremmel was imprisoned for the burglary. Perhaps Higgins realised it would only be a matter of time before he was caught, so he decided to change his name and the nature of his activities."

"Escaping to Egypt was a good way to evade the law."

"It was, wasn't it?"

"You managed to acquire a lot of information in exchange for five days of parole."

"Tremmel seemed quite happy to talk. His loyalty to Higgins appears to have waned over the years. I suppose it's not altogether surprising. He was serving a long prison sentence while Higgins was having a merry old time in Egypt. Having the name Robert Higgins is extremely useful to us. I'm sure some of my colleagues will have encountered him before."

"The question remains, though, how Robert Higgins came to meet the lady who calls herself Susan Hamilton."

"Tremmel knew nothing of her, which suggests to me that Higgins married her after Tremmel was imprisoned."

"Then her identity remains a mystery."

"It does. But we're getting closer, Penny, slowly but surely. There was something else quite interesting that Tremmel mentioned to me. When I told him the circumstances of Robert Higgins's supposed murder, he smiled."

"Really?"

"Higgins once confessed to him a plan he had devised for faking his own death. He predicted that sooner or later he would find himself in hot water and there would only be one way out."

"He told Tremmel that he planned to fake his own death?"

"Apparently so. But it would be rather tricky to pull off, wouldn't it? Unless someone else was in on it, that is. Another person willing to reinforce the idea that the individual really was dead."

"You mean someone like Beth Worthers?"

"We've been working on this case for a while now, Penny, and she is still our only witness."

CHAPTER 30

I sat at my writing desk the following morning and pondered the case. I watched Tiger lying on her side, gripping her knitted mouse between her paws. She gave me a mischievous look, sunk her teeth into the mouse's head, then kicked it furiously with her hind paws.

"Poor mouse!" I said. "What did he do to deserve that?"

Tiger stared at me, then began licking her shoulder. I looked at the brutalised mouse and thought of the time and care Beth had taken to make it. *Had it been a genuine act of kindness or an attempt to win me over as a friend?*

I turned back to my notepad, feeling ashamed of my doubts about her. I wanted to believe everything she had told me, and I hadn't yet found fault with anything she had said or done. *But was I a fool for trusting her?* A good deal of her work involved pretending to be someone else. *Was she really who she said she was?* She claimed Mr Hamilton had employed her to spy on his wife. *Had he actually employed her to help fake his death?*

I couldn't overlook the fact that Beth was the only person to have seen Mr Hamilton dead on the floor of his room.

There was no evidence at all that the incident had even happened; all we had was her word. I wanted to trust it, but I had made mistakes in trusting the wrong people before.

The maid I had spoken to at the hotel said she had heard Mr and Mrs Hamilton's voices in room 306 at half-past eight... forty minutes after Beth had reported finding Mr Hamilton dead. Perhaps the maid hadn't been able to confirm that the voices she had heard were those of Mr and Mrs Hamilton, but it was clear that someone had been in the room at that time. *Where had they been hiding while Beth was supposedly in the room?*

The story of Mr Hamilton's lifeless body disappearing within a few minutes of her seeing it was also difficult to believe. I had tried my best to do so, but it simply didn't make sense. There had been no sign of a disturbance in the room, and somehow the body had been removed from the hotel without anyone noticing.

The more I considered her story, the more improbable it seemed. *Was I a fool for believing everything she had told me?*

Mr Hamilton could have found himself in hot water, as James had put it, and decided to fake his own death. Presumably, his wife had not wished to do the same, so arrangements had been made for her to disappear somewhere. By employing Beth Worthers, Mr Hamilton had ensured that there was a witness to his supposed death, as well as someone who could potentially influence the investigation. *Had Beth approached me because she thought I could influence a Scotland Yard investigation?* Perhaps she hoped I would believe her story and persuade my police inspector husband to do the same.

I felt a bitter taste in my mouth as I considered how easily I had been fooled. Mr and Mrs Hamilton had probably been reunited abroad and were now living with new identities. *Perhaps Beth would disappear as well.*

As I ruminated, I wondered whether Mr Smollett could

also be in on the ruse. *Was it possible that Beth had brought him in to the fold to make the story more believable?* Mr Smollett was supposedly the reason why Beth had been employed by Mr Hamilton in the first place. I sighed and got up from my desk. I didn't know what to believe any more.

I decided to go out for a walk and get some fresh air. As I put on my hat and coat, there was a knock at the door. I opened it to find a messenger boy standing on the doorstep with a telegram from Mrs Miller.

She had news about the alabaster goblet.

CHAPTER 31

"Someone has responded to my advert," said Mrs Miller. She was dressed in emerald green and wore an elaborate hair decoration covered in painted shells.

"Who is it?"

"A Mrs Brown. We're to dine in a private room at the Café Royal this evening."

Could it be Mrs Hamilton herself? Would she be so brazen as to meet Mrs Miller in person?

"What excellent news!" I said. "Will you let me know if it's Mrs Hamilton who comes to meet you?"

She frowned. "Her name is Mrs Brown."

"But it could just be Mrs Hamilton pretending to be Mrs Brown."

"Oh, I see. Well, I can't really remember what Mrs Hamilton looks like, so I honestly wouldn't know."

"She's young and pretty with dark hair."

"So are half the girls in London! Can't you give me a better description than that?"

"I'm afraid not, as I've only ever seen a sketch of her.

You've met her, though, haven't you? Perhaps you'll remember her if you see her again."

Mrs Miller laughed. "I met the Hamiltons at a dinner, but I'm afraid she was perfectly forgettable. I remember him all right; he was quite a character. I shall report back on the appearance of Mrs Brown, and with any further information she decides to impart to me. Perhaps you'll be able to deduce from that whether she happens to be Mrs Hamilton or not. I must make it clear to you that I have no intention of buying the goblet. I shall tell Mrs Brown that I will merely consider the offer."

"It'll be rather difficult to determine whether or not Mrs Brown is truly Mrs Hamilton if neither of us knows what she looks like," I said. "I'll have to bring someone with me who knows her." I was thinking of Beth. "We can wait outside the restaurant, then once you've seen her you could make your excuses for a moment to come and find us."

"And what then?"

"If you think there's any possibility that she might be Mrs Hamilton, a friend of mine who knows her well can go inside with you and see for herself."

She pursed her scarlet lips and considered this for a moment. "All right, then. We're meeting at eight."

I sent a telegram to Beth asking her to meet me outside the Café Royal that evening. I knew it would be difficult to be my usual friendly self with her now that my suspicions had been aroused. *Should I confront her with my suspicions or keep them to myself for now?* I wondered. I felt sure that Beth would notice the change in my demeanour toward her either way.

"I hope it is Susan Hamilton!" enthused Beth when we met outside the Café Royal.

The exclusive restaurant occupied a sizeable section of the grand stone buildings at the lower end of Regent Street. The wide thoroughfare was busy with horses and carriages, and well-dressed people thronged the pavements. We stood beneath my umbrella in a heavy summer shower.

"I hope so, too," I replied. "Perhaps she'll be able to tell us exactly what has happened to her husband."

"She may not know!"

"But how is it that she vanished at exactly the same time he was supposedly murdered?"

"I don't know."

"And *why* did she vanish?"

"She must have thought people would suspect her of carrying out the murder."

"But there was only ever your word that he was murdered in the first place. No one else saw his body, did they?"

Beth shrugged. "Perhaps she panicked."

Her answer didn't make any sense to me. She gave me a questioning glance, as if she had noticed that I was beginning to doubt her story.

I broke her gaze by glancing up at the clock on the building opposite. It was almost a quarter-past eight. If Mrs Hamilton was inside the restaurant with Mrs Miller, we would surely have some answers soon.

A moment later, a doorman opened the restaurant door and a lady in gold and furs marched out through them. It was Mrs Miller.

Her look was stern as she strode toward me. "She's a total time-waster," she hissed. "Not the lady you're looking for at all!"

"Are you sure?" I replied.

"You'll see for yourself in just a moment," she replied. "Look out for an old lady leaving shortly. She may look a little sheepish, as I've already rebuked her for squandering my precious time." She called over to the doorman and asked him to summon her a cab. "I'm going home now. Good evening, ladies."

I thanked Mrs Miller for her time as she strode away, but I couldn't tell whether or not she had heard me. I knew for sure that I had no desire to be rebuked by her myself.

I watched the door cautiously, waiting for an old lady who appeared upset. An old lady did eventually emerge, but she seemed quite happy and relaxed. Her clothing was modest and she wore a large orange hat that had seen better days. She didn't look like the sort of lady who would have Egyptian antiquities to sell.

"Mrs Brown?" I said, approaching her.

"Yes, dear?" She grinned to reveal only a few teeth.

"Did you meet with my friend Mrs Miller just now?"

"She's your friend, is she? I found her quite rude."

"You had something to sell her, is that right?"

"I was thinking about it."

"An Egyptian goblet. by any chance?"

"That would be rather nice, wouldn't it?"

"Do you happen to be in possession of such a thing?"

"She asked me the very same question!"

"Do you know a lady named Mrs Hamilton?"

"Is that the friend I just met inside the restaurant? She was very rude indeed."

"No, that was Mrs Miller. Do you have the goblet, Mrs Brown?"

"Why does everyone want to know whether I have it? I certainly shouldn't mind having such a thing."

"Did you respond to Mrs Miller's newspaper advertisement?"

"Yes." She nodded. "Now, how do I get to Piccadilly Circus from here?"

"It's just further along that way," replied Beth, pointing down the street.

"Thank you, dear." She gave us both a wide grin. "Lovely talking to you."

"She's confused," I said sadly, watching her hobble away.

"Very confused," said Beth. "No wonder Mrs Miller was annoyed."

The disappointment at our continued failure to find Mrs Hamilton lay heavily on my chest. "None of this makes sense!" I snapped.

Beth was startled by my vexed tone. "What do you mean? What doesn't make sense?"

"All of it! You're the only person who saw Mr Hamilton dead. His body went missing within a matter of minutes and so did his wife. An ancient artefact is missing, which can only have been taken by Mr and Mrs Hamilton since their disappearance. Unless Mr Smollett isn't being honest with us and he took it himself. And Mr and Mrs Hamilton turned out to be criminals rather than Egyptologists. And Mr Hamilton also went by the name Robert Higgins."

"Robert Higgins?"

"Did you ever hear him use that name?"

"No."

"He burgled wealthy homes, apparently. And at some point, Mrs Hamilton, or whatever her real name is, helped him commit his crimes. Most of the items stored under that railway arch are stolen."

"Can you be sure of that?"

"Yes, my husband found records of them being reported stolen and has spoken to a former accomplice about him. Did Mr or Mrs Hamilton tell you any of this?"

"Of course not! I had no idea."

"You were working for a criminal."

"I knew nothing about that! I obviously wouldn't have taken on the work if I had!"

"Do you think Mr Smollett knew?"

"I wouldn't have thought so."

"You don't think he ever questioned why a storage area beneath a railway arch was crammed with treasures?"

"No, I don't think he did. Naive of him, of course, but he's quite a young man, isn't he?"

"I have no idea whether he's telling the truth or not. I really don't know who to believe any more."

"It's a complicated case."

"It certainly is, especially when you consider that the former accomplice James spoke to revealed that Mr Hamilton had previously planned to fake his own death."

"Is that so?"

"Yes, so it's very likely that he isn't dead at all."

"But I saw him!"

"Did you really?"

"Yes."

"Or are you just saying that?"

"I'm telling you I did!"

"Perhaps Mr Hamilton employed you to help him fake his own death. That would explain why you're the only person who ever saw him supposedly deceased."

Her brow crumpled. "Do you really think I've been lying to you, Penny?"

"I think a lot of people have."

"You don't trust me?"

I paused for a moment, aware that my words were hurting her feelings. *But if she was lying to me, surely there was no harm in saying how I felt.*

"I am struggling to trust you, Beth, if I'm honest. There are so many theories to consider, and I don't know what to think at this point. None of it makes any sense, and I think that's because Mr and Mrs Hamilton have manipulated the situation right from the off. It would have been easy for him to pay you to say that he was dead. As you pointed out to me and James when you first told us about this case, your work forces you to be a little duplicitous at times."

As I spoke, I saw Beth push her lips between her teeth, as if she were trying to suppress tears. There was a long pause when I finished.

"I'm sorry you feel that way, Penny." Her voice sounded timid and hurt.

I immediately felt a pang of remorse. *But was this just another act of hers?*

"Perhaps we'll never find them," she continued. "I feel we've done all we can."

Then she turned on her heel and walked away.

CHAPTER 32

"I feel awful," I said to James, after I had told him about my conversation with Beth. "I feel like I've lost a friend."

"She's not much of a friend if she's been lying to you."

"But has she?"

"You must have been fairly sure of it to confront her."

"But her reaction really affected me," I replied. "She looked so sad."

"Only because she's been found out!"

"But has she? Or has she been telling the truth all along?"

"Until we get to the bottom of all this, we really can't be certain. But we'd be wise not to take everyone at their word."

I nodded. "I've been caught out that way before."

"Exactly. It's always best to err on the side of caution, and if that means losing a few friends along the way, then so be it."

"But I don't like losing friends!"

"No one does. And at this moment in time, we don't know whether she's a true friend or not. If she is, perhaps she'll forgive you once all this is over."

"I don't feel as though it'll ever be over. I really can't see how we're going to find out exactly what happened."

"We're making progress, Penny."

"How? I really hoped Mrs Miller had managed to arrange a meeting with Mrs Hamilton, but it was just some unfortunate old lady who barely knew whether she was coming or going."

James laughed.

"What's so funny?"

"Investigations like this can be infuriating at times. The important thing is to keep trying."

"I don't know if I want to any more! If Mr Hamilton faked his own death, why should I even care about him and his criminal wife? I'd rather not waste any more time on it."

"Well, you don't have to, Penny. I do, however, now that we've discovered a horde of stolen items. But if there was never actually a murder, it makes our job a little easier."

"I hope you find the pair of them so they can both be locked up for wasting everyone's time!"

"That would be nice, wouldn't it? I'd like to speak to Mr Smollett and find out if he had any idea that Mr Hamilton intended to fake his own death. I like to think I've been making a little progress, however.

"I had a conversation with a colleague today, Inspector Powell. He was the man who arrested Jack Tremmel but never managed to find Robert Higgins, as he knew him. Apparently, Higgins had been arrested a number of times over the years by various divisions of the Metropolitan Police, but either he wasn't in possession of anything stolen at the time or he had a decent alibi. They had a good idea of what he was up to, but there was never enough evidence to charge him. Now that we've discovered his treasure trove, we've plenty of evidence. I just don't know how to go about finding him."

"It could take years," I responded. "He and his wife are probably overseas by now."

"Well, thank you for the encouragement, Penny." James smiled. "It's not like you to become so downhearted over a case. You're usually very optimistic."

"I'm still upset about Beth. I can't help it." Tiger jumped onto my lap and I stroked her smooth back.

"Inspector Powell also confirmed something Jack Tremmel told me. Higgins was reporting to someone else: a Mr Tom Scully. Scully was a crooked auctioneer who several criminals in his employ. The only crime they managed to convict him of was a minor fraud case, for which he served a year in prison. After that he changed his ways and apparently turned his back on his life of crime."

"Is there any chance he might know what has happened to Mr Hamilton?"

"I should think it unlikely, given that he's renounced his previous way of living. That said, I don't suppose there's any harm in tracking him down and finding out."

We were interrupted by the doorbell.

"Who can that be at this hour?" I said.

Mrs Oliver had already gone home, so James got up to answer it.

"So sorry to disturb you at this time," came Francis's voice from the hallway.

I got up from my seat to greet him as he entered the front room. He appeared flustered but was smiling.

"I apologise for the late hour, Penny, but I have some news that you may find rather interesting."

We took a seat while James went over to the drinks cabinet and poured out two whiskeys and a sherry.

"I've been trawling through various Egyptian reference books, as you well know," said Francis once he had a drink in his hand. "And when you mentioned the alabaster goblet,

Penny, I began looking for references to such items. There are a few, of course. Now, you might suppose that alabaster is a form of gypsum."

"Might I?" commented James.

"Well, in Europe it is generally considered so. It was a particularly popular material during the medieval period, when a great number of impressive religious carvings were made, especially in the Nottingham area. Gypsum was quarried in south Derbyshire, you see, not very far from Nottingham. Sadly, many of the carvings were destroyed during the Reformation, although some were taken to France."

"Have you called on us at this late hour just to tell us this?" inquired James.

"There will be a point to Francis's story," I responded. "Let him finish."

"Yes, there is a point," said Francis. "I'll get to it in time. Where was I? Oh, yes. I was about to say that the alabaster found in the ancient civilisations of Egypt and Mesopotamia is actually derived from calcite, not gypsum."

"Well I never," said James, suppressing a yawn.

I gave him a sharp look.

"It's a soft, attractive mineral that lent itself well to the many beautiful objects the Egyptians made from it. Now, the goblet you seek is particularly beautiful for the mere fact that it's carved into the shape of a lotus flower. It also has some attractive hieroglyphics etched into it. I searched for a mention of an object like this but found no match. I came across plenty of other alabaster goblets, as well as alabaster perfume bottles and canopic jars. But could I find a mention of this particular one? I'm afraid not. Then I researched Amenhotep IV and learned that he changed his name to Akhenaten."

"And founded Amarna," I added.

"Indeed he did!" Francis gave me a broad grin.

"How did you know that, Penny?" asked James.

"Mr Bagshaw told me."

"Akhenaten founded Amarna, and he and his wife, Nefertiti, introduced the worship of Aten, the sun disc," continued Francis. "Not all Egyptians were happy about this, and after his death they returned to their old worshipping ways as well as relocating the capital of the country back to Thebes. In fact, it was only after the rediscovery of Amarna that we began to learn anything about him. The goblet, therefore, must have been made during his reign but before he changed his name to Akhenaten.

"Anyway, I could go on about the fascinating things I've discovered about Egypt," he said, giving James a cautious glance, "but I must tell you my reason for visiting. When the books failed to answer my questions, I decided to visit the Department of Egyptian and Assyrian Antiquities at the British Museum and speak to the keeper of Egyptian antiquities. When I asked him about the goblet, he stared at me like a man bewitched."

"Why did he do that?" asked James.

"He took me over to a glass cabinet filled with a variety of ancient artefacts and there, standing proudly in the midst of them, was the very goblet you seek!"

"Are you sure?" I asked. "But how can it be the same one?"

"There must be more than one that matches its description," said James. "There are countless alabaster goblets and jars, as you said, Francis."

"I'll tell you why I suspect it's the same one, however. It's only been on display for a few days."

"But how did it get there?" I asked.

"It was left on the museum steps."

"When?"

"About ten days ago."

I pondered this. "The Hamiltons went missing three

weeks ago, so that fits with the timescale. One of them, or perhaps both, must have left it there. But why?"

"Or Smollett," said James. "He could easily have done it."

"Then why did he seem so surprised when he noticed it was missing? Surely he wouldn't have bothered bringing it to our attention. We had no idea of its existence until he mentioned it."

"That's a fair point. He could still have put it there, though I can't think of a good reason why at the moment. The person who left it there obviously had a good reason for doing so."

"They deliberately donated it to the museum," said Francis. "Whoever it was wanted it to be properly looked after."

"They had no interest in making money by selling it," I added. "It's rather lucky that no one stole it from the steps!"

"The keeper of Egyptian antiquities was extremely grateful for the gift," said Francis, "but I'm afraid there are no further clues as to how the goblet found its way there."

"Was there a note included with it?" asked James.

"None, I'm afraid."

"I should like to see it," I said. "Shall we all pay the museum a visit tomorrow?"

CHAPTER 33

"**I**f it truly is the goblet, I really can't fathom how it got here!" said Mr Smollett as we climbed the damp steps up to the British Museum.

James had called on him to accompany us so that Mr Smollett could confirm it was the goblet taken from Mr Hamilton's collection of treasures.

Francis met us at the top of the steps and led the way up to the Egyptian rooms, which were situated on the upper floor. Framed Egyptian papyri lined the walls of the staircase.

"These rooms are my favourite place to visit outside of Egypt itself," enthused Mr Smollett.

The first room we entered was lined with large statues on stone plinths, many with broken sections worn smooth over the intervening years. We passed recumbent lions, busts of pharaohs, a ram's head and seated figures that bore a close resemblance to the ones beside Mr Bagshaw's fireplace.

"How old are these?" asked James, his eyebrows raised.

"Between two and four thousand years old," replied Francis. "Quite spectacular, aren't they?"

We followed as he walked on, moving into a room where

167

rows of cabinets contained bound mummies lying on shelves above their colourful caskets. An Egyptian frieze was painted along the top of one wall, with tall cabinets displaying countless items and vessels recovered from Egyptian tombs.

"The Rosetta Stone," announced Mr Smollett.

I joined him in front of a large stone that stood at about three feet in height and two in width. Resting on a wooden plinth, it was covered in intricate script.

"Mr Bagshaw mentioned this to me," I said. "The British and French used it to translate Egyptian hieroglyphics."

"The same text is written in three languages," added Francis. "Egyptian hieroglyphics, Egyptian demotic and ancient Greek. It took about twenty years to work out the translation."

"What does it say?" I asked.

"It's rather a dull decree," replied Francis, "issued in the time of Ptolemy V. But its translation allowed us to interpret a language that had been lost to us."

"We'll have to visit again to get a proper look at all these objects, don't you think, Penny?" said James. "It's quite astonishing to see how many items have been shipped here from Egypt."

"The goblet is through here," said Francis, "in the third room."

"How many Egyptian rooms are there?" I asked.

"Six in all." He strode up to one of the wall cabinets. "And here it is."

I peered through the glass to view the cream-coloured goblet, which was about five inches high. Its surface was as smooth as pearl. It had clearly been carved to resemble a flower, and a neat rectangle along its side displayed intricate hieroglyphics. It stood among a range of small pots and jars, most of them a dusty red colour. The goblet looked very different from everything else around it.

"It's beautiful!" I exclaimed.

"What do you say, Mr Smollett?" asked James. "Is it the same goblet that was taken from Hamilton's cave?"

"Yes! And seeing it here..." His eyes grew moist. "I feel this is exactly where it should be."

"Good. The question is, who brought it here?" James asked. He turned to Francis. "Would it be possible for us to speak to the chap who looks after this section?"

"The keeper of Egyptian antiquities?"

"Yes, please. Can you ask him to bring the packaging this item was brought here in if he still has it? I hope he has."

"Of course."

Mr Smollett, James and I continued to look at the exhibits. For a brief moment I wished Beth were here to see the goblet before remembering that I had most likely been fooled by her. It seemed sensible to exclude her from our investigation for the time being, but I felt rather wretched about doing so.

"Ugh! I've just read the description for the canopic jars," said James. "Did you know they were used to store bodily organs of the dead?"

"Yes, I remember hearing that," I replied.

"Really? Where on earth would you have heard something like that? I can't say it's something I know much about. It says here that the brain was also removed. Goodness me!" He turned to look at one of the mummies lying in its case. "I can't say I'd like to be wrapped up like that after death and stared at in a museum. How about you, Penny?"

"I wouldn't like it, either. Not that I'd know anything about it, of course."

"You might be up in the heavens looking down on your-self. Then what might you think?"

"I really haven't ever considered it... Oh look, Francis has returned."

Francis had reappeared with a man wearing a top hat. He had thick, white whiskers around his face, a round nose and sharp, intelligent eyes. Francis introduced him as Dr Alexander Crossley.

"It's all a bit of a mystery as to who brought the goblet to us," Dr Crossley said, "but I'm delighted to be able to display it. Given its association with Akhenaten, we've chosen to display it in a case with other finds from Amarna. I like to think it's been reunited with its friends, as it were!" He chuckled.

"Is that the packaging in your hand?" asked James.

"Ah, yes. Mr Edwards here mentioned that you were interested in seeing it. Here you go." He thrust a bundle of brown paper at James. "I never throw anything out. Just a little habit we museum custodians have, I suppose!"

"Thank you." James unfolded the paper and examined it closely. "This was tied with string, was it?"

"Yes. I didn't bring the string with me, but it was perfectly ordinary string. I shouldn't have thought it would give you any clues."

"There was no note and no writing on the paper?"

"No writing at all."

"Does this sort of thing happen often?"

"No. I don't believe a valuable antiquity has ever been left outside the door like that before. It could easily have been lost or stolen! It might have been subjected to a night of bad weather or the whims of an opportunistic thief. It was rather careless of the person who left it there, really. We're lucky that no harm came to it."

"Have you any idea when it might have arrived at these shores?" Francis asked. "Perhaps there's a record of it being found."

"I can't recall it myself, but there may well be something written down somewhere. All finds should be catalogued."

"Where did the other finds in this cabinet come from?" I asked.

"There have been a number of digs in Amarna since it was happened upon by a Frenchman about one hundred and seventy years ago," replied Dr Crossley. "Most of these items have come from excavations carried out over the past fifty years. A good number are from Marmaduke Villiers."

"I've heard the name," said Francis. "I'm quite sure I came across Mr Villiers during my research."

"Is he an Egyptologist?"

"*Was*," replied Dr Crossley. "He died of malaria about fifteen years ago, after a fruitful career in the land of Egypt. A good number of the treasures in this cabinet were found by Villiers in Amarna."

"It's likely, then, that he found the goblet," I suggested.

"Not necessarily. A number of other gentlemen also worked in the area. And ladies, too, I should add."

"And somehow the goblet found its way into the hands of Charles Hamilton," I said.

"Ah, Hamilton," said Dr Crossley. "He's the chap who's gone missing, isn't he? This goblet was once in his possession, I believe."

"Yes. Mr Smollett here worked for him."

"I helped look after the goblet," Mr Smollett explained, "and then I realised someone had taken it. I really cannot begin to understand how it got here."

"Do you happen to know how Mr Hamilton came by it?" asked Dr Crossley.

"I have no idea, I'm sorry to say. I've only ever seen it sitting on the shelf in his collection."

"Could the theft of the goblet be linked to his disappearance?" asked Dr Crossley.

"If it is, we can't puzzle out how," I said. "It's awfully strange."

"We've found quite a few Egyptian artefacts in Mr and Mrs Hamilton's possession," said James. "Would you be interested in looking after them here at the museum?"

"Very much so! If Mr and Mrs Hamilton agree to it."

"If they ever turn up, that is," said James. "I think it most unlikely."

We left the Egyptian rooms and made our way back down the stairs.

"May I have a quick conversation with you, Mr Smollett?" asked James. "I should like to discuss a few things I've discovered about Mr Hamilton."

"All right, then." Mr Smollett's eyes were wide with concern.

Was it possible that he had been involved in Mr Hamilton's plan to fake his own death? I decided to leave the questioning to James.

"I'm going to see what I can find out about Marmaduke Villiers in the reading room," I said.

"Why's that?" asked James.

"To find out if he was the one who dug up that goblet. Some unknown person decided the goblet belonged in this museum. If I can understand its history, maybe it'll give us a clue."

When I reached the reading room, Francis returned my confiscated reading ticket and showed me all the reference books on ancient Egypt that mentioned Marmaduke Villiers. I sat at a desk and leafed through them, making notes as I went along.

Mr Villiers had travelled around Egypt during the 1850s and 1860s, exploring the pyramids at Giza as well as various ancient sites in Nubia. What caught my eye were two visits he had made to Amarna, where he had carried out work to improve maps of the area as well as conducting minor excavations. Mr Villiers had died of malaria in upper Egypt in 1871 at just forty-one years of age.

Perhaps it was the name Marmaduke that had piqued my interest. I liked it and was keen to learn more about him. An entry in one of the books stated that his father had been the fifth Baron Villiers. I turned to *Burke's Peerage* to find out more.

"Have you found out anything useful?" Francis whispered.

"Yes. The more I read about Mr Villiers, the more interesting I find him. He was the third son of Baron Villiers, but the title passed to his eldest brother, as you would expect. The records of the Villiers family interest me very much. Many of them have lived in Surrey, and even Epsom receives a mention."

"Epsom? It's a nice place, I suppose."

"Yes, it is. And I've heard it mentioned quite recently."

CHAPTER 34

"Smollett has no idea whether Hamilton faked his own death or not. And he has no idea whether Mrs Hamilton or Beth were in on the ruse," said James that evening.

We were standing in our little garden, the plants refreshed after the recent rain.

"I even asked if he took the goblet himself and left it on the steps of the museum," he continued. "He denied it, and to be honest I can't see why he would have taken it upon himself to do such a thing."

"You look as confused as I feel about this case," I said.

"I'm completely baffled! For some odd reason, I thought that finding the goblet would bring us a step closer to the Hamiltons, but that's not what's happened at all. I visited Dr Crossley after our meeting and asked him to find out if any of his staff had witnessed someone leaving the goblet outside the museum. But I'm not holding out much hope that anyone did, given that it was night-time and there would have been few people around."

"Do you think Mr Smollett is telling the truth?"

"It's hard to tell. He seems fairly honest to me, but perhaps that's just the mark of a good liar. Maybe my detective skills are beginning to fail me. Once upon a time I felt quite certain that I could tell when someone was lying, but I really am feeling confused in this case." He reflected for a moment. "I've a good mind to give that clematis a chop, you know. It's done very little this year; we've had no flowers at all. Sometimes it's best to cut everything back and give them a second chance."

Before James had readied himself with the secateurs, Mrs Oliver came to find us with a telegram for him. I watched his face as he read it, his brow furrowing.

"I've got to get down to Tooting," he said. "It sounds as though they've found Charles Hamilton."

CHAPTER 35

"Hamilton couldn't have chosen anywhere further from St John's Wood to be found," grumbled James as the cab trundled toward Chelsea Bridge.

He had asked the driver to move as quickly as possible, but the streets were busy. Tooting lay approximately three miles south of the river and it had already taken us half an hour to travel four miles.

"It would be quicker to run," he added.

"You could try," I replied. "I'll stay in the cab and cheer you on."

As the rain drummed down on the roof, I thought of the driver sitting at the back of the carriage, wrapped up in an oilskin cape. "At least you're not out there at the mercy of the elements," I commented.

"Are you trying to make me feel better about being stuck in this cab?"

"Yes. It's not working, though, is it?"

Having crossed the bridge, we passed Battersea Park. I was reminded of Beth presenting me with a tea cosy the last time we had walked there. I tried to ignore the pang of regret

I felt in my stomach and looked hopefully at the road ahead, which appeared to be a little less busy now.

"They was probably 'opin' an 'ouse would get built over 'im," said the foreman.

The light was fading in the overcast sky as we stood beneath our umbrellas on a newly laid road leading off Balham High Road. About a dozen spacious-looking terraced homes had recently been built along the street and another house had been half-constructed. Alongside this, an expanse of mud was being levelled for the next in the row. A short distance away, a group of men had gathered around a trench in the boggy ground. One held a large black bag, which presumably belonged to the police surgeon.

"It were a bit of a shock for our Bill, that's for sure," continued the foreman, "I told 'im 'e could go 'ome early, see. Shouldn't o' thought 'e'd go 'ome, though. 'E'll of gone for a drink!" He gave a dry cackle.

"I'll go and take a look at the burial site," said James.

I gave a sombre nod, feeling a twinge of nausea in my stomach.

"Would you mind holding my umbrella for me?" I asked a constable standing close by. "I need to get my notepad out of my bag."

He nodded.

I had no doubt that Mr Sherman at the *Morning Express* would be interested in an article confirming that Mr Hamilton had indeed been murdered. I readied myself with my pencil and addressed the foreman.

"At what time was Mr Hamilton's body found today?"

"Bill found 'im about four o'clock. White as a sheet, 'e was. Turned out the chap was wrapped in a white sheet, an' all!"

"The area where he was found... Had it been disturbed recently?"

"Nah. We been working on these ones 'ere." He pointed at the houses that had already been built.

"It's possible, then, that the body may have lain there undisturbed for three weeks?"

"I dunno 'ow long 'e's been there."

"Mr Hamilton went missing just over three weeks ago."

"Did 'e now? Well, 'e could of been there that long without us knowin' nothin' of it."

"Were there any obvious injuries on him?" I asked the constable.

"I'm afraid I don't know, ma'am. The police surgeon should be able to tell you that once he's finished his work. He'll want to do an autopsy, I should think."

"'E ain't a pretty sight," added the foreman. "But then neither would any of us be if we'd been lyin' in the mud for three weeks." He shuddered. "Never mind Bill; I'll be needin' a good few drinks meself after this."

"How did you know that it was Mr Hamilton?" I asked.

"We've checked 'is pockets and there was papers in 'em. They was damp, but we was able to read some of 'em. Then we called the coppers in and 'ere we are. Work 'ad to stop as soon as we found 'im, of course. Not that we'd of been gettin' much done today, anyways." He peered up at the dark clouds. "The weather's set in now."

I made some notes, then commented, "It's just as well someone found him. If your construction had continued, Mr Hamilton's body would never have been found."

"That's right," responded the foreman. "'E'd of been stuck in the foundations of someone's 'ouse. Can't say as it would of been a nice place ter live with a troubled spirit roamin' around!"

James returned a short while later with some soggy papers

in his hand. "I think these were originally photographs," he said to me. "Didn't Beth mention that Mr Hamilton had gone back to his room to fetch some photographs?"

"Yes, she did." I felt a pang of shame in my chest. Mr Hamilton hadn't faked his death after all, and she had clearly been telling the truth about the photographs. *Was it possible that she had been telling the truth all along?*

A black carriage pulled by a pair of black horses rounded the corner from the high road and came to a halt close by. We watched as two men lifted out a coffin shell and began making their way across the mud with it.

We were joined by a stocky sergeant from W Division whom I had seen talking to James by the trench.

"Whomever buried Mr Hamilton was most likely covered in this stuff," he said, looking down at his muddy boots and trousers.

"That's London clay for yer," said the foreman. "Always 'eavy goin'. And when the weather's 'ot and dry, it sets like concrete! Whoever's dug that 'ole to put 'im in must of worked 'ard."

"How long would it have taken one man to dig a trench that deep?" James asked the foreman.

"In this ground? Four or five hours, I reckon."

"About half a night," I said. "They could only have brought him here at night-time, couldn't they? They'd have been seen during the daytime."

"I suspect so," said the sergeant. "My men are knocking on doors around here to find out if anyone saw anything. My guess is that they didn't. With no one living in this immediate area, it was a good spot to choose."

"It was carefully planned," added James. "They must have had a cart or carriage of some sort, and at least one spade for digging. There would undoubtedly have been more than one; I can't imagine a single person managing this by themselves.

And they would have to have disappeared by dawn." He turned to the foreman. "What time do your men usually arrive here?"

"Sevenish. 'Alf six at the earliest."

"Therefore, if he was murdered at eight o'clock the previous evening, the murderer had almost eleven hours to bring him here and bury him," I said. "That would probably have been sufficient, wouldn't it?"

"Chelsea is about four-and-a-half miles away," said James. "The journey would have taken twenty or thirty minutes if the roads were quiet."

"But why Tooting?" I asked. "Perhaps the culprit lives near here."

"He must be fairly familiar with the area to know that this building work has been going on," said the sergeant. "They must have come down this road and seen for themselves that this was a good place to bury a body. They'd have seen these houses being built and must have assumed he would soon be covered up, only the building work has taken longer than they realised!"

"Mrs Hamilton is still missing," I said. "Will there be a further search for her body, just in case?"

James nodded. "Yes, we'll need to do that. I don't like to think of her meeting the same fate, but we must search all the same."

CHAPTER 36

"**S**o he *was* murdered after all!" said Edgar Fish when I visited the *Morning Express* newsroom the following day with my completed article. "And once again it's Mrs Blakely, who is no longer an employee of this newspaper, who has the most exciting story to write about it."

"I wouldn't call it exciting, exactly," said Frederick Potter. "It's rather grisly. I'd much rather cover the ongoing controversy over imported timber."

"No you wouldn't, Potter. What nonsense!" retorted Edgar.

"I'd like to hear you describe it as such to the Royal Commission, which is investigating the current industrial depression."

Thankfully, the conversation stalled when Mr Sherman entered the room, the door slamming behind him once again.

"Mrs Blakely! You have a report for me from the find at Tooting, do you?"

"Yes, sir." I handed him my article.

"Excellent." He skimmed through it. "Just the right number of words, too."

"Once again, Mrs Blakely has acquitted herself perfectly," grumbled Edgar.

"I can't see any comment from the manager of the Copeland Hotel," said Mr Sherman, his brow furrowing as he checked the article again.

"There isn't one, sir."

"There isn't? Why ever not? Now that it's been confirmed that this Hamilton chap was murdered, surely the hotel management must be feeling rather concerned."

"I'm sure they are, sir."

"Then please take yourself off to Chelsea and let's find out what they have to say for themselves."

"Of course, sir."

"Fortunately, there's still a fair amount of time before deadline." He checked his pocket watch. "Five hours. Will that be sufficient?"

"Yes, sir. While I'm here, I've also written another article about an ancient Egyptian goblet that was taken from Mr Hamilton's collection and then mysteriously reappeared at the British Museum. We're keen to trace its history." I handed it to him.

"Interesting... Are you appealing to the general public for help with this as well?"

"Yes. Perhaps someone knows something that might be of use to us."

"Unlikely, wouldn't you say?"

"There's a possibility."

Mr Sherman was clearly less impressed with this article.

"How about a picture to go with it?" I suggested.

He looked more interested all of a sudden. "Of what?"

"Of the goblet. Mr Hamilton's assistant is a skilled artist, and I'm sure he would be happy to sketch a picture of the artefact for us. Am I right in thinking that you wish to print more pictures?"

"Yes, you're right about that, Mrs Blakely. I think it could be quite eye-catching on the page if you can get a decent sketch from the chap."

"Thank you, sir. I'll see what I can do."

An hour later, I met with a flustered-looking Mr Fortescue at the Copeland Hotel. His lean face was flushed and his sharp blue eyes flitted about as he spoke.

"It's extremely inconvenient for us that Mr Hamilton's disappearance has been confirmed as a murder," he told me. "This place has been overrun with police officers and our guests are quite perturbed by it. I've had a number of cancellations followed by a long conversation with Sir Barnaby Gurridge this morning, who had convinced himself that he was about to be murdered in his bed!

"At the same time, we've received several enquiries from people with a ghoulish interest in staying at a hotel in which some poor chap has been murdered! It's all extremely troubling!" He pulled out a handkerchief and used it to remove a layer of perspiration from his thin moustache.

"Have you had any further thoughts as to who might have committed this crime?" I asked.

"None! I have had no further ideas since you were last here, Mrs Blakely. All I know is that I could have done without all this. Whoever decided to murder him should have gone and done it elsewhere!"

"You don't sound terribly upset about his death."

"I do apologise, Mrs Blakely. That wasn't my intention at all. Of course I'm upset about it. I only met Mr and Mrs Hamilton once, and I was annoyed, of course, that they had seemingly left without paying their bill. But now that I've learned of Mr Hamilton's death, I am deeply saddened and no longer annoyed, as that would be entirely unreasonable! There has been no word on Mrs Hamilton's whereabouts so far, has there? I imagine she, too, will be found in a miserable grave somewhere."

"I certainly hope not!"

"Oh, so do I! But what other possible outcome is there?"

"Perhaps she's the murderer."

"Ah, yes! There is that possibility. Yes, I suppose that would account for her sudden disappearance. She murdered her husband, then dashed off somewhere to evade the law. I can't say I envy the police this particular case. But much as I like and respect Inspector Gresham, I should really like them to leave my hotel very soon. Room 306 has been examined from top to bottom several times, and it's not likely to give up any of its secrets now. If only the walls could talk!"

"I wish they could. Surely a member of your staff must have seen something?"

"Let's hope so. Then the police will have something to go on. The staff are all being interviewed, along with all the guests we had with us at the time. It's a huge job, that's for sure. I'd much rather be a hotelier than a police officer. Although at the present time I'd rather be neither." He looked about him. "Inspector Gresham will be wanting another word with me in a moment. I'm afraid I'll have to go, Mrs Blakely."

I thanked him for his time and made my way toward Pimlico.

Mr Smollett's rented rooms were located within a terraced house on Ponsonby Place, a scruffy street adjacent to Millbank Prison. As I approached the address, I noticed a man in a dark coat step out through the door and stride up the street toward me. He paused, as if considering his next move, then strode off in the opposite direction toward the river.

It was Mr Bagshaw.

Had he recognised and deliberately avoided me?

I walked on, staring intently at the figure who was just rounding the corner onto Grosvenor Road. It wasn't a big surprise to me that Joseph Bagshaw should visit John Smollett, given that the two men had been on the dig together at Amarna.

But why was Mr Bagshaw hiding from me?

"I assume you've heard the news about Mr Hamilton?" I asked John Smollett after he had greeted me on his doorstep.

"Yes," he replied, his face downcast. "Very sad news indeed. I suppose it wasn't unexpected, seeing as Beth had always been adamant that he was murdered, but tragic all the same. At least he's been found. I'm even more worried about Susan now. I do hope she hasn't come to any harm. They searched the surrounding area, did they? Just in case... In case, she's buried there, too."

"Yes, they're still searching," I replied. "But I'm hoping that we'll find her safe and well very soon."

"So am I."

"What did Mr Bagshaw make of the news?"

"I haven't a clue."

"You didn't discuss it with him?"

"I haven't seen the man."

"But he left this house just a few minutes ago. He walked toward me, then changed his mind and headed off in that direction." I pointed toward the river. "It was him, I'm sure of it!"

Mr Smollett shook his head. "I didn't see him."

I stared at the sketch artist for a moment longer, trying to ascertain whether he was telling the truth. He returned my gaze, his eyes unblinking.

I began to doubt myself. *Had I really seen Mr Bagshaw?* It seemed there was nothing to be gained by pursuing it with Mr Smollett.

"I must have been mistaken," I said. "I came here to ask a favour of you. Might you be willing to sketch a picture of the goblet for the *Morning Express* newspaper?"

CHAPTER 37

I felt sure that Mr Smollett had something to hide and hoped to find out what it was in due course. In the meantime, the deceased Egyptologist, Marmaduke Villiers, remained in my mind. I returned to the British Museum and visited the goblet in the Egyptian rooms once again.

Opening a new page in my notebook, I made my own sketch and copied down the hieroglyphics as best I could. My drawing was nowhere near as good as one of Mr Smollett's, and was quite clearly asymmetrical and out of proportion, but I hoped I had captured a good enough likeness.

After leaving the museum, I walked to Chancery Lane and took an omnibus to Victoria station. From there, I travelled a short distance by train to Battersea Park station before making my way to Beth Worthers's home.

I hadn't visited Beth before, but I remembered her telling me that she lived in rooms at number four, St George's Street. After making a few enquiries outside the station, I found the street quite close by. The terraced houses were tall and narrow, and the viaduct of a railway line ran diagonally across the street.

The sun was emerging from behind the clouds as I knocked on Beth's door, and I hoped this was a good omen that our friendship could be rekindled.

The smile on Beth's face was faint when she finally answered the door.

"I apologise, Beth," I said immediately. "I'm so very sorry for doubting your word."

"I see."

"I don't expect you to forgive me; in fact, I'd quite understand if you can't. I just became rather frustrated with the case and my imagination got a little carried away."

"That's one way to describe it. I suppose you'd better come in."

I followed Beth up to her rooms on the third floor. Her front room was small, yet neatly furnished. Her knitted work was on full display in the antimacassars and arm covers on the chairs. Even the potted plants sat on colourful knitted doilies.

I stood beside a large sash window that stood level with the railway viaduct. "I miss living near a railway line," I said to fill the silence. "I used to enjoy the sounds of the trains coming and going from Moorgate station when I lived in Cripplegate. There was something rather soothing about it."

"Would you like some tea?" Beth asked. She was standing beside a small stove similar to the one I'd had in my rooms at Mrs Garnett's place in Cripplegate.

"Thank you."

I watched her fill the kettle from a jug of water. "Mr Hamilton's body has been found," I said. "It had been buried on a construction site in Tooting."

"So that's what made you realise I hadn't been lying to you," replied Beth. "It wasn't a pang of conscience, then."

"I did feel that, too," I said. "As soon as I accused you, I questioned whether what I had said could possibly have been right."

She made no reply to this and instead busied herself with the tea making.

I watched a train pass over the viaduct, smoke and steam swirling around it. "I suppose the trains go on to Clapham Junction from here," I said. "Isn't it the London, Brighton and South Coast Railway? I believe they go all the way down to the sea." My futile attempts at conversation were leaving me with an unpleasant sense of shame, and I felt my face redden a little. "Something else has turned up," I said. "We found the alabaster goblet."

Beth looked up, more interested this time.

"It's at the British Museum," I continued. "Someone left it on the steps. It could only have been Mr Smollett or Mrs Hamilton, don't you think? We can obviously rule Mr Hamilton out. There's no way he could have had anything to do with it."

"I don't see why Mr Smollett would have left it there," she said, pouring hot water into the teapot. "He seemed genuinely surprised to find that it had gone missing. It must have been Susan, which gives me hope that she's alive. I suppose she's hiding herself away in case people suspect her of murder." She gave me a pointed glance, as if I were one of Mrs Hamilton's accusers.

"I'd like to find out how Mr Hamilton came to have that goblet in his possession," I said. "I think Mrs Hamilton retrieved that particular item and donated it to the museum for a reason. If I could just find out where the goblet came from, I'd be able to learn more about it. It's currently sitting in a case with a number of other items from Amarna. They've been collected by various Egyptologists over the past forty years or so, but many were collected by a man named Marmaduke Villiers. Have you heard of him?"

"No."

"I'm not sure why he interests me – perhaps it's the name – but he spent a good deal of time in Egypt twenty or thirty years ago. What intrigues me further is that the Villiers family comes from Surrey and has, at times, lived in Epsom. That's one of the areas Mr Hamilton, or Robert Higgins as he was then known, carried out his burglaries. In fact, it was the burglary at Lord Manningham's home in Epsom that led to the conviction of Mr Hamilton's accomplice, Jack Tremmel."

"That sounds like an interesting connection," said Beth as she poured out the tea.

"Mr Villiers was a son of the fifth Baron Villiers, and according to the latest edition of *Burke's Peerage*, Marmaduke Villiers's widow is still alive. I'd like to travel down to Epsom to find her."

"If she still lives there."

"I'm sure someone in the locality will be able to tell me where the Villiers family lives. The baronetcy dates back to the fourteenth century, when an ancestor assisted Edward I with a battle of some sort. I forget exactly what now."

"Sounds like an important family. I'm sure you'll find them easily enough."

"I think it's possible that Mr Hamilton stole the goblet from them. That's what I'd like to ask Mrs Villiers about."

"And if he did? What would that tell you?"

This was a good question, and I wasn't quite sure of the answer. "I want to find out why it was so important to Mrs Hamilton," I replied. "Will you come with me?"

"To Epsom?"

"Yes."

"I'm afraid I can't. I've just taken on a new job, and it

looks as though it'll be keeping me busy for the next few weeks."

"Oh."

I had hoped she would say yes, but her solemn expression as she handed me my cup of tea suggested she had no immediate intention of forgiving me.

CHAPTER 38

"The post-mortem revealed that Mr Hamilton died from strangulation," said James when he returned home that evening. "There's no sign of the ligature used, which explains why it wasn't visible to Beth Worthers when she found him. His body was wrapped in what appears to have been a cotton bed sheet. I suspect it was taken from the hotel. He was still wearing the dinner suit that witnesses remembered him wearing at the drinks reception.

"There were no other obvious injuries on his body; not even from any attempt he might have made to defend himself. My guess is that the assailant crept up behind Mr Hamilton and surprised him, so he barely had any time to respond. The drink would also have slowed his reaction, no doubt. Here are the photographs found on him."

James laid out numerous crumpled pieces of paper. Damage from the damp had caused significant clouding of the images, but it was just possible to make out the desert scenes with dark figures standing in the sand alongside palm trees and broken walls.

"Rather underwhelming now that they're so damaged, aren't they?" he said. "But he was intending to show them to someone. I wonder if that someone planned to make sure he went back to his room so an ambush could be sprung."

"If only we could find out the identity of that person," I replied.

"Inspector Gresham and his men at T Division are questioning everyone who was at the drinks reception," said James. "They're putting all their men on the case now it's been confirmed that Mr Hamilton was murdered. Perhaps someone will mention a conversation about the photographs in passing."

"I do hope so."

"Are you all right, Penny? You don't seem your usual self this evening."

I told him about my failed attempt to make amends with Beth.

He sighed. "You did accuse her of something quite devious, I suppose. I can't say I'm very surprised that she's still upset about it."

"But you thought she might have been lying, too!"

"Yes, I did. But confronting her about it is another matter entirely. She was bound to be upset by it."

"You think I was unreasonable with her, don't you?"

"I don't think anything of the sort. It was quite understandable, especially given that you've been fooled by people like Beth in the past. There might have been a more tactful way of discussing it with her—"

"You *do* think I was being unreasonable!"

"I didn't say that, Penny. Nothing can change what you said to her, but you've paid her a visit to explain yourself and apologise. That was a completely reasonable thing to do. Now it's up to Beth to decide whether she wants to forgive you or not. Sometimes people enjoy having a little time to sulk after a disagreement like this."

"I suppose you would know all about that."

"What's that supposed to mean?" His offended expression quickly turned into a smile.

"I imagine we'll soon have Mr Hamilton's murder solved now that Inspector Gresham and T Division are involved," I said.

"It's certainly possible. I've been thinking more about John Smollett, and I think there's a strong possibility that he had something to do with Hamilton's death."

"Really?"

"He was having a love affair with Hamilton's wife, and she was unhappy in the marriage. Perhaps she had even been forced into a life of crime by her husband. She and Smollett may have conspired to have Hamilton murdered. Perhaps Smollett knew that Hamilton was fetching the photographs from his room and lay in wait for him there. We don't have an alibi for Smollett yet. We know Mrs Hamilton briefly remained at the drinks reception after her husband left, but soon after that she disappeared. Did she go up to the room to help Smollett with the terrible deed? Or did she run off, so it would appear as though she had no association with it? Her disappearance makes her look rather guilty. T Division can question all the guests they like, but I think the two chief suspects are the most obvious ones: John Smollett and Susan Hamilton."

"I agree," I said, "and we know that Mrs Hamilton was involved in her husband's criminal endeavours. Despite Beth's fondness for her, she may have been an unpleasant person deep down. But Mr Smollett? I really can't imagine him strangling Mr Hamilton. He seems too good-natured. I can't imagine him causing harm to anybody."

"Murderers aren't always big and scary, Penny. You know

that. Perhaps Mrs Hamilton implored her lover to commit murder. Perhaps he was led to believe that it was the only way they could be together. When passion seizes a man's heart in that way, he may find himself capable of anything."

"But if she promised herself to him, she broke her promise," I said. "She ran off without him!"

"Can we really be sure of that? Perhaps the two have been meeting in secret. If they'd run away together it would have been a little too obvious that they had planned Mr Hamilton's murder, don't you think?"

"Yes, I can see that. I just can't imagine it..."

"The good news is that a lot of people are working on this case now. And gentle as he is, Mr Smollett would likely confess under interrogation."

"You don't intend to be cruel to him, do you?"

"He's our main suspect now, Penny. Or one of them, anyway. And if he has been meeting Mrs Hamilton in secret, his arrest might bring her in, too."

"Please don't be too harsh on him, James. You might be mistaken about him, just as I was mistaken about Beth."

"Very well. I shall let you know how we get on with questioning him."

"Funnily enough, I called on Mr Smollett earlier today, but before I reached his home I saw someone familiar leaving."

"Who was it?"

"Joseph Bagshaw."

"How interesting."

"And stranger still, Mr Smollett refused to admit to the meeting."

"That's very odd indeed. I shall have to ask him about it."

"In the meantime, I intend to visit the widow of Marmaduke Villiers."

"Whatever for?"

"To ask her about the goblet."

"Do you think she might have left it outside the museum?"

"I don't know what to think at the moment, but I'm hoping she can confirm whether it was her husband who originally found it."

"What would that achieve?"

"I honestly don't know quite yet."

CHAPTER 39

It was another sunny, late-summer morning as I travelled by train from Waterloo station. Open countryside lay beyond the carriage window once the train had passed Wimbledon. Cows and sheep dotted the fields, and the trees had a hint of autumn colour about them.

Passing hamlets and villages, we soon reached the larger settlement of Epsom. I knew the place for its famous horseracing course on the Epsom Downs, but I had never visited before.

On arrival in Epsom, I made enquiries with a local green-grocer and discovered that the Villiers family lived a short walk up West Hill.

As I made my way up there, I felt pleased that it had been so easy to locate Mrs Villiers. *But was I being too hopeful too soon?* I had to remind myself not to assume that my visit would be completely straightforward. *Perhaps Mrs Villiers would be rude, or maybe she was away from home. There was no certainty that I would make any progress even if she agreed to speak with me.*

Beyond the hedge on the right-hand side of the road appeared the impressive frontage of a wide, three-storey red-brick house. As I drew nearer, I surmised that it was the sort of place that might well have appealed to Mr Hamilton the burglar. Or Robert Higgins, as he had formerly been known.

I reached the tall iron gates and tentatively made my way up the path toward the house.

"Egypt?" responded Mrs Villiers. "I never went to the place! Marmaduke wouldn't have wanted me there, either." A large lady, she was draped in colourful silk shawls. She walked with a stick and had a stern face with a twinkle of humour in her eyes. "Where's our tea got to?" she said, glaring at the doorway through which the maid had exited a few minutes earlier.

We were seated in her morning room, which was pleasantly furnished in yellow. Tall windows overlooked well-tended gardens.

"Marmaduke simply adored the place," she continued. "So much so that he died there!" She gave a hollow laugh. "It was the malaria that got him."

"I'm very sorry to hear it."

She dismissed my concern with a wave of her hand. "He died doing what he loved best. Egypt was his first love; his family came second."

I nodded, indicating far more sympathy than she realised. As the daughter of a plant-hunter, I knew only too well what it was like to have a family member who was obsessed with visiting foreign lands.

"You say you're a journalist," she commented. "A very impressive role for a young lady. What made you choose such a profession?"

The maid brought in the tea tray as I told Mrs Villiers about my work on Fleet Street. She asked a lot of questions, but my patience was rewarded when we eventually came to discuss the reason for my visit.

"I'd like to know whether you and your husband ever had anything stolen," I said. "Was your home burgled at any time?"

Her jaw dropped. "Why yes, it was. And I must say that the police didn't do a particularly good job of investigating it. In fact, they were perfectly hopeless!"

"Lord Manningham," I ventured. "Does he live near here?"

"Not especially near. He's over by the Downs." She waved an arm in that direction.

"I understand that his home was burgled about four years ago."

"Yes, that's right. Whoever it was got to us about six months later. They only took Marmaduke's Egyptian finds, though, leaving behind the silver and my jewellery. It was most odd."

I took my notebook out of my carpet bag and turned the pages to find the sketch I had made of the goblet. I got up from my seat to show it to her.

"Was this goblet taken during the burglary?" I asked.

There was a long pause as she screwed up her eyes, then opened them wide again.

"My sketching isn't very good, I'm afraid," I added.

"It doesn't help that I'm not wearing my spectacles." She rang the bell and asked the maid to fetch them for her.

A short while later, Mrs Villiers peered intently at my drawing with her spectacles perched on her nose. I suddenly felt ashamed of my artistic ineptitude.

"Is it a cup?" she asked.

"Yes. An Egyptian goblet, to be precise. It's made of alabaster and carved to resemble a lotus flower, and—"

"I remember it now!" she enthused. "It has some sort of Egyptian writing on it, doesn't it? Marmaduke gave it to our daughter Louisa, but it was stolen. Where is it now?"

"In the British Museum."

She pulled her glasses off. "Is it really? How marvellous! I take it they've arrested the men who took it?"

"They haven't, I'm afraid."

"Why doesn't that surprise me? They're completely hopeless! How did the museum come by it?"

"Someone left it on the doorstep."

"Did they now? Having second thoughts about his wicked ways, I suspect. What about the other things that were taken from us?"

"The police have discovered a storage area in south London that contains a large number of stolen items. They may be among those. Do you have a list of what was taken?"

"I gave it to the police here in Epsom... not that they did anything with it. I hope they still have it. I could write another, I suppose, but my memory isn't what it used to be. I'll call Louisa. She'll want to know that the goblet has been safely found."

Mrs Villiers rang the bell for the maid once again and asked for her daughter to be summoned.

"I'd like to find out what else is in that storage area in London, as they stole rather a lot from us. Almost everything Marmaduke brought back from his travels, I would say."

"Didn't Scotland Yard help with the investigation?"

"No. I know that they helped with the burglary at Lord Manningham's place, but that's because he's a lord, I suppose!" She laughed. "Poor Marmaduke was only the third son of a baron."

I heard footsteps from beyond the doorway, then a young

woman stepped into the room. Her dark hair was pinned back behind her ears and she wore a blue damask dress.

I knew in an instant that I had seen her somewhere before. *But where?*

I thought about this for a moment.

In John Smollett's sketchbook.

CHAPTER 40

"Ah, there you are, Louisa," said Mrs Villiers. "This is Mrs Blakely, a journalist. She has discovered the whereabouts of that Egyptian goblet your father gave you. The one that was stolen, remember?"

Louisa blinked a few times, and I noticed her chest rise and fall.

"Is that so?" she replied.

As her dark eyes rested on mine I detected wariness; perhaps even fear.

I tried to remain calm as I addressed the woman who I had quickly realised was Susan Hamilton.

"Yes, I've been investigating the murder of Mr Charles Hamilton," I replied, keen to demonstrate my knowledge of the case.

"Murder?" cried out Mrs Villiers. "You never mentioned a murder to me, Mrs Blakely. All you spoke of was the goblet!"

I noticed Louisa Villiers swallow uncomfortably, then compose herself again.

"Mr Hamilton owned the storage area in south London I told you about, Mrs Villiers," I said. "We believe he may have been responsible for burgling your home, along with many other properties. His body was found two days ago."

"How awful! He doesn't sound like a particularly pleasant man, mind you. Has anyone been arrested yet?"

"Not yet."

I glanced at Louisa, but her face had become impassive.

I decided to address her directly. "As the rightful owner of the goblet, Miss Villiers, I imagine you're entitled to request that it be returned to you," I said. "Would you like me to inform the museum of your wishes?"

"If it's safely stowed in the British Museum, that's where it should stay," she replied. "Many of the artefacts my father found are already there, so I believe that's the rightful place for my goblet."

I felt quite certain that she was the person who had taken the goblet from beneath the railway arch and left it outside the museum.

Her mother, on the other hand, appeared to have no awareness of Mr Hamilton's former existence at all. Presumably her daughter had concealed the marriage from her. Although it was tempting to tell Louisa Villiers everything I had discovered about her right there and then, I sensed it would cause a rift between mother and daughter.

Was I being too lenient on her? Surely it was my duty to confront her if she were a murderer.

"Mr Hamilton went missing almost four weeks ago," I said, "and his wife vanished at the same time. It's been a puzzling case for everyone involved."

"Well, at least you've found his body," said Mrs Villiers. "I imagine the wife will turn up somewhere soon. Was she murdered as well?"

"I don't think so," I said. "She merely vanished."

"That is a puzzle." Mrs Villiers chuckled. "But as long as

the rightful owners can be reunited with the items he stole, I don't suppose we need worry much more about it."

"Perhaps you'd like to visit the British Museum and see the goblet in its case, Miss Villiers," I suggested.

"Yes, I should like to do that."

"The Egyptian rooms there are fascinating. Have you ever visited Egypt?"

"Of course she has!" Mrs Villiers laughed. "My daughter is quite the budding Egyptologist, Mrs Blakely. She only recently returned from spending three years there."

"Is that so?"

"She's only been back for three weeks. Isn't that right, Louisa?"

Her daughter gave a cautious nod.

"Did you happen to encounter Mr and Mrs Hamilton while you were out there?" I asked, wondering how she would find a way to reply.

"It's rather difficult to avoid the British in Cairo," she replied. "Everybody stays at Shepheard's Hotel."

"Did you speak to them at all?"

"No."

"I met with Joseph Bagshaw recently. He told me he had undertaken a dig with Mr and Mrs Hamilton in Amarna."

She nodded.

"Did you come across Joseph Bagshaw?"

"Of course. He's very well known."

"Mr John Smollett," I said.

Miss Villiers started blinking rapidly again. "I've met him a few times, yes. Did you come across him during your investigation?"

"Yes. I believe he was Mr Hamilton's assistant."

She spoke calmly of the two men, displaying no obvious emotion.

How was she able to do so without giving anything away?

"Unfortunately for me, I shan't have Louisa with me for much longer," said Mrs Villiers. "She's planning to return to Egypt soon. Isn't that right, Lou?"

Her daughter's eyes moved toward the carriage clock on the mantelpiece. "I'm sorry," she said, "but I've just noticed the time. I'm late for an appointment."

"With whom?" asked her mother.

"With Angela. We arranged to take a walk on the Common together." Miss Villiers turned back to me. "Thank you for notifying us of the goblet's return, Mrs Blakely. I shall visit it at the British Museum first thing tomorrow morning." She smiled. "I can't wait to see it again!"

CHAPTER 41

I willed the train to move more swiftly as I travelled back to London. *Whom should I speak to first... James or Beth?* I settled on Beth, knowing I would reach Battersea more quickly.

Mrs Villiers clearly had no knowledge of her daughter's marriage to Mr Hamilton. And she hadn't a clue about her daughter's criminal activities, either. I found myself smiling as I considered how brazen Louisa Villiers had been. She had fooled her mother as well as Beth and John Smollett.

Would she attempt to fool me, too? And the police?

I felt sure she knew that I had uncovered her fake iden-tity. *Was she also aware that I suspected her of murdering her husband?*

There was a risk that my visit to her home would prompt her to vanish once again. Her mother had mentioned she was planning another trip to Egypt soon. *Maybe she would bring her plans forward in order to make her escape.*

I recalled the way she had looked at me when she told me she would be at the British Museum first thing in the morn-ing. Her eyes had locked with mine as she said the words, and

I wondered whether she had intended this to be some sort of clue.

Was it possible that she wished to meet me so she had a chance to explain herself?

I knew James would want to speak to her the moment he discovered where she was, and T Division would also be after her. *Perhaps I could persuade them to wait until I had met with her.*

I changed trains at Clapham Junction, and a short while later I found myself knocking at Beth's door once again.

There was no invitation into her home when she opened it, neither did she greet me with a smile.

Nevertheless, the words tumbled out of me before I was able to explain myself properly. "I've found her! Susan Hamilton! But she's really Louisa Villiers – the daughter of Marmaduke Villiers. They live down in Epsom!"

"Are you sure it's her?"

"She looks just like the woman in John Smollett's drawing!"

Beth reluctantly invited me inside and I related the conversation I'd just had with Mrs Villiers and her daughter.

"We should meet her tomorrow," I added. "I think she wants me to. And you should come with me."

"But then I would have to explain that I wasn't who I said I was. That I wasn't a proper friend."

"She lied to you, too! You were both pretending, so how could one of you possibly hold that against the other? I think she wanted to explain herself, Beth, but she couldn't say anything in front of her mother. I think she's been hiding for so long that she just wants to talk to someone about it."

"Can you be sure of that?"

"I'm not absolutely certain, but I'm hopeful. Why else would she say that she would be at the British Museum first thing tomorrow? If she wanted to avoid me she never would have said such a thing."

"All right, then," said Beth. "I'll come along." Her shoulders relaxed a little. "Thank you for finding her, Penny. I'm relieved to hear that she hasn't come to any harm."

***

"I must get down to Epsom right away," said James when I called on him at Scotland Yard. "I'll notify the police station that I'm on my way. Well done for finding her, Penny! Excellent detective work. How I wish we could employ you here. Perhaps one day we'll be allowed to hire lady police detectives."

"Oh, please wait until I've spoken to her, James!" I begged.

"What?" He scowled. "Wait? I've already got Smollett in custody with T Division. Why on earth do you want me to wait?"

"I think she wanted to talk to me."

"Oddly enough, I'd like to speak to her, too!" replied James. "That woman is a suspect in the murder of her husband, Penny. It's vital that we arrest her as soon as possible. I don't want her getting away again!"

"I'm certain she'll be at the museum tomorrow. She wants to see the goblet in its rightful place."

"You feeling certain just isn't enough. There's a high risk that the woman will attempt to dash off again. I think you're falling for more of her nonsense."

"I'm not, James. I'm confident she'll be there."

"I'm sorry, Penny, but I simply can't wait that long. Now we know where she is, we must pounce. I need to send a telegram to Epsom police station right away." He moved toward the door.

"Can't you just ask them to watch her for now?"

"What do you mean?"

"Just have a constable watch the house overnight and make sure she doesn't attempt to run off."

He sighed. "There may not be a man spare to do it."

"I'm convinced that she'll be more honest with me and Beth than she would be with a bunch of humourless police officers."

"Humourless?"

"James, this is the best way, I'm certain of it. Please! I managed to find her, so at least let me speak to her before she's arrested. It's so important that we hear her side of the story."

"How the murderess conspired with her lover to murder her husband, you mean?"

"Perhaps that's what she'll say, or maybe she has an entirely different story altogether."

"You expect a man to stay up all night carrying out sentry duty so you can have one of your cosy chats with her in the morning?"

I felt a flip of anger in my chest. "This may seem a lot to ask, but please don't patronise me like that," I snarled.

James seemed a little taken aback by my retort. He scratched his brow, shook his head and then examined his fingernails for a moment. "If that woman escapes justice because I've allowed this..."

"She won't! I'm convinced that she wanted to speak to me."

"I hope you're right, Penny. Because if you're wrong and she slips through our fingers... This could be our last chance to catch Hamilton's killer."

CHAPTER 42

I met Beth on the steps of the British Museum long before the doors opened. There was a cool dampness in the air, with a hint of autumn about it. We made stilted conversation and watched the pigeons strut about. I wasn't sure whether Beth was still upset with me or just nervous about meeting Louisa Villiers again. Perhaps it was a combination of both.

The museum forecourt grew a little busier as the opening time of ten o'clock approached. Sightseers, students and a few familiar faces from the reading room climbed the steps and passed us by. I felt my heart thud a little faster as each minute passed.

Was it possible that Louisa Villiers had vanished again?

I tried to calm my breathing, hoping I had made the right judgement about her.

Then, at about ten minutes after ten, I saw her approach the steps. She wore a simple travelling cape with a matching hat.

"Here she comes," I whispered to Beth.

I felt a warm sense of relief in my stomach and Beth gave an audible gasp.

"She won't be expecting to see me here!" she said. "Oh, how will I explain myself?"

But Louisa was already too close for us to discuss the matter any further. Her eyes met mine as she climbed the steps. And when she saw Beth, she stopped altogether.

"Good morning!" Beth called out, her voice wavering a little.

Louisa gave a slight smile, then climbed the rest of the steps to join us. "You know each other?" she said. "I had no idea."

"Beth asked for my help when you went missing," I said.

The two women exchanged a smile.

"I'm afraid to say that I haven't been completely honest with you," Beth said to Louisa.

"It's all right," she replied. "Neither have I."

It took a while for Beth to explain who she really was and why she had been employed by Mr Hamilton. Louisa listened calmly, without appearing too upset by the revelation. I considered that her own crimes were potentially far worse.

Could this demure young lady really have murdered her husband, though?

For the time being, I needed to remain on friendly terms with Louisa and resist the temptation to accuse her of anything. Nevertheless, I was eager for her to explain the baffling case that had been occupying my time for almost four weeks.

It was Louisa's turn to talk. "I do apologise for my rudeness during your visit, Mrs Blakely. There's a great deal about my life that my mother knows nothing about. Perhaps you noticed that."

I nodded.

"I felt terrible that I was unable to be truthful with you," she continued. "I'd like to explain exactly what has happened. Firstly you must understand how I felt about my father. I loved him very much, you see. He wasn't at home a great deal when I was young, but whenever he returned he related such wonderful stories of his travels in Egypt that I was enraptured. I longed to visit the country myself one day, and he assured me that he would take me there. How I looked forward to that day! I counted the years until I would be able to travel with him. Unfortunately, it never came to pass, as he died before the day arrived. I was ten years old at the time of his death."

Beth and I said how sorry we were to hear it.

"About four years ago, our home was burgled," she continued. "The police believed our home had been specifically targeted because the thieves someone knew about the treasures we owned. Father had donated most of his finds to this very museum," she gestured up at the facade, "but there were a few he was particularly fond of, one of which he gave to me. It was a beautiful goblet; elegantly carved and smooth to the touch. Father told me it was carved from stone, but it didn't feel like stone to me. It was so light and had such a translucent quality to it that it practically glowed. There were some ancient hieroglyphics carved into it, but I never knew their meaning.

"What I found most spellbinding of all was its age. Father told me it was more than three thousand years old! Yet when I held it in my hands, it seemed as though it could have been carved just yesterday. I often thought of the craftsman who had spent so much time making it. Compared with many of the treasures uncovered in Egypt, it's not such a remarkable item. But it was remarkable to me, and it felt all the more special because my father had given it to me. It was of great comfort to me after he died. And when it was stolen..." Her voice trailed off and she looked away as she composed herself.

"I was extremely upset," she continued, "and angry, too. How dare someone break into our home and take something so precious?"

"How did you discover that Mr Hamilton had stolen it?"

"That took some time. After the burglary I decided to embark on my first trip to Egypt. It was something I'd wanted to do since I was a child, and when I reached the age of twenty-one I felt the time had come. Mother wanted me to travel with a companion, of course, but I discovered that the Thomas Cook tours were well suited to unaccompanied ladies, so that seemed to be the solution. I soon made friends with the other ladies when the tour group met in London. We travelled down to Brindisi in Italy together by train, then took the steamboat from Brindisi to Alexandria. Even the journey was such wonderful fun, as I had never left the shores of Britain before.

"I first encountered Charles at Shepheard's Hotel in Cairo. He enjoyed seeking out antiquities and collecting them. He had read a great deal about ancient Egypt and spent a lot of time with other people who had done the same. He was no fool, and he had gleaned a lot of information very quickly. By the time I met him in Cairo he had been there for six months, and he had already convinced many people that he was a genuine Egyptologist. He wanted to spend time with acclaimed Egyptologists, such as Joseph Bagshaw, and he took a special interest in me because of who my father was.

"He could be quite amusing and had a certain charm about him, but I thought little more of him as I took a wonderful trip up the Nile with my tour group. By the time I returned to Cairo about a month later, I knew that I wanted to stay in Egypt. I'd fallen in love with the place, just as my father had. I hoped to find some companions at Shepheard's Hotel whom I could travel with. Charles was there at the time and paid me a great deal of attention. I suppose I was flattered, and I also admired his extensive knowledge of ancient Egypt and his passion for it.

"We started spending a good deal of time together. We visited interesting sites and made several excursions up the Nile. I realised he wasn't a gentleman in the truest sense of the word, but he was funny, clever and kind. He often gave money to beggars; in fact, he carried a little purse of silver piastre coins just for that purpose. He certainly wasn't the sort of man my mother would have liked, but I was quite drawn to him.

"It was then that a waiter at the hotel told me an extraordinary story about Charles. He told me that when he was the worse for drink one evening, Charles had boasted about the criminal life he led back home in England. He told me Charles had supposedly acquired some significant wealth, and that he was hoping to get his hands on more antiquities and make even larger sums of money.

"I refused to believe it to begin with. I simply couldn't imagine him being a criminal. But then I considered how little Charles had really told me about his life in England. I resolved to ask him about it, but when I did so I found that his replies were often vague. Sometimes he avoided the questions altogether and changed the subject completely. I began to wonder whether there was some truth in what the waiter had told me after all.

"I thought then of the burglary at my family's home and how the thieves had only taken Father's Egyptian artefacts, leaving behind the other valuables. Did Charles know something about it? It was something I wished to find out, but I was wary of asking the question directly."

"Why?" I asked.

"He had a temper, especially when he'd had a drink. And he liked to drink quite often."

"Didn't the hotel staff alert the police in England when they heard about his criminal past?" I asked.

"They obviously didn't consider it their duty to do so. Travel attracts a broad range of people, Mrs Blakely. Some simply wish to see the world, while others are seeking a new life overseas. They may be escaping upset or wrongdoing at home, and I think staff in these tourist hotels see a good number of people like that walk through their doors. And besides, he never confessed to any specific crimes. He merely boasted about the lifestyle he had been so proud of prior to travelling.

"If he hadn't left England when he did, the police would almost certainly have caught up with him. Perhaps they assumed he felt at least a little regret, given his generosity and the fact that he was trying really hard to become a respected Egyptologist. Despite all his talk of money, I think respect was what he truly sought. He had been born into lowly circumstances and had always wanted to lift himself out of them.

"Then one day he suddenly proposed marriage to me. It wasn't something I had wished for at all. I certainly wasn't in love with him! However, I was still a little fond of him, and I was desperate to find out more about Father's stolen treasures. Having already spent a good deal of time with him, there was a risk that my honour would be called into question. This meant I had to make a decision to either marry him or leave fairly swiftly.

"It was foolish of me to agree to it, but marriage brought an air of respectability to both of us. We were invited to grand parties and events, and I have to admit that I began to enjoy myself a little. I loved exploring the country and was learning a great deal. After a year, I considered myself quite proficient in Egyptology and had met a great number of interesting people. I hoped my father would have been proud of me and willing to overlook the fact that I had married a man who wasn't a gentleman by anyone's standards. I didn't tell anyone about my past, of course. I couldn't risk word getting back to my family about what I had done."

"Which is why you told me your father was a clergyman from Rochdale," said Beth.

"Yes, I'm sorry about that. I was trying to protect my family."

"What happened between Charles and Joseph Bagshaw?" I asked. "He claims Charles stole from him."

"In truth, he did. The dig in Amarna was fraught with arguments between the two of them. Charles took three precious items from Joseph, partly out of spite and partly because he wanted them for his own collection. He had them smuggled back to London illegally. I chose to turn a blind eye, I'm afraid. I disagreed with my husband's actions, but I wasn't keen on Joseph, either."

"Mr Smollett was with you by this time, wasn't he?"

Her face coloured. "Have you spoken to him?"

"Yes. He'll be ever so relieved to hear that you're safe."

"How is he?"

I didn't want to be the one to tell her that he was sitting in a police cell on the King's Road in Chelsea.

"He's concerned about you."

"I doubt he'll be able to forgive me for running away as I did. I'm very fond of him, and he made my last winter in Egypt a good deal easier. We spent a lot of time together and we're closer in age than Charles and I were. I knew Charles was jealous, of course, though I'm surprised to hear that he went to the lengths of employing Beth. No one expects to be spied upon by an undercover lady detective! I understand you were only doing your job, Beth." She gave a gentle laugh. "It's quite funny now to think that we were both pretending to be people we weren't!"

"When did you discover that Charles was in possession of the goblet?" I asked.

"Just a few months ago. As you know, he kept a secret storage room beneath a railway arch not far from our home in Camberwell. He'd hinted at its existence but never told me exactly where it was. On our return from Egypt, he wanted to show me the treasures he'd taken from the dig at Amarna. He was so proud of himself for adding them to his collection. He also wanted John to begin documenting the items he kept there.

"John and I were sworn to secrecy about its location, of course. Charles had been renting the storage room for many years and had acquired a lot of items, most of which I felt certain had been stolen. John wasn't so sure. He always tried to see the good in Charles because Charles had given him the opportunity to travel.

"My heart skipped a beat when I saw the goblet there, but as I was never allowed to visit the storage room without Charles, it was difficult to see whether any of my father's other treasures were there."

"Surely Mr Hamilton realised you would see the goblet he had stolen from your home," I suggested.

"Perhaps he did, but I don't think it really mattered to him. He'd probably forgotten what he'd stolen and from where by that time."

"Did you ever ask him about the burglary at your home?" I asked.

"Yes, I eventually plucked up the courage."

"And what did he say?"

"He laughed and told me that his memory was beginning to suffer due to his age. I asked for the goblet back and he told me it would be my reward after our first child was born. He was very impatient for me to bear him children."

"Couldn't you have just taken the goblet there and then?"

"No, I was too frightened to. He would have noticed it was missing and lost his temper with me. I decided I had to come up with a plan. I'd achieved my aim of discovering the whereabouts of the goblet, and all I had left to do was determine where the rest of Father's treasures were. It wasn't easy to look for them when Charles was always at the storage room with me. I asked John to help me get a copy of Charles's key. Then I resolved to find the stolen items and make my escape."

"From the marriage?"

"Yes. I was determined to leave him."

Although Louisa Villiers's story was an unusual one, it all sounded quite believable so far. The real test was about to begin.

"What happened on the evening of your disappearance?" I asked.

CHAPTER 43

Louisa's demeanour changed, and she pulled her cape a little tighter around her. She cleared her throat before speaking again.

"The evening began perfectly normally. There was no indication that it was about to go horribly wrong. The drinks reception was perfectly pleasant and the events of the weekend had been quite enjoyable. I had no idea that my marriage was about to come to an abrupt end that evening. Shortly before dinner, Charles returned to our room because John had asked to see some photographs in order to make sketches from them."

"Mr Smollett asked to see the photographs?"

"Yes."

"Do continue."

"Then Beth said she needed to return to her bedroom before dinner. I know now that she planned to tell Charles she no longer wanted to work for him. While the two were gone, I chatted with a lady named Mrs Chilton. I felt a tap on my shoulder and turned around, but I couldn't see who had tried to attract my attention. Whoever it was, I got the impression that they had walked around me quickly. I thought it was someone playing a joke; Charles after returning from his room, perhaps. It all happened so quickly. I turned back to face Mrs Chilton, and that's when I noticed the note in my drink."

"In your drink?" I asked.

"Yes. The end of it was dipped in my wine. I pulled it out quickly and saw just a few words written on it: 'Leave now! Your life is in danger!'. Aware of the criminal activities Charles had been involved in, I realised there could be a very real threat to my life."

"What did Mrs Chilton make of it?"

"I didn't show her what was written on the note, but she was quite baffled by the whole situation. She told me a young man in a dark suit had knocked into her, but neither of us could work out exactly what had happened. We were purposefully distracted so the note could be dropped into my drink, of course."

"Did you attempt to return to your room at that point?" I asked.

"I wanted to, but I was worried about what might be happening there. I could only imagine that the threat was related to Charles, and I knew that he had gone back to our room. My instinct told me not to go up there, so instead I made my excuses to Mrs Chilton and said that I needed to attend to the message. I think she was rather confused by it all.

"I left the hotel and walked around Cadogan Square for a bit, the drink still in my hand. Then I hailed a passing cab and asked to be taken home."

"To your house in Camberwell?"

"Yes. I was so scared that I swore the housekeeper to secrecy when I got there. I thought somebody was about to come after me, you see. I told her she must never tell anyone she had seen me that evening, and that Mr Hamilton and I were in grave danger. I packed up a few personal belongings and then left again. I took a cab to east London and checked into a hotel there, wondering what on earth to do next.

"I returned to the house the following day and spoke to the housekeeper again. She told me she had received no word from Charles and I began to suspect that something terrible had befallen him. I felt sure that whoever had harmed him would come after me next, and I just couldn't get that note out of my mind. I filled a few trunks with as many of my belongings as I could and then returned to the hotel in east London."

"Why didn't you go to the police?"

"I thought about it, and although I had nothing to hide, I had been associating with a criminal for quite some time. I felt they would assume that I had taken part in his crimes, or at least known about them. I'm sure Joseph Bagshaw considers me partially responsible for the theft of the items Charles took from the dig in Amarna. It just felt easier and safer to hide out at the hotel for a few more days.

"It was then that I decided to retrieve the goblet from the storage room. With Charles missing, I hoped he would never get wind that I had taken it. I went at night, just as we had always done. Charles didn't want anyone to see him visiting the place and getting an idea of what might be stored there. I tried to avoid staying at the storage room too long because I was worried that someone would see me there, so I didn't get a chance to look for the other things Charles had taken from Father. But at least I had the goblet.

"I continued to hide out at the hotel, and then I read a newspaper report stating that Charles and I had mysteriously vanished. I decided then that my days of living as Mrs Hamilton were at an end. I could return home to Mother and she'd be none the wiser. I could hardly show her the goblet, so I left it at the British Museum. She would have wondered how I'd come by it if I'd kept hold of it. The whole thing has been a terrible fiasco, but all I can say is that I'm truly relieved it's all over."

"Did your mother really believe that you had only just returned from Egypt when you arrived home?"

"Yes, I think so. I had all my travelling clothes with me and the battered trunks and cases with luggage labels still attached. I felt very guilty about keeping the truth from her. Perhaps one day I shall tell her what really happened, but I'm so worried about what she'll think of me."

"How did you learn of Mr Hamilton's death?"

"I read about it in the papers two days ago. I had already begun to suspect that he was dead, and I'll admit there was some relief to see it confirmed. I felt desperately sad, too. Although he was a criminal who stole from my family, I don't believe that he deserved to suffer that awful fate."

"Have you any idea who might have murdered him?"

"None at all."

"Do you think his murder might have been linked to his criminal activities?"

"I suppose it must have been. He must have found himself caught up in something, but he didn't mention anything about it to me."

"Some people might wonder whether you murdered Mr Hamilton yourself," I suggested.

She scowled. "Why should I do that? I wouldn't even be capable of such a thing!"

"You wanted your goblet back and the other items he stole from you. Perhaps you also wanted revenge."

"The only revenge I sought was to get those treasures back! And I still only managed to find one of them. I could never have harmed Charles, much as I disliked the man. There was no reason for me to murder him."

"Here comes your husband, Penny," warned Beth.

I had been so absorbed in Louisa's story that I hadn't noticed James marching up the steps, accompanied by several uniformed police officers.

Louisa turned and saw them approaching. "Your husband, Mrs Blakely? A police officer?"

"Not now, James!" I called out to him. "Miss Villiers is just telling us her story."

"Perhaps she can enlighten us, too," he replied as he reached the top of the steps. "Good morning, Miss Villiers. I'm Inspector Blakely of Scotland Yard, and this is Inspector Gresham of T Division." He pointed to his companion, who had downturned eyes and a drooping moustache. "I'm arresting you for the murder of Mr Charles Hamilton, otherwise known as Robert Higgins."

"But I've done nothing wrong!" she protested.

As two constables took her arms, her eyes darted back to me. "You told them I'd be here," she hissed. "You betrayed me!"

"Mrs Blakely has done nothing of the sort," said James. He turned to the constables. "Take her to the Black Maria, please."

"Why are you doing this?" I asked him as Louisa Villiers was marched down the steps. "Why now?"

"You were able to meet with her, Penny, and you've had the conversation you wanted. Now the police need to hear what she has to say for herself."

"But you can't just take her away like that!"

"She's been arrested. What did you expect?"

"But now she believes that I'm behind it."

"I'm sorry, Penny, but Miss Villiers is the chief suspect in a murder inquiry. We'll talk more about this later."

He strode back down the steps, following the police officers and Louisa Villiers as they walked over to the black police carriage parked just beyond the gates.

"Did you really arrange for your husband to do that?" asked Beth, visibly shocked.

"No!"

She turned to look me in the eye. "I'm not sure I believe you."

CHAPTER 44

I retreated to the reading room and tried to distract myself with *Voyage dans la Basse et la Haute Egypte*. I was in no mood to translate the text, so I browsed the pictures instead.

Although I understood why James considered Louisa Villiers a suspect, I felt that her arrest had been too hasty. *Surely she should have been given the opportunity to explain herself first.* It had been an unnecessary course of action at that time, and now she believed I was behind it.

You betrayed me.

Her words repeated over and over in my head. Having just managed to gain her trust and confidence, I had immediately lost it. And I had also lost Beth's for the second time.

Tears sprung into my eyes and I tried to blink them back. I just about managed to quell them, but not before one large teardrop had dropped onto my page of notes, dispersing the ink into a large smudge of blue.

"Penny?" Francis's concerned whisper sounded from just over my shoulder.

I quickly wiped my eyes and forced a smile.

"Are you all right?" he asked.

"No. James has just arrested someone and she thinks I set her up!"

He gave me a puzzled glance. "Presumably he had good reason to arrest her."

"Yes, but that's not the point. He should have waited!"

"I see. I suppose that's the trouble with being married to a police inspector."

"It's usually no trouble at all, but he has really angered me this morning!"

"I'm sorry to hear it." Francis glanced around, aware that we might be disturbing those around us. Then he turned back to me, pushing his floppy hair away from his spectacles. "Do you want to talk somewhere else?"

He held my gaze, and I recalled the moment when he had readied himself to propose marriage to me many moons earlier. I felt warmth in my face and averted my eyes. I suddenly felt a pang of guilt for grumbling about James.

"I'm all right. Thank you, Francis."

"Of course."

I tried to concentrate on my work when I returned home, but my mind was too restless. Instead, I sat at my writing desk and twisted a piece of blotting paper in my fingers.

Why had James been so hasty? Why couldn't he have waited just a little while longer?

Mrs Oliver entered the room and informed me that my father had called and was waiting for me in the front room. My stomach turned. He was awaiting an answer about accommodating his family, but I wasn't in the mood for such a conversation at this point in time.

I re-pinned my hair, smoothed out my dress and headed down to meet him.

"Penny! How are you?" he asked. "I hadn't heard from you for a few days so I was beginning to wonder how you were."

"Is that the real purpose of your visit?"

"Yes! Well, part of it, anyway."

I sat down, and he followed suit.

"Actually, I'd been expecting to hear from you about your offer..."

"My offer?"

"Yes. Your offer to house my family for a short while. They'll be arriving into Liverpool in a few days."

"I never made you an offer, Father."

"Really? I thought you'd said that you just needed to ask James."

"It wasn't an offer as such. I merely said that I would ask him."

"And what did he say?"

"That it wouldn't be a good idea." The fact that I was angry with James at that moment made it relatively easy to lay the blame on him.

"Oh dear. I hope you tried to talk him round!"

"Actually, I didn't."

"Why ever not?"

"Because I agree with him, Father. We simply don't have the space."

"But you have this enormous house!"

"It's not enormous. We have three bedrooms, one of which I use as my writing room."

"They'd be quite happy in just one room, Penny. That would still be a luxury to them! They're accustomed to very primitive living conditions, of course. Just a simple hut and no furniture."

"We couldn't possibly accommodate six people in one bedroom, Father. That's total nonsense! They need proper accommodation, and I'm afraid you'll need to arrange that for them yourself."

"That's exactly what I'm doing, Penny. I've explained all this before, haven't I? When the money comes in from the tour—"

"And when will that be?"

"Soon!"

"You haven't even started it yet."

"No, but it's all happening. And..." his voice trailed off, as if he realised there was little use in trying to persuade me. "They'll be here in just a few days' time. Where on earth am I supposed to put them?"

"I don't know, Father. But you were the one who decided to produce a new family and then ship them over here. I'm afraid that's something you'll have to sort out yourself."

"You're beginning to sound rather heartless, Penny. The youngest child is only two years of age!"

I drew in a deep breath, feeling desperately sorry for this child I had never met. I felt sorry for all his children. They were moving to a country that was completely different from their own. However, I tried not to allow sympathy to affect my judgment.

"You'd be happy for a two-year-old to sleep in the doss house, wouldn't you?" barked my father.

"No, I would not!" I retorted. "But you should have thought about this properly before you decided to bring them here."

"I thought I had more money. And I hoped my family would support me, at the very least. I suppose I shall have to ask Eliza."

"Don't you dare! She's just had to endure a divorce, and she has her own children to worry about."

He got to his feet and leaned on his stick, suddenly appearing rather old and frail. "It's all such a terrible shame. I accept full responsibility for my actions, of course, but I also believe in a society in which we all help one another, and when a chap and his young family find themselves in dire straits..."

I felt tears fill my eyes. "Father, I can't continue this conversation any longer. It's been such a terribly busy time, and I have a lot to think about—"

"I understand," he said. "I'll show myself out."

⚜

James returned home late that evening.

"Have you been interviewing Miss Villiers all day?" I asked.

"Not all day, no. I was called down to Camberwell."

"Why?"

"Someone's emptied the Aladdin's cave."

CHAPTER 45

We continued our conversation in the garden. Dusk was falling and a blackbird was singing happily close by. "They told P Division they were from the Yard," said James, describing how a group of well-organised men had carefully loaded the artefacts into a smart carriage while the men from P Division looked on. "How could trained officers have been so foolish?"

"The men were clearly very convincing," I said.

"Clearly. But who are they? And how did they know about the storage room? There was someone else there, too. That chap Bagshaw."

"Joseph Bagshaw?"

"Yes. He had a great pile of papers supposedly proving that some of the Egyptian artefacts were his. I'd told him proof of ownership was needed, hadn't I? I had no idea how he was going to manage, that but somehow he's managed to falsify some papers.

"He's clearly up to no good, though. He told the constables at P Division that he'd agreed with the Yard to retrieve his belongings, and that's obviously not true. Apparently, he had sketches of himself unearthing the treasures in Amarna. Why he wasn't able to show them to us sooner, I really don't know."

"John Smollett!" I exclaimed. "That's what Mr Bagshaw must have been arranging the other day. Mr Bagshaw didn't want me to see him leaving Mr Smollett's house, and Mr Smollett denied that Mr Bagshaw had ever been there. He must have asked Mr Smollett to produce those sketches and perhaps draw up some fake documents, too!"

"Sounds likely."

"It would explain why he was suddenly in possession of all those papers when he had never shown them to us before."

"Not only did P Division allow him to take the artefacts away, but the chaps pretending to be from the Yard did, too. Some of them were even wearing uniforms! Where on earth did they get those from? They gave P Division the name of my colleague, Sergeant Wilcox. The poor chap knew nothing about it, of course."

"Why did the criminals pretending to be from the Yard allow Mr Bagshaw to take some of the items?"

"I imagine he must have colluded with them. It can be no great coincidence that they were all there at the same time, can it? The storage area is now completely empty, and all those belongings recovered from robberies have been stolen again. I can't even begin to imagine what Lord Manningham will have to say about it." He rubbed his brow. "I've asked some of my men to arrest Bagshaw, and I shall go and speak to Smollett again myself. He may have conspired with Miss Villiers to murder Hamilton. And Bagshaw's somehow involved in it all, too."

"What do you think of Louisa Villiers's story?" I asked him. "Do you think it's credible?"

"She seems genuine when she talks, but her story seems a little far-fetched. I'll need to check some aspects of it with the housekeeper, but given that she's already lied to us once, I'm not sure we can trust her."

"I'm still unhappy about the way you arrested her, James. It looked like I had set her up."

"Miss Villiers may well be a murderer, Penny! I've never known you protest so much when I've arrested suspects in the past."

"But now it seems as though I had something to do with her arrest."

"Well, you are married to a police officer."

"But that doesn't mean I work for you! Nor do I always agree with the actions of the police. I need people to trust me, James. Sometimes suspects are more willing to speak with someone who's not a police officer. And sometimes they're more willing to speak with a woman. Don't you see how valuable that is to me? It's how I've always done my work, and I don't want to compromise it now that I'm married to you."

James gave a sombre nod. "I hear you, Penny. I'm sorry my actions upset you."

I wanted to remain angry with him, but I could see that he was sincerely sorry. "Please don't do it again," I said, embracing him.

"I'm sorry," he said as we disentangled from our embrace, "but you know how much I enjoy arresting people!"

He gave a playful smile, which vanished the moment he saw my reprimanding look.

He scratched the nape of his neck. "Anyway, back to Miss Villiers," he continued. "I'll need to verify her story with the hotel she claims to have stayed at in east London. She's given me the name of it."

"I suppose we ultimately need to find evidence that she didn't murder Mr Hamilton."

"Or evidence that she did. She had a strong motive,

Penny. She was desperate to get away from him, and she wanted to retrieve the items that had been stolen from her father. Smollett and Bagshaw may have carried out the murder on her behalf. We always knew there had to have been more than one person involved, didn't we?"

"Did she tell you it was John Smollett who had asked to see Mr Hamilton's photographs? That was why Mr Hamilton returned to his room."

A smile spread across James's face. "No, she didn't mention that. That was a bit of a slip-up, wasn't it? Smollett's request ensured that Hamilton fell into the trap, in that case. I'd wager that Bagshaw was hiding in that bedroom with the garrotte. And the note that was dropped into Miss Villiers's glass... It had to have been written by Smollett. He didn't want her to be harmed. He warned her away."

"Which suggests to me that she wasn't involved in the plot," I said. "If she had helped arrange her husband's murder she wouldn't have needed warning, would she?"

"That's a good point, Penny." James rubbed his chin. "Unless the note in her drink was a complete fiction! Perhaps she made that part of the story up to make herself look innocent."

"Mrs Chilton would know."

"She's the lady Miss Villiers was speaking to at the time, was she? We'll have to find her and ask about the note. There's a lot of following up to do here. Mrs Chilton might be fictitious as well, mightn't she?"

"I suppose so..." I considered this carefully. "I still think Miss Villiers is telling the truth, James. I don't think she murdered her husband. In fact, I can't imagine John Smollett or Joseph Bagshaw doing it, either, if I'm honest. Strangle a man, cart his body down to Tooting and then bury him in a shallow grave? I just can't see it."

"That's why murderers are so hard to catch, Penny. They're rarely obvious about it, are they?"

"I suppose not."

"I feel like we're making good progress. By this evening we should have all three main suspects behind bars. All we need to do then is verify their stories. I'd feel a lot happier if P Division hadn't allowed Hamilton's storage room in Camberwell to be emptied. Exceptionally poor police work! The superintendent will have a lot to answer for after this." He paused in thought. "I'm going to chop that clematis down now in the hope that it'll make me feel better."

CHAPTER 46

I slept poorly that night. My thoughts about my father swung between anger and pity. Then a fear began to creep in that I might never see him again. *After all, he'd left me once before. Might he leave me again because I had refused to help him?*

I told myself it didn't matter, given that his behaviour was so selfish and unreasonable, but this left me with such great sadness that I was almost tempted to visit him the following morning and offer to host his family. *He may have been far from perfect, but he was my father. How could I turn my back on him?*

My lost friendship with Beth also weighed on my mind. Not only had I doubted her, but she now believed that I had worked with James to have Louisa Villiers arrested. It was unlikely that she would ever trust me again. I came to the conclusion that it was perhaps impossible to combine true friendship with my work.

James left early for work in the morning, keen to learn whether Mr Bagshaw had been successfully apprehended.

"Is there something wrong with your egg?" asked Mrs Oliver as I absent-mindedly toyed with my breakfast.

"No, it's very good. Thank you." She gave me a knowing smile and glanced down at my middle. I had noticed her doing so a good deal recently. As I was newly married, she no doubt expected that I would soon be with child. The thought ruined my appetite altogether.

Something didn't feel right about the case. James seemed happy to be rounding up the chief suspects, but I still wasn't convinced we were on the right track. However, I was beginning to doubt my judgement these days. *Perhaps James was right after all and I should leave the rest of the work to him and his colleagues.*

For almost four weeks I had been working as hard as possible to discover the fate of the Hamiltons, and I felt enormously tired. Beth no longer needed my help and the police had three suspects to be going on with. It was time for me to rest and leave the remaining work to James and his colleagues. My work on the case was done.

After breakfast, I picked up a biography of Mary Wollstonecraft, which had been sitting on my reading table for some time, and took a stroll up Primrose Hill.

There was still some warmth in the breeze, but a few golden leaves had already been blown from the trees. I paused at the top of the hill to watch the clouds scud over the spires and chimneys of London. Patches of light and shadow passed over the metropolis in gentle waves. There was almost something soothing about the motion.

I found the bench with the best view and sat there with my carpet bag on my lap. My book remained unopened inside it.

The events of the past few weeks ran through my mind. It

had been a confusing time. The untruths and fake identities had made our work complicated.

I tried to push these thoughts from my mind, and instead focused on naming the church spires I could see. I began with the most obvious of all landmarks; the dome of St Paul's.

Yet it seemed there was a voice in my mind that wouldn't be silenced. Although my work was finished, it didn't feel complete. I lacked the sense of satisfaction I had felt when working on previous cases.

There was still more to do.

I picked up my bag and got to my feet.

It was time to go back to Chelsea.

CHAPTER 47

I hoped that by returning to the scene of the crime I might discover something new about Mr Hamilton's murder. As I approached the Copeland Hotel, the brown-and-cream-brick Excelsior Hotel next door caught my eye. Once again, it struck me as odd that two hotels stood side by side.

I walked into the wood-panelled foyer of the Copeland, where the desk attendant was occupied with a loud customer in a stovepipe hat. Crossing the tiled floor, I followed an engraved sign pointing toward the ballroom and turned left into a long corridor.

The ballroom was where the drinks reception had been held that fateful night. Its heavy double doors were closed, which was to be expected during the daytime. After checking there was no one else around, I pushed open one of the doors and peered inside.

The large windows were shuttered and the room's contents were barely discernible in the gloom. I had expected nothing different, but I felt that orientating myself here would enable me to get as close as possible to the events of that night.

Turning away from the ballroom, I made my way back to the foyer and the main staircase, just as Mr Hamilton and Beth had done that evening. On my way, I passed a blank door. There was no sign on it, nor even a handle. Presumably it was for staff use only.

I paused and walked back toward the door. *Was it a store cupboard or did it lead somewhere?* I gently pushed against it and it gave way, opening out into the stairwell of a stone service staircase. A folding metal door was pulled across a lift shaft beside it.

I climbed three flights of stairs, thankfully encountering no one else as I did so. On reaching the third floor, I carefully pushed open the door and found myself standing opposite room 312. *How had I not noticed this door before?* There were so many along the corridor that I must have walked past it without giving it any thought. I turned right, and a few strides brought me to the door of 306. I estimated that it had taken less than two minutes to get there from the ballroom.

Had Mr Smollett run up the service staircase as soon as Mr Hamilton left the room? If so, he would have reached room 306 ahead of his employer. Perhaps he had joined Joseph Bagshaw and the two had lain in wait.

I knocked on the door of room 306. I didn't expect the occupant to admit me, but I felt that even just a glance inside the room might help.

There was no answer.

The squeak of a wheel sounded along the corridor, and I turned to see a chambermaid pushing a large trolley toward me. As she drew nearer, I saw that it was the same maid I had spoken to previously.

"Can I help you, madam?" She gave me a quizzical look, as if she recognised me. "Weren't you a friend of 'is?" she asked.

"That's right."

"D'you wanna see inside 'is room?"

"I should very much like to, if at all possible."

"I seem to remember you 'ad a shillin' last time."

I smiled in response to her boldness and pulled my purse out of my bag.

There was nothing remarkable about room 306. It contained a large bed, a washstand and a wardrobe. There was an attractive view from the window and the accommodation was spacious, but it had the plain, impersonal appearance of the average hotel room. Perhaps I had expected to feel an uncomfortable tingle in my bones as I stood in the room where a man had been murdered, but I felt nothing.

"Sorry for yer loss, madam," said the maid. "We've 'ad a lot o' folk comin' down 'ere since they've found 'im. It's only jus' calmin' down again."

"I can imagine."

"Anythin' else you wanna see?"

"No, I think that's everything. Thank you."

The maid followed me out of the room, locked the door and bid me farewell as she pushed her trolley away. She seemed pleased to have made a shilling for just a minute of her time.

I returned to the foyer via the main staircase and felt reassured that this was definitely a longer route.

I almost managed to leave the hotel without encountering Mr Fortescue again, but not quite.

"I thought we'd seen the back of all the reporters," he commented on spotting me there. "Especially now that arrests have been made."

"Are the police keeping you informed?"

"Absolutely! I need to be able to reassure my guests, don't I? This whole sorry business is beginning to calm down now, but I fear my hotel will always have the unfortunate reputation as the location where a recent murder took place."

I stepped outside into sunshine, which was swiftly blotted out by the cooling cloud. I turned and looked back at the two hotels, then walked toward the Excelsior Hotel and stepped inside.

CHAPTER 48

"There's no sign of Bagshaw anywhere," fumed James when he returned home that evening. "We've got John Smollett and Louisa Villiers down at King's Road station, but Bagshaw's vanished!"

"Along with the artefacts?"

"Yes! He must have left London in the carriage he used to collect the items from Camberwell. We've alerted all the ports to keep an eye out for him. This is rapidly turning into a wild goose chase! Meanwhile, Smollett has confessed to forging the sketches and papers for Bagshaw. It didn't take much to make the chap crumble."

"He's admitted to forging the papers but denies murder?"

"Yes."

"You'd think that if he crumbled so easily on one count he'd also admit the other."

"Not necessarily." He peered at me more closely. "Why do you have that look on your face, Penny?"

"What look?"

"A sort of faraway, distant look, as if your thoughts are

completely elsewhere. Are you no longer interested in the case?"

"I decided I was finished with it earlier," I replied, "but then I changed my mind. In fact, I returned to the Copeland Hotel today."

"Whatever for?"

"To get some fresh ideas."

"We don't need any new ideas, Penny. We just need to find Bagshaw! And we need someone to draw confessions out of Smollett and Villiers."

"John Smollett may have a case to answer, but I don't believe Louisa Villiers has done anything wrong." I paused for a moment. "Anyway, I need your help with something."

"What is it?"

"I need you to find the title deeds to the Copeland Hotel."

"Why so?"

"I'll explain once you have them. I think they may lead us to the last piece of the puzzle."

He rubbed his brow. "Penny, I really don't have time—"

"I know, James. Perhaps you could ask a constable to fetch them. Here's the name of Mr Fortescue's lawyer." I handed him a slip of paper with the name and address written on it. "I'd ask myself, but the lawyer would have every right to refuse my request. However, if there happened to be a particularly intimidating constable who could go, we might just have some luck."

James took the piece of paper from me. "Are you sure this is worth our while, Penny? I really can't see the relevance of it."

"I'm not completely sure it'll be worthwhile, James. All I can do is hope that the papers will provide some answers."

"And if they don't?"

"Then I will wash my hands of this case once and for all!"

. . .

I sat down at my typewriter that evening and wrote an article about the treasures that had been stolen from Mr Hamilton's storage room beneath the railway arches and the subsequent disappearance of Mr Bagshaw.

The following morning, I handed it in to a grateful Mr Sherman.

CHAPTER 49

Two days later, James and I found ourselves sitting in a drab room at King's Road police station in Chelsea, where Louisa Villiers and John Smollett were being held. I very much hoped I would be able to visit Louisa and explain that I hadn't been complicit in her arrest.

"There's been a report of a man resembling Joseph Bagshaw staying at an inn in Woodford, Essex," said Inspector Gresham of T Division. "I've sent a man out there, but at the same time we've had another report from Twickenham. That's meant having to send another man there! And there's no way of knowing how reliable these reports even are!"

"It's extremely tricky," said James. "Mrs Blakely here has written an article for the *Morning Express* newspaper appealing for information about Joseph Bagshaw's whereabouts."

"And that's another part of the problem!" protested Inspector Gresham. "The great unwashed read these things and then convince themselves they've seen him. And we're expected to follow up on everything."

"I'm sure it'll be worth your while, Gresham."

"It had better be!"

"My wife has been doing a lot of work on this case," continued James. "She would appreciate a few minutes of your time, if possible."

The inspector acknowledged me with a glance, but I wasn't important enough for him to turn in my direction. I sensed he was the sort of man who had no time for ladies getting involved in his work. I felt sure that if I hadn't been James's wife, he wouldn't have paid me any heed at all.

"We have a lot to do," he responded, "but proceed all the same, Mrs Blakely."

"I don't believe that Joseph Bagshaw committed murder, sir," I said to Inspector Gresham. "Nor do I believe that Louisa Villiers did."

"Hamilton stole from Bagshaw," replied the inspector. "We have a motive right there."

"I agree, and Bagshaw hasn't helped himself by taking off with the artefacts he believes are his. I can't claim to like the man, but I'm not convinced he's a murderer." I paused briefly to allow him to consider this. "I also believe that Miss Villiers implicated herself by not speaking to the police sooner. By taking matters into her own hands in a bid to retrieve the items taken from her, she has brought suspicion upon herself."

"If I'd received a note in my drink telling me to run away, the first thing I would have done is take it to the nearest police station," added Inspector Gresham.

"Yes," I agreed. "I think most people would have done that. But Miss Villiers was very frightened. Once she learned what had happened to Mr Hamilton, she feared the police would hold her responsible. And she wanted to keep her true identity under wraps because she didn't want her family finding out what she had been up to."

"Hardly the best course of action," said Inspector Gresham. "Not only did she complicate matters for us, but her family have found her out anyway. Her mother has been haranguing my men, petitioning for her daughter's release."

"I can't say that I blame her," I replied.

"Are you saying it was John Smollett who did it?" he asked.

"Let me explain a few things first," I replied.

The inspector checked his watch and gave a contemptuous sniff.

I took a deep breath and began, aware that he wasn't very interested in anything I had to say. "Mr Hamilton's murder and disappearance was so swift that someone powerful and organised must have been behind it," I said. "That would explain why only one witness saw the body before it was discovered in a shallow grave in Tooting three weeks later.

"Mr Hamilton was murdered in his room while a drinks reception was taking place in the ballroom downstairs. He had gone up to fetch some photographs that Mr Smollett had asked to see. Mr Hamilton's murderer must have been lying in wait for him there. The murderer knew that Mr Hamilton would be returning to his room, so either Mr Smollett told the murderer he intended to do so, or the murderer commanded Mr Smollett to come up with a reason that would compel Mr Hamilton to return to his room."

"John Smollett was in on it either way, then," said Inspector Gresham.

"Yes, I think he was. By committing the murder while the drinks reception was taking place, the murderer had plenty of time to carry out the act. He presumably thought there would be nobody around to disturb him. He couldn't have known that Beth Worthers would choose the very same moment to speak to Mr Hamilton about terminating her employment.

"Mrs Worthers entered the room before the body could

be removed. The people responsible were no doubt hiding in the room at the time, perhaps under the bed or in the wardrobe." I shuddered. "It's fortunate that Mrs Worthers was completely unaware of their presence when she walked into that room. She's also very fortunate that she wasn't murdered herself to prevent her from telling anyone about the body."

"Why wasn't she?" asked Gresham.

"Because that would have created even more problems for the murderers. There would have been two bodies to dispose of and much more uproar. They must have reasoned that Mrs Worthers's account would be disbelieved. If there was no evidence of a murder, her claims would easily be dismissed as mad ramblings."

"A tactic that worked wonders," added James.

"She's lucky to have escaped with her life," I said.

"You seem to be suggesting that there was more than one murderer," said Inspector Gresham.

"Yes, I think there must have been. I also believe John Smollett may have reached room 306 before Mr Hamilton by using the staff staircase."

He looked puzzled for a moment. "Smollett asked Hamilton for the photographs, then watched him leave, you mean? Then as soon as he was gone, Smollett dashed up to the room to help with the murder?"

"I think it's possible, though I'm not sure if he was involved in the murder itself. I am convinced that there was more than one person in the room with Mr Hamilton, however."

The inspector nodded. "It does make sense when you consider how quickly they managed to get the body out of there. My money was on Smollett and Bagshaw, but I can see that you have more explaining to do, Mrs Blakely."

"I've spoken with a maid at the hotel on a couple of occasions," I said, "and I noticed that she pushes a large trolley filled with housekeeping items. It's like a cupboard on wheels. There are shelves inside with folded towels and linen—"

"Yes, I know the type of trolley you mean," he interrupted.

"The thought occurred to me that such a trolley could be adapted to conceal the body of man," I said. "It would allow the body to be removed from the room without rousing anyone's suspicion."

The inspector raised an eyebrow. "Mr Hamilton's body, you mean?"

"Yes. The trolley could have been taken to the service lift located next to the staff staircase. My guess is that the service lift runs down to a level in the basement where the housekeeping trolleys are kept, and perhaps the laundry is also taken down there."

"That makes sense," said the inspector. He seemed to be taking my theory a little more seriously. "But how on earth would someone adapt a housekeeping trolley? And I don't see how he would have gained access to the service lift or the basement without the hotel staff becoming suspicious. Then there's the question of the horse and cart that must have quickly conveyed Hamilton's body down to Tooting. Presumably it was waiting near an external door that led down to the basement."

"It must have been."

"Somehow Hamilton's body was removed from the maid's trolley and loaded onto the cart, all without anyone suspecting anything. I like your theory, Mrs Blakely. The idea of a housekeeping trolley being used is imaginative, yet not improbable. But this is where we come unstuck every time we attempt to work out what happened. It's impossible to imagine how anyone managed to get Hamilton out of that hotel without a single person noticing!"

"Not if the staff at the hotel were involved," I replied.

CHAPTER 50

"The hotel staff?" queried Inspector Gresham incredulously. "Why would the hotel staff be involved?"

"Some weeks ago I spoke with Mrs Palmer, who founded the Ancient Egypt Society," I replied.

The inspector pinched the bridge of his nose in exasperation. "What does this have to do with the Copeland Hotel?"

"Mrs Palmer told me she had been approached by Mr Fortescue, the hotel manager, who asked if she would consider hosting an event with him. He offered her such discounted prices that she suspected he was looking to create loyal customers from among the society members. Apparently, there was competition between him and the manager of the Excelsior Hotel next door, and it was her opinion that Mr Fortescue was losing out a little."

"Your point being, Mrs Blakely?"

"The event was proposed by Mr Fortescue. It was all his idea. He planned the event... and he also planned the murder."

"Mr Fortescue? But he's a respectable hotelier! Why on earth would he be involved?"

"I've met him a number of times since the Hamiltons disappeared," I replied, "but I only recently remembered something strange about my very first conversation with him."

"What was it?"

"He was very dismissive of the idea that Mr Hamilton had been murdered. In fact, he was adamant that Mr Hamilton must have run away to avoid paying his bill. Yet when he described the size of Mr Hamilton, he referred to him in the past tense, as if he already knew that Mr Hamilton was dead."

The inspector gave this some thought. "That doesn't make him a murderer."

"No. But it's odd, don't you think, to insist that a man must still be alive and yet refer to him in the past tense?"

"It is rather odd," he conceded.

"I agree that these facts alone don't make Mr Fortescue a murderer," said James, "and I was sceptical myself until Penny asked me to acquire the title deeds to the Copeland Hotel."

"What do they have to do with anything?" asked the inspector.

"I paid a visit to Mr Hambridge, who runs the neighbouring Excelsior Hotel," I said. "He and Mr Fortescue have been feuding for a good while. The Copeland Hotel has only been open a few years; it was a large house previous to that. When the property came up for sale, Mr Hambridge wished to purchase it in order to extend the Excelsior Hotel. He was outbid, however, by Mr Fortescue, who bought the building and constructed another at the rear to create a larger establishment than the Excelsior. Apparently, he was keen to become more successful than his neighbour and perhaps even put him out of business.

"Mr Hambridge explained some of the lengthy legal

proceedings that took place between the two men, though I can't pretend that I understood all the details."

"That's lawyers for you," commented the inspector.

"But what has interested me throughout this case," I continued, "is the number of people who are not who they said they were. Beth Worthers pretended to be someone else when she was working for Mr Hamilton. Louisa Villiers pretended to be someone else once she was married to Mr Hamilton. And while it may prove difficult to discover Mr Hamilton's true identity, we do know that he called himself Robert Higgins for a long time.

"Although exceptionally dull, legal documents often provide fascinating insights for anyone patient enough to read through them," I said. "I spent much of my weekend doing so after my husband kindly acquired the title deeds to the Copeland. He obtained them from Mr Fortescue's lawyer, whose name Mr Hambridge was kind enough to share with me. It turns out the owner of the hotel named in the title deeds is not Mr Fortescue, who receives no mention at all. Instead, it's a gentleman named Mr Thomas Scully."

"And who might he be?"

"A corrupt auctioneer Robert Higgins once worked for."

"According to a colleague of mine, Inspector Powell, he once had a number of criminals in his employ," said James. "Then he was convicted of a minor fraud, for which he served a year in prison. It was widely believed that he changed his ways after this brief period of imprisonment and turned his back on his life of crime. That belief has been proven to be incorrect, however. Mr Fortescue is, in fact, Mr Scully."

"How do you know this?"

"The two men are the same age and have the same physical description. I shall confirm it with Inspector Powell to be absolutely sure. He was well acquainted with Thomas Scully."

"They do say that a leopard never changes his spots," said

Inspector Gresham. "But I still can't see any hard evidence that Fortescue committed the murder."

"We need to get his staff to speak to us honestly," said James. "I think some may have lied to protect him."

"How many?" asked Inspector Gresham.

"I suspect only a couple assisted him with the murder, but one or two others must have been intimidated into keeping their silence. That's why we found no witnesses who had seen Hamilton's body being removed from the hotel."

"I suspect the maid I spoke to had been ordered to lie about the events of that evening," I added. "Her account differed from Beth Worthers's. I know now that Beth was telling me the truth."

"And then there's John Smollett," said James. "I'm sure he knows something. He was the one who arranged for Hamilton to return to his room, and he may also have ensured that Miss Villiers was warned off. Perhaps he insisted on being allowed to do so in return for his help. Someone approached him about the murder, and I think he'll admit his involvement once we've arrested Fortescue. Once everybody knows they are no longer in danger, I think they'll start talking. In the meantime, I'd like to begin with Mr Smollett."

"I have a request, too," I added. "Can Louisa Villiers be released?"

"She's still a suspect," said James.

"I don't see why," I retorted. "You said you were going to check out her story with the housekeeper and the hotel in east London. If they're able to verify her story, I think we can safely assume that she's telling the truth."

"Very well, I'll see what I can do," said James. "How does that sound to you, Gresham?"

The inspector shrugged. "It seems Fortescue is now your chief suspect."

"You're not convinced?" James replied.

"Who am I to question an inspector of the Yard?" Inspector Gresham followed this with a sidelong glance in my direction. "Or his wife."

"Edward Fortescue *is* Thomas Scully," said James, "and he needs to be arrested. I'm also fairly sure that he colluded with Joseph Bagshaw to empty Hamilton's storage room in Camberwell. The men who carried out that work were professional about it. They even fooled the officers from P Division."

"Not too tricky, I imagine." Gresham gave a derisory laugh. "If you're certain about all this, leave it to me and my men," he added. "We've got to know Fortescue quite well over the past few days, so I'll pay him another visit. What with that and trying to find Bagshaw, we won't have a great number of men left for the rest of our work. Can't be helped, I suppose."

"I'd like to speak to John Smollett as well, please," I asked.

Inspector Gresham sighed heavily, as if this really was asking too much. "Right, we'll have him brought up from the cells, and I'll ask Sergeant Collis to join you. I was going to send him down to Twickenham to follow up on the supposed sighting of Bagshaw, but I suppose that'll have to wait."

Although he was a young man, John Smollett's face appeared lined when he was led into the room to talk with us. There was a greyish hue to his dark skin and his eyes were downcast. I felt sorry for him being confined to a cell, but I couldn't be sure how innocent he was.

He had created false sketches and papers for Joseph Bagshaw. What else was he capable of?

Sergeant Collis was a bored-looking man with a wispy moustache. He made notes throughout but said very little.

"It's about time we heard the full truth from you, Mr

Smollett," said James. "We know who the murderer is and Inspector Gresham is on his way to make the arrest."

Mr Smollett's eyes flickered wide open. "Who is it?"

"Perhaps you can tell us."

"But I don't know who did it!"

"Perhaps you can tell us what you do know. Why did you ask Mr Hamilton to fetch those photographs that evening?"

Mr Smollett looked down at his fidgeting hands and a long pause followed.

"We know far more than you realise, Mr Smollett," said James. "It will be far better for you if you can give us your version of events. If you've done anything unlawful you will be shown greater leniency if you talk than if you remain silent and unhelpful."

"Someone asked me to request the photographs," he muttered.

"Who?"

"I don't know." He looked up. "I honestly don't know. It was a man, quite smartly dressed. He approached me that afternoon. He didn't tell me his name, but I assumed he worked at the hotel."

"Why did you assume that?"

"He seemed to know his way around and he knew my name."

"What did he say to you, exactly?"

"He told me they needed Mr Hamilton to be up in his room for a meeting at around eight o'clock that evening. I had no idea they intended to murder him!"

"Thank you, Mr Smollett," said James. "You're being incredibly helpful now. What was his specific request?"

"That I come up with a way of enticing Mr Hamilton back to his room. I really didn't know what to think, so he suggested that I ask Mr Hamilton to fetch something. All I could think of were the photographs I'd been wanting to make sketches from. So that's what I asked for, and I..." He swallowed hard. "I led a man to his death."

"But you didn't know that was what you were doing," said James.

"I'm still responsible for his murder!"

"Not necessarily. Out of interest, why did you comply with the man's request? Did he offer you money?"

"No. I don't really know why... Actually, I do. I was scared. I know it sounds foolish to admit it, but I was afraid. To begin with I was perturbed because he knew my name and quite a few details about me, but I soon realised he was an intimidating man. And he kept mentioning 'we', so I knew there were more people involved. I envisaged a whole group of them, in fact. I was too scared to say no. I realise now how cowardly that makes me."

"You're no coward, Mr Smollett."

"I had no idea that Mr Hamilton would be murdered, but I sensed there was danger afoot. I managed to negotiate a little. I said that I would do it, but only if he could guarantee that Susan would be safe. I didn't want her to be caught up in their meeting or whatever it was they were planning."

"That was a good suggestion, Mr Smollett."

"Do you think so? I hear she's in the cells here as well. The inspector told me who she really is. It's some story, and I admire her all the more for it! I do wish I could see her."

"I'm sure you will in due course," James said reassuringly.

"She had no idea they intended to murder Mr Hamilton. She's innocent, truly she is! Will you ask them to release her?"

"I shall speak to Inspector Gresham about it."

"Yes, Inspector Gresham must be consulted," added Sergeant Collis.

"The cells are awful," continued John Smollett. "Certainly no place for a woman! It's cruel."

"I'm sure Miss Villiers won't need to be detained here for much longer."

"I do hope not. How much trouble am I in? I know I shouldn't have drawn those sketches for Mr Bagshaw, either. I had no idea what he intended to do with them. I'm always allowing people to push me around. I just don't feel able to stand up to them. If only I had! Now look at me."

"I'm very grateful to you for being so forthcoming today, Mr Smollett," said James. "May I ask why you didn't tell us any of this sooner?"

"I was too frightened. I felt sure they'd come after me. But now I know the murderer is to be arrested, I feel confident that I shall be safe after all. Who is it?"

"Mr Fortescue, the owner of the Copeland Hotel."

"The hotel manager?" His mouth hung open.

"Your hunch about the man who approached you was probably right; he may well have worked at the hotel. He certainly worked for Mr Fortescue."

"What could the hotel owner have had against Mr Hamilton?"

"That's something we are yet to discover."

"What will happen to me now?"

"I'll have to speak to Inspector Gresham, but I don't really see the need to detain you any longer."

"Inspector Gresham must be consulted," interjected Sergeant Collis.

I was beginning to wonder whether the man ever said anything else.

CHAPTER 51

I left James at King's Road police station and, in a final attempt to make amends, called on Beth at her home in Battersea.

"I've asked them to release Louisa Villiers," I said as soon as she had greeted me. "And I promise I didn't arrange for James to arrest her the other morning. He just turned up!"

"You told him you were meeting her, though." She looked pale and tired.

I nodded.

"Then I don't see why you were so surprised by his actions."

"I'd asked him to wait a little longer."

Beth sighed. "She's been in custody for two days now. It must be so awful for her."

"I know, and I'm doing my best to get her out. May I come in and explain something to you?"

"How's the new job you've taken on?" I asked Beth as she made tea.

"There isn't one..." A pause followed. And then, "That was just an excuse I came up with because I was so angry with you."

"I see."

We both fell silent.

I watched a train rumble past the window. "Are you still angry with me?" I ventured.

"I'm not altogether happy about what's happened between us, but I realise friendship can be difficult in this sort of employment."

"My thoughts exactly. I want you to know that I trust you now, and I'm sorry for ever doubting you."

"It's not just that. I feel as if I betrayed Susan – I mean Louisa – too. She appears to bear me no grudge for lying about my identity, but I feel terrible about it all the same. It's made me question whether I can continue in this line of work."

"Of course you can. You must! You're so good at it."

"I shall have to think about it. What is it you wished to explain to me?"

"I think I know who the murderer is."

I proceeded to tell her everything I had explained to Inspector Gresham.

"I think that all sounds very plausible," she said once I had finished. "It explains how Mr Hamilton's body was so swiftly removed. Mr Fortescue conspired to make everyone believe I had made it all up. And he was almost successful, I might add. I'm glad I came to you, Penny."

"It's not fully resolved yet, though," I replied. "Let's not start celebrating until Mr Fortescue has been arrested."

"And Louisa Villiers is set free."

"Exactly!"

A telegram arrived the following day from the antiquities dealer, Mrs Miller. She requested that I pay her a visit, so I travelled by omnibus to Mayfair, wondering all the while what she could possibly want with me.

I pulled the rope beside the plaque that read 'Mrs. L. J. Miller, Antiquities', then waited. *Was she still annoyed with me following her meeting with the confused old lady at the Café Royal?*

"Mrs Blakely!"

She didn't seem at all annoyed when her assistant showed me in. Dressed in a tangerine and gold bustle dress, she was her usual buoyant self.

"Sherry?"

I reluctantly agreed.

"Now, tell me," she began as she poured me a glass, "are you still on the hunt for missing Egyptologists?"

"Well, we found one," I replied, "but lost another. Joseph Bagshaw is now missing."

"Ah, yes. That's the one." She handed me my glass. "I read in the paper the other day that he'd vanished after clearing out a secret storage hold in Camberwell. Lots of treasures, I believe."

"Yes, that's right. I think he took those that belonged to him along with various others. Some of the items have probably been stolen several times over. I can only hope they'll eventually be recovered and reunited with their original owners."

"If he doesn't try to sell them first, that is."

"Why did you ask me to come here, Mrs Miller?"

"Finish your drink, Mrs Blakely, then come with me."

I drained my glass, then carefully rose to my feet. I was unaccustomed to drinking sherry at such an early hour, and particularly at such speed.

Once outside, Mrs Miller led me along a street of smart, red-and-cream-brick buildings to an elegant Georgian building in brown brick with a cream porch.

"This is the Imperial Hotel," she said. "And hiding inside it is Mr Bagshaw."

"Really? But the police received reports that he'd escaped to Essex! And apparently there was another sighting in Twickenham."

"Well, I can tell you now that he's inside that small hotel awaiting a meeting with me, and he has various items to sell. He tried to do some sneaky deals and swear me to secrecy, but that's not how I like to work. Now, what do you think? Is this a matter for the police?"

"Very much so!" I grinned. "Let's find a constable."

We found one stationed on the corner of Charles Street and John Street. Once we had alerted him to Joseph Bagshaw's whereabouts, he dashed off to Vine Street police station to summon help.

Mrs Miller and I walked back to the hotel.

"I think it's best if I go in there and meet him as we

arranged," she said. "That way he won't grow suspicious, and I can make sure he stays put until the police arrive."

Having encountered him while working on previous cases, I recognised Inspector Paget of C Division as he climbed out of the police carriage that pulled up a short while later. He was a wiry man with a wispy moustache.

"Are you the lady who summoned me?" he asked. "I've met you before. Miss Green, isn't it? News reporter?"

"Yes, only I'm Mrs Blakely now."

"Ah, yes. You married Blakely at the Yard, didn't you? Well, congratulations. Now, tell me where Joseph Bagshaw is, will you? I've heard there's a warrant out for his arrest."

"He's inside that hotel with Mrs Miller, an antiquities dealer. Trying to sell her some of the items he stole last week, apparently."

"Excellent. We'll get in there and nab him." He turned to a couple of constables standing behind him. "Come along!"

A short while later, Joseph Bagshaw was led out of the hotel in handcuffs. He curled his thick upper lip when he saw me.

"Happy now, Mrs Blakely? I did my best to help you, and this is how you repay me?"

I chose not to say anything in response. I simply watched as Inspector Paget shoved him inside the police carriage.

Mrs Miller joined me.

"Thank you," I said.

"My pleasure. I'm awfully pleased I was able to help. Has Mr Hamilton's murderer been apprehended yet?" she asked.

"I sincerely hope so."

CHAPTER 53

"**W**ell done, Penny," said James that evening.

A silver crescent of moon was just visible in the darkening sky above the rooftops as we stood chatting in our garden.

"I had a good look around the hotel room Bagshaw had been staying in, and it was filled with Egyptian artefacts! I don't know how he thought he would get away with it. He couldn't possibly have a viable claim to all of them."

"He must have thought Mrs Miller was as crooked as he was."

"He certainly made a mistake there. Some of the artefacts were most likely stolen from Marmaduke Villiers. Hopefully we can reunite his family with them soon. Speaking of which, Miss Villiers has been returned to her home in Epsom."

"That's wonderful news! I shall send a telegram to Beth tomorrow morning and let her know."

Tiger mewed and rubbed her head against my skirts. I bent down to make a fuss of her.

"What will become of John Smollett, do you think?" I asked.

"He faces the serious charge of abetting a murderer at the present time. I hope the police court can be persuaded that he was coerced into doing so. But even if he's shown some leniency in that respect, there may be a lesser charge related to the fact that he withheld crucial information from the investigation."

"He may receive a prison sentence, in that case."

"I should think it quite likely. Perhaps only a few months if his case is treated with an understanding of the pressures placed upon him."

"And what of the other items taken from Hamilton's storeroom?"

"No sign of them as yet. I've no doubt that Fortescue was behind the robbery. And that's where the problem remains."

"Which problem?"

"Inspector Gresham has informed me that Mr Fortescue is proving rather elusive."

"He hasn't arrested him yet?"

"Not yet, no. He's having a bit of difficulty finding him."

We heard the distant chime of the doorbell and headed back inside the house. Mrs Oliver had left for the evening, so James went to answer the door while I waited in the front room.

A moment later my father walked in, leaning heavily on his walking stick. I gave him a cautious greeting.

"Don't look so concerned, Penny. I'm not here to ask you for anything or to create any further disagreement between us. I've come to apologise."

"Thank you, Father. Perhaps you'd better take a seat."

"I will do, thank you."

"Would you like a drink, Mr Green?" asked James as he entered the room.

"Yes, thank you. A whiskey would be just perfect."

I wondered what had caused my father's change of heart since our last meeting.

"Have you found suitable accommodation for your family yet?"

"Not yet, but I shall have plenty of choice."

"What do you mean?"

"I've had a wonderful offer, Penny, and I have you and dear James to thank for it."

"Really?"

James handed me a glass of sherry.

"Yes. I received a visit from a very pleasant gentleman today, and he's offered my family a large sum of money."

"That doesn't sound right, Father," I said. "Who is he?"

"You know him. And apparently you've been doing him a great favour!"

"We both know him?" asked James, passing my father a glass of whiskey.

"Apparently so! He's a charming chap who recently came to one of my performances. We spent a good deal of time talking about that. He was very impressed by it, you know."

"Why did he offer you money?" asked James.

"Because of you. He told me you've been so generous toward him."

"This isn't making any sense, Father," I said. "I don't recall us being so generous to anyone that they should offer you a large sum of money. Just tell us who it is."

"His name is Edward Fortescue." My father beamed. "And he really is a delightful chap!"

"He is nothing of the kind!" replied James sharply. "He's a criminal who has been evading arrest! When did you see him?"

My father's face fell. "He visited me just now..."

"Where?"

"At my home."

"He knows where you live?" I exclaimed.

"Yes..."

"Do you know where he is now?" asked James.

"Well, actually... He told me he wished to thank you himself. So he's... he's just outside."

"Outside here?" asked James, leaping up from his seat.

"I'm sure there's no need to panic," said Father, looking thoroughly confused. "He's a perfectly pleasant fellow."

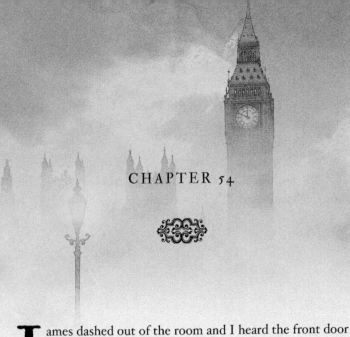

CHAPTER 54

James dashed out of the room and I heard the front door open. My heart began to thud.

"Penny," said my father, his face drawn. "I'm sorry, but I don't understand what's happening here. He's a criminal, you say?"

"Yes. And he's wanted for murder."

"Murder?" His mouth opened and closed as he attempted to find the right words. In the end, he could only repeat the same one. "Murder?"

"Get out of my house!" came James's voice.

I stood to my feet just as Mr Fortescue came striding into the front room.

"Mrs Blakely!" he said with a wide grin. "Has your father told you the good news?"

James barged into the room. "Edward Fortescue, I'm arresting you for the murder of Mr Hamilton!"

Mr Fortescue laughed. "Put your handcuffs away, Inspector, and let's talk about this like proper gentlemen. The first thing you must do is calm your temper. I'm not here to cause any trouble."

James gave me a look that suggested I should go and summon help. I was confident that I could run to St John's Wood police station within a few minutes.

"Stay where you are, Mrs Blakely," said Mr Fortescue, sensing that I was about to leave the room.

"Don't you speak to my wife in that manner!" ordered James. "You're only making matters worse for yourself by resisting arrest."

"I'd like to know what you think of my offer," said Mr Fortescue.

"We're not talking about any offer," retorted James, positioning himself in front of the doorway.

"You're not? Well, that's a great shame. I usually find police inspectors much more amenable."

"Do you mean Gresham? He allowed you to escape, did he?"

"I simply explained that I needed a little time to put my affairs in order. Now, Mr Green here is in need of some assistance. If his wife and children have nowhere to live when they arrive in the country, they may end up in the workhouse!"

"Why should that be any concern of yours?" I asked.

"Oh, I can't bear to see families suffer," he said, placing one hand on his chest. "I like to do what I can to help. By accepting my offer, Mr Green and his family needn't ever worry about money again. They'll be able to live in a comfortable house and the children will receive an excellent education. They'll never want for anything."

"I don't need your charity," said Mr Green. "I can pay the money back—"

"No, Father!" I snapped. "This man is offering you money in return for James agreeing to let him walk free!"

"Oh, is that so?" queried my father. "I'm so sorry... I didn't realise. Well, I don't think that would be right if he's committed a crime."

"You're happy to allow your father's children – your own brothers and sisters – to live like paupers, are you, Mrs Blakely?" asked Mr Fortescue.

"They won't be paupers!" said Father.

"But they have nowhere to live when they arrive," said Mr Fortescue. "And you owe money, Mr Green. Wouldn't it be wonderful to pay off all those debts?"

"Yes, but not under these circumstances," said my father. "You didn't fully explain who you were when we talked earlier. You said my daughter and her husband had done you a great favour; I didn't realise the favour was still expected of them."

"Your offer is firmly refused, Mr Fortescue," said James. "Now, consider yourself under arrest and accompany me down to the police station."

"How are you going to persuade me to do that?" retorted the hotelier.

"You're legally obliged to obey a police officer."

In one swift move, Mr Fortescue reached beneath his jacket and pulled out a revolver. The moment I saw the gun, I fully expected it to be pointed at James. But instead, it was pointed at me.

I stood stock-still, my heart pounding in my chest.

James did the same, while Father sat immobile in his chair, his mouth hanging open.

"You're to let me walk out of here a free man, Blakely," said Mr Fortescue.

"Point that gun at me, not my wife."

"I'm no fool." He gave a sickening laugh. "The gun remains as it is. Now, let me out of here."

James's revolver was locked in the writing desk drawer. There was no chance of either of us reaching it in time.

"Why are you doing this, Mr Fortescue?" asked James.

"You didn't need to offer Mr Green money and you didn't need to come to our home. If Gresham let you escape, why didn't you just run away?"

"Because I want to be free to carry on with my business here in London. It's taken me a long time to build it up again after my time in prison. I don't want all my hard work going to waste again."

"Perhaps you should have thought about that before you committed murder."

"I'm asking you to overlook a misdemeanour in return for your family's happiness. Surely your family comes first, Mr Blakely?"

"That's *Inspector Blakely* to you," retorted James. "Now put down your weapon. Comply with me now and you'll be treated with greater leniency. You know that. If you're willing to confess, you'll make it even easier for yourself. Waving a gun about in my home and threatening my wife will make matters far, far worse for you. There's no escape, Fortescue. Put the gun down and come quietly."

I wondered whether I could tackle Mr Fortescue while he was looking at James, but his gaze was darting so rapidly from one of us to the other that I realised there would be little opportunity.

"Few people were upset by the passing of Charles Hamilton," said Mr Fortescue. "Or Robert Higgins, as I knew him. Did you know that the man stole from me and then eloped with my sister? After just two months she was left destitute, her reputation ruined."

"Are you admitting to his murder?"

"No, but I want you to understand that it's not worth risking the life of your wife on behalf of a man like him. He's not worth any of the time you've spent on this case. Just let me walk free. I can just change my name again."

"Everyone gets found out eventually, no matter how often

they change their name," I said. My voice sounded feeble and my mouth felt dry. "Listen to my husband, Mr Fortescue. He knows what he's talking about."

"I'm starting to lose my patience," warned Mr Fortescue. "One more word from either of you and I'll pull the trigger. I intend to remain a free man, whether I achieve that through finance or force. If you refuse to listen to me, you'll regret it for the rest of your days. Now, let me leave!"

I noticed his finger move on the trigger. I took a sharp intake of breath and held it inside.

James must also have noticed the slight shift. He moved to one side, giving the hotel owner space to pass through the doorway.

Mr Fortescue stepped forward, still pointing his gun at me.

I slowly released the breath I had been holding, but my heart was thumping heavily.

He could still change his mind. He may go ahead and shoot me. All of us, even.

All of a sudden a primal roar split the air and Father was up out of his chair. I saw his arms rise above him and heard a dreadful crack as Edward Fortescue fell to the floor.

"No one points a gun at my daughter!" my father yelled at the crumpled form.

Mr Fortescue groaned. Father's walking stick lay broken in two by his side.

James jumped forward and stamped on the hand that was, by now, only loosely holding the revolver. He picked it up, opened the cylinder and emptied the cartridges out onto the floor. Then he knelt on Mr Fortescue's back, pulled his arms into position and fastened handcuffs around his wrists.

"Where on earth did you learn a trick like that, Mr Green?" James puffed.

"The jungle," replied Father, panting. "I had to do it to a

leopard once." He swayed a little as he attempted to stand without his walking stick.

I dashed over and helped him into his chair.

"Thank you, Father." My body was shaking and tears blurred my vision.

I fell into his lap and locked him in a long embrace.

CHAPTER 55

"I really can't believe you involved Father in one of your scrapes, Penelope," my sister scolded as we travelled in a four-wheeler cab with James and Francis the following day. "He's an old man! We're lucky he's still with us."

James and I exchanged a glance and said nothing. We had tried to explain what had happened to Eliza but she seemed intent on holding me responsible.

"Your father is a brave man," James said to Eliza. "Even I would think twice about hitting a man over the head with a walking stick while he was holding a gun."

"I think the word is *foolish* rather than brave," said Eliza. "He's always been prone to it. I suppose that's where Penelope gets it from."

The cab stopped on Milton Street and we disembarked.

Mrs Garnett answered the door and welcomed us in. "It's not the best time to visit him, I'm afraid," she said. "We've just been having the most terrible row."

"Oh dear! What about?" I asked.

"You'll see."

We followed her into the parlour, where Father was just standing to his feet. He leaned on the back of his chair for support.

"How are you, Father?" Eliza's voice was filled with concern.

"Absolutely fine! How lovely of you all to come and visit me."

"I've been ever so worried," said Eliza.

"There was no need!"

"I think you look perfectly well, Mr Green," said Francis. "And well done for tackling the assailant."

"Oh, it was nothing."

"Excuse me while we settle something once and for all," said Mrs Garnett, turning to address my father. "Just take this stick from me, Mr Green, before I hit you with it!"

"What?" exclaimed James.

Mrs Garnett pointed at the handsome walking stick by her side. It was made of dark wood, with a carved seated figure forming its handle. "Mr Green needs a new stick," she said, "and I've told him to take this one."

"But I couldn't possibly use the one that belonged to your father," Father replied. "It's so very precious to you."

"All it's done is sit in the attic for the past forty years," she retorted. "I don't need it and you do. It's made of ebony, so it's even stronger than your last one. A proper African stick! It certainly won't break in two the next time you have to hit a man."

"I hope there won't be a next time!" protested Eliza.

"Mrs Garnett," said my father. "This stick is of great sentimental value to you, and it came all the way from Arochukwu—"

"And so it must pass from one traveller to another," interrupted Mrs Garnett.

"Where's Arochukwu?" asked Eliza.

"In the country we now call British West Africa," replied Francis.

"That's right," said Mrs Garnett proudly. "My family are Igbo people. I just sense that my father wants Mr Green to have his stick."

"I think you need to stop arguing about it, Mr Green, and accept the stick," said James.

Father sighed. "All right, then. If you're sure…"

Mrs Garnett picked up the stick and presented it to him. "It was made to last," she said, "and it should last you until the end of your days."

"Excellent," said my father. "Thank you very much, Mrs Garnett. And thank you to your father, too."

"Now don't you go using that stick too much just yet, Father," said Eliza. "You need to rest."

"Rest? I don't want to rest!"

"You have to!"

"But I can't."

"Why not?"

"I have to travel to Liverpool."

"Liverpool?"

"Yes. I need to be there to greet my family." He gave a proud smile. "I can't wait for you all to meet them."

CHAPTER 56

A few days later, James, Francis, Beth, Louisa and I gathered inside the Egyptian rooms at the British Museum to view the latest additions to the display.

"Marmaduke Villiers collected some extremely interesting items for the British Museum," said Dr Crossley, the keeper of antiquities, "and we're very pleased to have become the custodians of even more now! Thank you, Miss Villiers, for donating them."

"My father would have been so pleased to see them here," Louisa said with a smile. "Everyone can visit them now that they're no longer hidden away."

"I think it's wonderful," said Francis. "The more I read about ancient Egypt, the more it fascinates me."

"Me too," said Beth. "I've found myself borrowing quite a few books on the subject from the library recently."

"Have you read *Voyage dans la Basse et la Haute Egypte* by Mr Vivant Denon?" Francis asked her.

"Not yet. I'm afraid my knowledge of French may not quite be up to it."

"How about *A Thousand Miles Up the Nile* by Amelia Edwards? No relation of mine, by the way."

"I'm reading that one right now!"

Alongside Marmaduke Villiers's finds stood the blue glass vase, the yellow fragment of a woman's face and the limestone torso fragment; the three pieces Mr Smollett had been so excited to show me in Mr Hamilton's cave of treasures. I felt a pang of sadness that he would be punished for his actions, as I felt sure that he hadn't meant any harm. If only he had been brave enough to tell us the truth sooner.

"I should certainly like to come here and look at everything properly someday," said James. "I just never seem to find the time."

"You're here now," said Francis.

"Yes, but I shall have to dash off again shortly."

"Perhaps you'll find more time when winter comes," I said. "There'll be much less to do in the garden by then."

"Very true, Penny. For a garden so small it takes up a huge amount of my spare time."

Out on the steps of the British Museum, Beth handed me and Louisa each a soft package wrapped in brown paper.

"Have you knitted something else, Beth?" I queried.

"Open it and see."

Louisa and I did so, and soon discovered that Beth had knitted us identical red-and-yellow shawls.

"Look closely at the pattern," said Beth. "It's not perfect, but it's supposed to resemble hieroglyphics."

"So it does!" said Louisa with a laugh.

"I've no idea what they mean," continued Beth. "I copied them from a book."

"It's beautiful," I replied, draping the shawl across my

shoulders. "Thank you very much! This will be perfect for keeping the chill off on a boat sailing up the Nile."

"Are you planning on doing that sometime soon, Penny?" asked James.

"Yes, I think we should."

"*We?*"

"I think we need to go on an Egyptian adventure."

"To be perfectly honest with you, I feel as though I've just been on one."

"So do I, but I'm quite sure the next one will be a little more enjoyable!"

THE END

HISTORICAL NOTE

'Egyptomania' in nineteenth-century Europe and America began with Napoleon's invasion of Egypt in 1798. While he waged his military campaign, French scientists and scholars explored and surveyed the country, documenting and publishing their finds. After the defeat of French troops in 1801, many of their acquisitions - including the Rosetta Stone - came into British possession. This increased interest in ancient Egypt sparked the rise of the 'Egyptologist' - a profession which attracted amateur scholars as travel to Egypt became easier during the late nineteenth century.

In 1870, the British travel agent Thomas Cook began offering tours of Egypt. It was the first time his company had provided holidays outside Europe or America. His tours were reasonably priced which made them accessible to middle-class tourists as well as the upper-class. They also provided the first opportunity for women to comfortably travel alone.

Amelia Edwards made the most of this opportunity to travel and first visited Egypt in the winter of 1873–1874. Her account of the journey, *A Thousand Miles up the Nile* – which she illustrated herself – sold very well when it was published in 1877. Interested in preserving Egypt's monuments and treasures, Edwards co-founded the Egypt Exploration Fund in 1882. The organisation funded a number of excavations including some by the pioneering archaeologist Flinders Petrie.

Shepheard's Hotel in Cairo was founded by an Englishman, Samuel Shepheard, in 1841 and first opened under the name Hotel des Anglais. The hotel became known for its hospitality and luxury and was popular with European and American tourists (Amelia Edwards stayed there) as well as celebrities and military and government officials. The hotel burned down in the Cairo fire in 1952.

Egyptology remained Edwards' passion for the rest of her life and she toured America giving lectures on the subject in 1889-90. She died in 1892 and left her collection of antiquities and a sum of money to University College London to set up the Edwards Chair of Egyptology: a position which was held by Flinders Petrie for forty-one years and is still in existence at the university today.

Many well-heeled Victorians enjoyed holidays in Egypt and the Thomas Cook company enjoyed a boom time there until the First World War. 'Egyptomania' experienced a resurgence in 1922 when Howard Carter discovered Tutankhamun's tomb.

The British Museum is the most visited museum in the United Kingdom, attracting around six million visitors a year. It was founded in 1753 by an Act of Parliament which purchased a collection of more than 70,000 objects which had been amassed by the physician Sir Hans Sloane. The museum was rebuilt to accommodate its swiftly growing collection and the present classical style building was completed in 1852. According to the British Museum's website, the museum holds the largest collection of Egyptian objects outside Egypt. The Rosetta Stone has been displayed at the museum since 1802. In recent years, Egypt's Supreme Council of Antiquities has made requests for the Rosetta Stone to be repatriated to Egypt. These requests have been refused because the British Museum Act of 1963 forbids the museum from disposing of its holdings. This controversy is no doubt set to rumble on.

Cleopatra's Needle sits on the Victoria Embankment, close to Embankment tube station, and has little to do with the Ptolemaic queen. It was originally erected in Heliopolis in 1450 BC before being moved to Alexandria in 12 BC. It was gifted to Britain by the ruler of Egypt and Sudan in 1819 but it didn't arrive in London until 1877 when a sponsor was willing to pay for its transportation.

During its transit, the boat was caught in a storm in the Bay of Biscay and six crew members on a rescue boat sadly lost their lives.

Today Cleopatra's Needle is flanked by two bronze Egyptian-style sphinxes and is accompanied by a plaque commemorating the men who lost their lives in its transportation.

The United States didn't want to miss out! In 1877, the US Consul General in Cairo, judge Elbert E. Farman, secured another Cleopatra's Needle from Alexandria for New York. It was placed in Central Park in 1881.

The late nineteenth century saw an increasing number of women, like Mrs Worthers, working as lady detectives such as undercover store detectives or female inquiry agents. Uncovering evidence of adultery in divorce cases provided a steady flow of work and women were sometimes employed by male private detectives or police forces when needed, for example obtaining information while disguised as a domestic servant.

Battersea Park was laid out on reclaimed marshland in the 1850s and 1860s. *The Dickens's Dictionary of London 1888* describes it as:- "One of the youngest of London parks, it is certainly the prettiest. No park or garden in London can compare with the sub-tropical garden, which is emphatically one of the sights which no visitor should fail to see."

If *The Egyptian Mystery* is the first Penny Green book you've read, then you may find the following historical background interesting. It's compiled from the historical notes published in the previous books in the series:

Women journalists in the nineteenth century were not as scarce as people may think. In fact they were numerous enough by 1898 for Arnold Bennett to write *Journalism for Women: A Practical Guide* in which he was keen to raise the standard of women's journalism:-
    "The women-journalists as a body have faults... They seem to me to be traceable either to an imperfect development of the sense of order, or to a certain lack of self-control."
    Eliza Linton became the first salaried female journalist in Britain when she began writing for *the Morning Chronicle* in 1851. She was a prolific writer and contributor to periodicals for many years including Charles Dickens' magazine *Household Words*. George Eliot – her real name was Mary Anne Evans - is most famous for novels such as *Middlemarch*, however she also became assistant editor of *The Westminster Review* in 1852.
    In the United States Margaret Fuller became the *New York Tribune*'s first female editor in 1846. Intrepid journalist Nellie Bly worked in Mexico as a foreign correspondent for the

Pittsburgh Despatch in the 1880s before writing for *New York World* and feigning insanity to go undercover and investigate reports of brutality at a New York asylum. Later, in 1889-90, she became a household name by setting a world record for travelling around the globe in seventy-two days.

The iconic circular Reading Room at the British Museum was in use from 1857 until 1997. During that time, it was also used as a filming location and has been referenced in many works of fiction. The Reading Room has been closed since 2014 but it's recently been announced that it will reopen and display some of the museum's permanent collections. It could be a while yet until we're able to step inside it but I'm looking forward to it!

The Museum Tavern, where Penny and James enjoy a drink, is a well-preserved Victorian pub opposite the British Museum. Although a pub was first built here in the eighteenth century much of the current pub (including its name) dates back to 1855. Celebrity drinkers here are said to have included Arthur Conan Doyle and Karl Marx.

Publishing began in Fleet Street in the 1500s and by the twentieth century the street was the hub of the British press. However, newspapers began moving away in the 1980s to bigger premises. Nowadays just a few publishers remain in Fleet Street but the many pubs and bars once frequented by journalists – including the pub Ye Olde Cheshire Cheese - are still popular with city workers.

Penny Green lives in Milton Street in Cripplegate which was one of the areas worst hit by bombing during the Blitz in the Second World War and few original streets remain. Milton Street was known as Grub Street in the eighteenth century and was famous as a home to impoverished writers at the time. The street had a long association with writers and was home to Anthony Trollope among many others. A small stretch of Milton Street remains but the 1960s Barbican development has been built over the bombed remains.

Plant hunting became an increasingly commercial enterprise as the nineteenth century progressed. Victorians were fascinated by exotic plants and, if they were wealthy enough, they had their own glasshouses built to show them off. Plant hunters were employed by Kew Gardens, companies such as Veitch Nurseries or wealthy individuals to seek out exotic specimens in places such as South America and the Himalayas. These plant hunters took great personal risks to collect their plants and some perished on their travels. The *Travels and Adventures of an Orchid Hunter* by Albert Millican is worth a read. Written in 1891 it documents his journeys in Colombia and demonstrates how plant hunting became little short of pillaging. Some areas he travelled to had already lost their orchids to plant hunters and Millican himself spent several months felling 4,000 trees to collect 10,000 plants. Even after all this plundering many of the orchids didn't survive the trip across the Atlantic to Britain. Plant hunters were not always welcome: Millican had arrows fired at him as he navigated rivers, had his camp attacked one night and was eventually killed during a fight in a Colombian tavern.

My research for The Penny Green series has come from sources too numerous to list in detail, but the following books have been very useful: *A Brief History of Life in Victorian Britain* by Michael Patterson, *London in the Nineteenth Century* by Jerry White, *London in 1880* by Herbert Fry, *London a Travel Guide through Time* by Dr Matthew Green, *Women of the Press in Nineteenth-Century Britain* by Barbara Onslow, *A Very British*

Murder by Lucy Worsley, *The Suspicions of Mr Whicher* by Kate Summerscale, *Journalism for Women: A Practical Guide* by Arnold Bennett, *Seventy Years a Showman* by Lord George Sanger, *Dottings of a Dosser* by Howard Goldsmid, *Travels and Adventures of an Orchid Hunter* by Albert Millican, *The Bitter Cry of Outcast London* by Andrew Mearns, *The Complete History of Jack the Ripper* by Philip Sugden, *The Necropolis Railway* by Andrew Martin, *The Diaries of Hannah Cullwick, Victorian Maidservant* edited by Liz Stanley, *Mrs Woolf & the Servants* by Alison Light, *Revelations of a Lady Detective* by William Stephens Hayward, *A is for Arsenic* by Kathryn Harkup, *In an Opium Factory* by Rudyard Kipling, *Drugging a Nation: The Story of China and the Opium Curse* by Samuel Merwin, *Confessions of an Opium Eater* by Thomas de Quincy, *The Pinkertons: The Detective Dynasty That Made History* by James D Horan, *The Napoleon of Crime* by Ben Macintyre and *The Code Book: The Secret History of Codes and Code-breaking* by Simon Singh, *Dying for Victorian Medicine, English Anatomy and its Trade in the Dead Poor* by Elizabeth T. Hurren, *Tales from the Workhouse – True Tales from the Depths of Poverty* by James Greenwood, Mary Higgs and others, *Sickness and Cruelty in the Workhouse - The True Story of a Victorian Workhouse Doctor* by Joseph Rogers, *Mord Em'ly* by William Pitt Ridge, *Alice Diamond And The Forty Elephants: Britain's First Female Crime Syndicate* by Brian Macdonald, *The Maul and the Pear Tree* by P.D. James, *The Five* by Hallie Rubenhold, *Sister Sleuths* by Nell Darby, *A Thousand Miles up the Nile* by Amelia Edwards, *Ancient Egypt: the Glory of the Pharaohs* (audiobook) by David Angus, *Egypt : handbook for travellers, 1885 - 92* by Karl Baedeker and *Dickens's Dictionary of London 1888*. The *British Newspaper Archive* is also an invaluable resource.

GET A FREE SHORT MYSTERY

Want more of Penny Green? Sign up to my mailing list and I'll send you my short mystery *The Belgrave Square Murder*!

A wealthy businessman is found dead in Belgrave Square on a foggy November night. Was the motive robbery? Or something more personal? Penny Green tries to report on the case, but no one wants to cooperate. How can she investigate when there's so little to go on?

Visit my website for more details:
emilyorgan.com/the-belgrave-square-murder

Or scan the code on the following page:

THE CAMDEN SPIRITUALIST

A Penny Green Mystery Book 12

A woman shot dead on her doorstep. A killer who disappears into the fog.

News reporter Penny doesn't believe in spirits, so she's unimpressed with the young medium who claims to communicate with the dead. Is it harmless entertainment or something more sinister?

When the spiritualist's performance is interrupted by a protestor, Penny finds an ally. Two days later, her new friend is dead. As Penny investigates, the mystery deepens. Could family money lie behind the murder? Or an affair?

Soon, Penny suspects the spiritualist isn't who she claims to be. There's another puzzle to solve and increasing conflict with her police inspector husband. A second death puts a twist on the case, but Penny's running out of time. Then there's news which changes her life forever...

Find out more:

mybook.to/penny-green-camden

THANK YOU

Thank you for reading this Penny Green mystery, I hope you enjoyed it!

Would you like to know when I release new books? Here are some ways to stay updated:

- Join my mailing list and receive a free short mystery: *The Belgrave Square Murder:* emilyorgan.com/the-belgrave-square-murder
- Like my Facebook page: facebook.com/ emilyorganwriter
- Follow me on Goodreads: goodreads.com/emily_organ
- Follow me on BookBub: bookbub.com/authors/emily-organ
- View my other books here: emilyorgan.com

And if you have a moment, I would be very grateful if you would leave a quick review online. Honest reviews of my books help other readers discover them too!

You can discover more about the Penny Green Series by scanning this code:

ALSO BY EMILY ORGAN

Augusta Peel Series:

Death in Soho
Murder in the Air
The Bloomsbury Murder
The Tower Bridge Murder
Death in Westminster
Murder on the Thames
The Baker Street Murders

Churchill & Pemberley Series:

Tragedy at Piddleton Hotel
Murder in Cold Mud
Puzzle in Poppleford Wood
Trouble in the Churchyard
Wheels of Peril
The Poisoned Peer
Fiasco at the Jam Factory
Disaster at the Christmas Dinner

Christmas Calamity at the Vicarage (novella)

Writing as Martha Bond

Lottie Sprigg Travels Mystery Series:

Murder in Venice
Murder in Paris
Murder in Cairo
Murder in Monaco
Murder in Vienna

Lottie Sprigg Country House Mystery Series:

Murder in the Library
Murder in the Grotto
Murder in the Maze
Murder in the Bay

Printed in Great Britain
by Amazon

41429471R00172